DESPITE THE DUKE

The London Vices
Book 1

Kathleen Ayers

© Copyright 2026 by Kathleen Ayers
Text by Kathleen Ayers
Cover by Dar Albert

Dragonblade Publishing, Inc. is an imprint of Kathryn Le Veque Novels, Inc.
P.O. Box 23
Moreno Valley, CA 92556
ceo@dragonbladepublishing.com

Produced in the United States of America

First Edition March 2026
Trade Paperback Edition

Reproduction of any kind except where it pertains to short quotes in relation to advertising or promotion is strictly prohibited.

All Rights Reserved.

The characters and events portrayed in this book are fictitious. Any similarity to real persons, living or dead, is purely coincidental and not intended by the author.

AI Statement: No AI or ghostwriting was used in the creation of this story, or any story, published by Dragonblade Publishing. All text, structure, content, ideas, and concept are 100% human generated solely by the author whose name appears on the cover. It is prohibited to use this material, or any copyrighted material, for AI engine training.

ARE YOU SIGNED UP FOR DRAGONBLADE'S BLOG?

You'll get the latest news and information on exclusive giveaways, exclusive excerpts, coming releases, sales, free books, cover reveals and more.

Check out our complete list of authors, too!

No spam, no junk. That's a promise!

Sign Up Here
www.dragonbladepublishing.com

Dearest Reader;

Thank you for your support of a small press. At Dragonblade Publishing, we strive to bring you the highest quality Historical Romance from some of the best authors in the business. Without your support, there is no 'us', so we sincerely hope you adore these stories and find some new favorite authors along the way.

Happy Reading!

CEO, Dragonblade Publishing

Additional Dragonblade books by Author Kathleen Ayers

The London Vices Series
Despite the Duke (Book 1)

The Five Deadly Sins Series
Sinfully Wed (Book 1)
Sinfully Tempted (Book 2)
Sinfully Mine (Book 3)
Sinfully Yours (Book 4)
Sinfully Wanton (Book 5)

The Arrogant Earls Series
Forgetting the Earl (Book 1)
Chasing the Earl (Book 2)
Enticing the Earl (Book 3)
The Haunting of Rose Abbey (Novella)

PROLOGUE

Devil's Acre, London 1811

MARIANNE VICEROY, DUCHESS of Roxboro, clutched at the enormous mound of her stomach, panting and terrified as she stumbled on the filthy cobblestones, covered with filth and lord knew what else. Tripping on the edge of her gown, she braced herself against the side of a building, before venturing further down the darkened alley, hand tracing along the worn stone, alert for any sign of her pursuers.

A sudden flare of pain struck her midsection. Biting her lip so hard she tasted blood, Marianne struggled to remain silent, knowing no sound could escape lest she alert the men following in the darkness to her location. Those horrid men. Thugs who had—

Charles. He's dead. He—

Another pain constricted the lower half of her body, nearly as painful as the one in her heart. She'd witnessed the brutal murder of her beloved husband with her own eyes. The villains who'd overtaken the carriage first shot John, the duke's driver. Thrown Robbs off the back of the carriage, bludgeoning the poor footman until Marianne saw the sheen of blood in the street.

I am the Duke of Roxboro. Unhand me.

Charles, so certain of his place in the world, had been more furious than anything. He was the Duke of Roxboro and one did not stop a duke's carriage as it pulled away from Parliament. Her husband hadn't realized the danger, until John fell from his perch, a pistol ball lodged in his forehead.

Pressing herself closer to the stone of the building, Marianne crouched down, terrified when footsteps, at a run, approached. Clamping her lips shut, she covered her mouth to keep from screaming in terror.

"She couldn't have gotten far." A harsh, lisping voice, dripping with the worst streets of London, reached Marianne's ears. "Lord, she's as big as a sow."

"Leave 'er to the vermin here," another voice declared before spitting, "The Devil's Acre will eat her alive. There's plenty who want to mount a woman with a rounded belly. She won't survive the night."

"She had diamonds in 'er ears, you bloody idiot." The smack of a hand hitting flesh sounded. "I want 'em. Promised any jewels on their person."

Marianne shrank further into the shadows, attempting to make her form as tiny as possible as she curled behind a pile of rags and foul smelling trash. Another pang ripped through her body, leaving Marianne clutching at the stone wall.

"Besides, I want a go at 'er. Never fucked a duchess," a gurgling sort of laugh came out. "Specially not one big with child."

"Nice teats too from what I could see. We'll find 'er." The other man belched. "Maybe down that way. I see somethin' moving around."

The next, fierce pain was so sharp that Marianne's head swam for a moment, but she blinked and forced her eyes open. Fainting in this hellish alley was not an option. Nor could she give up. She must find safety, if not for herself, for the child she carried. The child she and Charles had so dearly wanted. There had been so many…miscarriages. But she'd finally conceived when she and Charles went abroad for nearly a year. Not daring to share their happy news until Dr. Howard declared Marianne and the child to be healthy after their return to London. And now—

She held her breath, praying for divine deliverance.

One of her assailants hollered some distance away. "Here!"

"Sounds like Yorrick found her." The heavy footsteps of the

two men who'd been close, hurried away, back in the direction they'd come. "Don't forget the duke's signet ring. 'E's asked for proof or we don't get paid."

Marianne's breath left her lungs in a shocked hiss.

Proof?

Her heart beat that much faster. This was no accident. No random robbery. But a planned attack against the Duke of Roxboro.

Charles was well-liked. Respected. But he did have enemies, a handful. He was outspoken on a number of contested bills, ones he defended passionately. A fiery orator, Charles was known to be intractable at times when trying to prove his point. Even so, that was hardly a reason to want him dead, was it? A disagreement over the rights of miners? Or how best to fix the price of corn?

But who else could it be but a political opponent?

Mariane pressed closer to the wall.

She was alone. The baby was coming. And she was running for her life and trapped in The Devil's Acre, a desolate part of London known for vice, murder, populated with thieves and prostitutes, ironically located close to Parliament.

Which would make it easier to murder a duke, firmly placing the blame on the denizens of The Devil's Acre. Could it have been Cotswold? The earl blamed Charles and his platform for inciting the workers at his mine to riot.

Yes. It could be Cotswold.

Charles had been delayed in arriving to the carriage where Marianne awaited him. He'd been so pleased to see her, pressing a kiss to her rounded stomach, before cursing Cotswold for the barbaric treatment of the working class. Mere seconds later, the vehicle rocked violently. A shot was fired, followed by the terrible groan of John as he fell to the ground. The door had been flung open so forcefully, it had nearly been ripped from its hinges. Hands reached inside, grabbing Charles and pulling him from the carriage. Knives flashed in the light of the streetlamps, as their assailants stabbed him over and over, blood spreading across his coat.

Marianne hadn't even screamed.

She had pushed herself into the furthest corner of the carriage, her mind unable to comprehend what was happening, knowing there was nothing she could do to save her husband. Charles fell to the ground, head lolling in her direction, his eyes meeting hers one last time.

Run. He mouthed. *Run, Marianne.*

Her fingers had grasped the handle of the door at her back as Charles continued to struggle, distracting the assailants so they wouldn't—

Charles. A tear slipped down her cheek.

She had slid from the carriage as quietly as possible, knowing that she must save the heir to Roxboro. The thieves were so busy killing her beloved—well, they disregarded Marianne. Never glancing inside the carriage, likely assuming she'd fainted.

Cocking one ear, Marianne listened for any sign those awful men would return, but the nearby streets were quiet. Carefully, she stood, pressing a hand between her thighs as a great maw of agony leeched through her. Her fingers came away wet, the coppery tang of blood filling the air.

This child, all that was left of her sweet Charles, was choosing to arrive at the worst possible time.

"Mama will save you," she whispered to her stomach. "I will."

A dog barked in the distance. Shadows danced along the walls of the buildings surrounding her. A drunk sang a song off key. Taking a deep breath, Marianne darted down a small alley nearly hidden behind a half-dozen barrels. A soft light glowed, beckoning her towards a dilapidated house standing alone at the end of the alley. Music and laughter sounded from a street or two over, but here, everything was quiet. The light came from a lamp, sitting in the window. Marianne could make out the sagging porch and the small pot of geraniums blooming beside the chipped wood of the front door.

Marianne focused her gaze on that door. Murderous thugs wouldn't bother with geraniums, would they? Surely someone inside would come to her aid.

She half ran, half stumbled to the house, the scent of her own blood filling her nostrils, mixing with the unpleasant smells of the alley. She gagged at the scent, before another pain struck, forcing Marianne to her knees. Panting, she crawled up the steps, blood dripping down her legs. Flinging herself at the door, Marianne pounded with her fist as loud as she dared, gaze darting back down the blackness of the alley.

"Please," she cried, her strength waning. "I beg you. Help me." She collapsed against the door, ears and eyes alert for any sign of her pursuers. "Please," she whimpered as another stab struck her midsection.

The door opened a crack, which given the part of London Marianne found herself in, made a great deal of sense. These were not the manicured streets of Mayfair, geraniums or not.

A gasp came from somewhere above her, followed by a loud creak as the door jerked open.

Marianne fell through the opening, a scream on her lips as she took in the long, homely face hovering over her. Pale as a wraith. Pinched, tiny features. Wide, dark eyes.

Perhaps I am already dead.

"Lordy," the ghostly creature whispered. "Oh lordy. Mrs. Bean! Come quick."

Heels clicked across the wooden floor as Mariane struggled to pull the rest of her body inside the humble foyer. "Please," she begged. "Help me. I was attacked." A sob caught in her throat, wondering how much she should say. For all she knew, the attackers lived here. But she had little choice. A tiny scream left her throat as she clutched her stomach. "My child—please."

An older woman appeared, graying hair tightly plaited and wrapped around the crown of her head, a pair of spectacles perched on her nose. Shrewd, pale eyes took in Marianne's crumpled form, the lamp in her hand raising higher. "What's this?"

"She was bangin' on the door, Mrs. Bean," the wraith answered.

"And you opened my home to trouble. Haven't I taught you better?" She lightly cuffed the back of the wraith's, who was no more than a girl of fourteen, head. "We don't care what reason is given. The door stays closed to strangers."

"But," the girl stuttered.

"Please," Marianne whispered. "I will pay you whatever you wish. I—" A moan of pain escaped her lips. "A fortune. No amount is too large." Inhaling at another wave of pain, she said, "send word to my husband's brother, I beg you. He will pay whatever sum you require for offering aid. Lord Damon Viceroy. Mayfair. Number fourteen, Brook Street. Gray brick house. The door is green with a large, golden knocker of a bull's head—

"I don't know a Lord Damon," Mrs. Bean interrupted with a roll of her eyes. "Is he your protector?"

"No, he's my brother-in-law," Marianne choked.

"You're a harlot who's lost her protector, I'll warrant." Mrs. Bean pushed with one foot, trying to dislodge her from the doorway before inhaling sharply at the sight of Marianne's bloodied skirts and writhing mound of stomach. "And now you're bleeding all over my rug."

"I," Marianne snarled in a coldly patrician tone, "Am the *Duchess of Roxboro*. Most definitely not a trollop. Nor do I resemble one."

The serving girl's eyes widened.

"Well, I suppose not," Mrs. Bean raised a brow at Marianne's tone. "Not in that gown at least. Nor with those earbobs."

"They are yours if you help me. And whatever gold you ask for," Marianne panted as black spots appeared in her vision. "Send for Lord Damon, I beg you. He'll reward you handsomely." Marianne struggled to her knees, fingers digging into the rug as another pang struck. "I give you my word."

"We've not been formally introduced, Your Grace, but as you've overheard, I am Mrs. Bean." She waved a hand at the young girl. "This is Louisa. And you'll forgive me for being cautious but most of the girls who roam these streets come to me for aid at such times. Though, much sooner." She pointedly looked at the mound of Marianne's stomach, lips drawing back at the blood soaking her rug. "And they use the entrance to my establishment."

"I am not a trollop."

"Don't suppose you are. But I don't know this Lord Damon or any Duchess of Roxboro," she said. "But I will take those fancy diamonds," she flicked at the diamond hanging from Marianne's left ear. "And the gown, if I can get the blood out. Possibly your slippers."

"You can have all of it." Mrs. Bean could strip Marianne naked for all she cared, as long as the woman helped her.

"A new rug as well, Your Grace."

"I can have one sent from Axminster. The same that graces the home of the Prince Regent," Marianne sputtered. Axminster made the finest rugs in all of England and any one of them was likely worth more than this woman's house.

Mrs. Bean nodded. "I suppose that will suffice." Snapping her fingers, she said, "Wilkes."

A massive form appeared from shadows, looming over Marianne and the two other women. "Yes, Mrs. Bean?"

"I need you to lift the duchess," Mrs. Bean ordered, with some mockery, clearly not truly believing Marianne. "Gently. Place her in the spare room, the one my sister uses when she visits. Louisa," she said to the girl, who hadn't stopped staring at Marianne. "I need linens. Clean ones. Hot water. Soap."

"Yes, Mrs. Bean."

"And send Matty to find—this Lord Damon." She leaned over Marianne. "I do hope you aren't making this up or things will go poorly for you, *duchess*."

"Lord Damon Viceroy." Marianne managed to get out. "If he

is not at home, his servants will know where to find him." More black spots crowded her vision. Mrs. Bean, grimace still on her lips, grew blurry.

I'm dying.

Marianne grew more certain of that by the moment. But with her last breath, she would save her child. Even now, he was moving about inside her, begging to be free. The heir she and Charles had so dearly wanted. Prayed for. Finally. And he wasn't here to see it.

A sob left her as strong arms lifted her, carefully cupping her head.

"Wait a moment," Mrs. Bean said, placing her palm over Marianne's massive stomach. "How far along are you?" Concern flashed in her pale eyes, there and gone in an instant.

"Nearly seven months," Marianne whispered.

Mrs. Bean clucked her tongue. "Too soon and…either the babe is quite large or…" she shook her head. "Hurry, Louisa. Now."

The girl jumped and rushed off to do her bidding.

"The babe," Mariane struggled to say as she was carried away. "Save it. No matter what."

The older woman gazed down at Marianne with something that resembled pity before it was gone.

"You believe me."

Mrs. Bean didn't answer. "I'll do what I can. I promise."

THREE. THREE DAMNED babies.

Delores Bean, proprietor of a small brothel which catered to gentlemen with unusual tastes, looked at the poor dead woman lying on the bed before her. She'd done all she could, but Delores knew, since she'd once been a midwife before coming to London, that there had been too much blood for the mother's survival. Even had she lived, the duchess, as Delores was now fairly certain

the woman happened to be, would likely have died of fever.
Not hardy in the least. Few fine ladies were.

Childbirth, Delores mused, was a great equalizer. She wasn't quite sure what to make of the woman's story that she and the duke had been set upon by unknown assailants, but Delores supposed it was none of her business. Bad things happen when you stick your nose into things that you shouldn't. She'd lived in The Devil's Acre a long time.

And in that time, Delores had helped to birth dozens of children or prevented them from coming into the world at all.

But never, in all her sixty years, had she witnessed the birth of more than one child save a pair of twins two decades ago.

Certainly not…. three. All boys. All identical. Mostly.

The first boy born, was, as expected, the strongest of the three. He'd come out squalling; face wrinkled in consternation at having to face the world. And though he was small, he seemed sturdy enough.

But the other two?

Tiny. Far too small to survive. One nearly blue before she smacked his back. That one had a freckle on the end of his nose. Barely a sound came from the other boy, only tiny mewls, like a kitten. He had a birthmark on his shoulder that reminded Delores of a heart.

Again, it didn't matter. Neither was likely to survive.

She'd ordered Louisa to take them from the room and out of sight of the dying duchess lying in a pool of her own blood. A small kindness. There was no sense in her seeing the other two boys since both would likely soon be joining her in death. The duchess should be allowed to pass in peace without a heart laden with grief.

Delores knew that sort of grief well. She'd lost three of her own children.

A squall met her ears, coming from the basket at the foot of the bed.

Alexander, the duchess had whispered, touching his cheek, a smile of pure happiness pulling at her lips before her eyes closed. Barely conscious.

A blessing. Delores thought it unlikely the duchess ever felt the birth of the other two infants.

Poor lamb.

Charitable isn't how most in Devil's Acre would describe Delores Bean. Life was hard. Cruel. She knew firsthand. But—she smoothed down the duchess's matted hair before taking the diamond earbobs from her ears—every now and again she allowed herself a moment of weakness. As she had tonight.

"Mrs. Bean." Louisa ran into the room, averting her eyes from the bed, pursing her thin lips at the scent of all that blood.

"Has Lord Damon arrived?"

"No." Louisa shook her head. "Another gentleman. Mr. Philpot. He was at Lord Damon's home, awaiting his arrival to inform him…of the duke's…demise," she sputtered. "He's a solicitor."

Another wave of pity struck Delores for the duchess. The woman had been screaming for Charles, half out of her mind with pain. Muttering about being chased. Something about knives.

Not my business.

Louisa looked at the infant in the basket, before turning to the sound of whimpering coming from the room just across the hall. "Should I—bathe them and—"

"No." Delores took a deep breath, tasting the tang of blood on her tongue. "Let us not burden Mr. Philpot or Lord Damon with any more terrible news. The two babes," she sighed. "Will likely not live the night. Far too small. I would imagine the death of the duke and duchess is tragedy enough for this Mr. Philpot and Lord Damon. Try to comfort the babes, Louisa. A bit of sugared water in a napkin should quiet them. Hold and rock them, if you choose. Say a prayer for the duchess."

"Yes, Mrs. Bean." Louisa nodded and rushed from the room, likely surprised to find that her employer had a heart.

Bothersome, having a heart.

Mrs. Bean tucked the blanket more fully around little Alexander who waved his fists at her. Hungry, no doubt, though there wasn't any way for her to feed him. Mr. Philpot, as the duke's man, would see to it.

"I'm sorry about your mum," she whispered. "Truly. But she was going to die no matter what I did. Lost too much blood. But I saved you. A future duke."

"The Duke of Roxboro. Address him properly, if you please, Mrs. Bean."

A spare gentleman with narrow shoulders, appeared at the bedroom door, looking out of place in his rich garments. He spared a glance at the dead woman in the bed, closed his eyes for a moment, whispering something mournful under his breath. "I am Mr. Philpot." Two flat, black eyes snapped open to appraise her. "The Duke of Roxboro's solicitor." He nodded to the basket. "*His* solicitor."

"Mr. Philpot." Delores inclined her head. "I did what I could to save her. The duchess promised—"

"You will be amply rewarded for your efforts." Philpot's eyes pierced her with a grief-filled stare. "Lord Damon is not in London at present but has been sent word of the death of the duke and duchess," the words trembled from him. "I was awaiting his return when the lad in your employ found me."

"Lucky."

"If you say so, Mrs. Bean. I will take possession of His Grace." His voice cracked just slightly before glancing over his shoulder at two burly footmen in livery, followed by a somber gentleman garbed in black. "My wife will care for the duke until his uncle's return." He waved the other gentleman forward. "Mr. Switch will...take Her Grace." His throat bobbed once more, obviously distressed.

The duchess had been loved, that much was clear from Philpott's reaction. One of the footmen wiped tears from his eyes. The other stared at the floor.

Delores handed the basket containing the tiny duke to Philpot. Given their reaction, it was a good thing she'd done, keeping the news of the other two infants from the solicitor. The man was so stricken. "He's small, but healthy. Hungry. You'll need a wet nurse."

"Mrs. Philpot will make arrangements," the solicitor assured her.

She nodded, hating that she cared for the little duke, though he was assuredly no longer her problem.

"She named him Alexander," Delores thought to add.

"After the duchess's father, Lord Manville," Philpot murmured, fingers curling around the handle of the basket. "A good name. Lord Damon will be pleased."

Sticking out her palm, Delores raised a brow. "My payment for services rendered. And Her Grace insisted I have a new rug. From Axminster."

Disdain colored Philpot's features, but he reached into his coat, producing a heavy bag of coins. "For your trouble, Mrs. Bean. And your care of the duchess. The rug will be delivered within the week." He looked towards the bed, his eyes watery with emotion.

"Mr. Philpott," she inclined her head as the footmen and Mr. Switch prepared the body of the duchess. "I bid you good evening."

"Mrs. Bean." He gave a short bow. "I thank you on behalf of the Duke of Roxboro."

Chapter One

London, 1840

Lady Sophia Simmons hopped away in time to avoid having her toe crushed by one of the overly amorous suitors surrounding her sister, Lady Mara. There were always gentlemen swirling around Mara.

Ugh.

Sophia, as a general rule, didn't care much for the cloud of simpering dandies surrounding her sister, or their overblown infatuation. She found their behavior intolerable. Pushing further into the wall, she pulled her skirts up, barely managing to escape one gentleman's clumsy, overly large feet. Mama would have a fit if she tore the hem of this lovely blue gown or created any sort of what she deemed "a fashion incident."

Mara let out a soft peal of laughter and swatted one young man playfully on the shoulder with her fan.

Artfully done. Mara has been practicing.

Sophia plucked at her pale blue skirts. Tugged at the bodice, *discreetly*. Tried not to frown at her sister, who looked over one creamy shoulder with a smug smile. It would only encourage further poor behavior.

Mara was often declared one of the great beauties of London. The very flower of English womanhood. Some whispered how the other apple, namely Sophia, could have fallen so far from the Canterbell tree.

Constantly being considered…inferior had a way of prompting Sophia to behave in the exact *opposite* manner of her sister.

Mara The Beautiful, who was permitted to be in her third Season because Lady Canterbell was holding out for a marquess or a duke.

I would be thrilled for you to attract any sort of attention, Sophia.

Unfortunately, Sophia did draw attention, though not the sort Mama approved of.

Another deep sigh came from her as she attempted to appear enthralled at the sight of the Perswick ballroom, watching half the men in London fawn around her sister. Sophia longed for...oh, an apple. A tiny pebble. Or one of those tiny cakes she'd seen at the refreshment table. Anything at all to throw at Mara's inflated head. She'd once placed two beetles in her sister's bonnet at a garden party because she'd been particularly *insufferable* that day. Sophia had quite enjoyed the screeching while Mara danced about swatting at her head.

"Lord Wilde," she heard Mara whisper, loudly, to the gentleman not two paces away. "I shall save my last dance for you, but first," she shot Sophia a look of false sympathy. "Could you spin my sister about for the next set. She hasn't danced at all this evening. Poor dear."

I would give anything for some sort of flying insect to launch itself at Mara's head.

Turning her eyes to the ceiling of the vast Perswick ballroom, Sophia begged for deliverance. Why not merely place a sign on her back announcing her inadequacy and lack of appeal to the entire crowd of London's finest all gathered here tonight?

Wilde took her in with a weak smile and, as expected, murmured a polite excuse about returning later to dance with Lady Mara's sister. He wouldn't. They never did. Not that Sophia minded, overmuch. The sort of men Mara attracted were vastly uninteresting. Conversations limited to the weather, horses and who they'd seen walking in the park. Dreadfully dull. Overly polite. And Wilde had a loose thread on his coat, button dangling and about to fall off, something she would have ordinarily pointed out to him as a courtesy.

"I tried, Mama," Mara said softly, sounding far too innocent.

"You did your best," Mama replied.

Good grief.

It wasn't as if Sophia was some sort of troll. Or possessed a horrid skin condition like Miss Andrews. She'd been told she was pretty. Slightly plump, but many gentlemen appreciated an overabundance of curves. True, her hair didn't shine like bits of spun gold, as Mara's did. Nor did she have her sister's modest, demure manner and dulcet voice.

Dulcet? What did that even mean?

But Sophia was intelligent. Quick witted. Had interest in the world around her. Read a great deal whereas Mara cracking open a book was more accidental in nature.

Her sister was a bit of a pea-hen.

I should live in a constant state of disappointment were that my daughter. Poor Lady Canterbell. Perhaps if Sophia possessed an ounce of Mara's charm.

Lady Perswick's exact words, whispered behind the exquisitely painted fan she held to another finely dressed matron of the *ton*. She didn't even have the decency to wait for Sophia to be out of earshot before relaying her opinion. Was it any wonder that all of Mama's hopes and dreams were solely focused on Mara? Her sister was held up as an example of everything Sophia *should* be and was not.

The more Mama insisted, the more her youngest daughter…resisted.

The battle lines had been clearly drawn with no winner in sight.

"Sophia." Mama took her arm. "You aren't even trying. Not one gentleman caller this entire Season. No dances at all. You must engage in conversation."

"I've no idea what to say."

Mama made a puffing sound. "Gentlemen adore speaking about themselves. Encourage them to do so. Then you can merely nod at the appropriate times."

"Terribly dull." Sophia lifted her chin. "Should I not share my thoughts? My opinions?"

"I would prefer you do not." Mama fanned herself. "Gentlemen find your forthright manner far too honest."

"Honestly is a desirable trait."

"Not when you are pointing out that an excess of pomade is perfuming the air. Or a straining waistcoat could benefit from being let out and suggesting a tailor."

"I'm only trying to help. The pomade was overpowering." Sophia only sought to help Lord Richardson. Several young ladies had whispered complaints that while they liked the viscount, the scent of him was rather off-putting. And in the case of Mr. Soames, well, how could he not notice that the straining of his waistcoat would cause a button or two to pop off?

"Look at Mara." Mama tilted her head. "See how she pretends great interest in whatever is being said? Blushes in a most ladylike manner? Refrains from unwanted candor?"

"Mara is entirely full of herself." She waved a hand at her sister, who smiled, head thrown back, as a handsome man spun her about. "It is embarrassing for her to beg dances for me as if I'm some sort of diseased rat who cannot possibly—"

"That is quite enough," Mama gave a dramatic gasp. "Where do you get such notions? A diseased rat? Who says such things? You've become a bluestocking, surrounding yourself with mounds of books. As if finding you a husband will not be difficult enough."

"I quite agree. Imagine, if I were as dumb as Mara—"

Mama's fingers bit into her arm. "Silence. I do not know why I was burdened with such an argumentative, unbiddable child. Combative, your father calls you. If I were to tell you the sky was blue, you would say the opposite, merely to spite me." Her lips drew tight as she plucked at the sapphire bracelet on Sophia's wrist. "Did I give you permission to borrow this?"

"I thought you had."

A complete lie. Sophia had snatched the sapphire bracelet

from Mama's jewelry box after seeing how well it went with her gown.

"The clasp is loose. Don't you dare be careless. I adore this bracelet." Another puffing noise came from Mama. "I've advised your father that we should marry you off to Mr. Hemming and be done with it."

Sophia's mouth popped open in horror. "You would not."

As a threat, Mr. Hemming was a good one. He was a distant cousin of some sort and Papa's designated heir. Also, he was quite terrible.

Mama's features were triumphant. "Do not challenge me further. Make some effort. Else you find yourself wed to Mr. Hemming."

"Mr. Hemming is the unfortunate recipient of a great many warts, Mama. I liken him to a toad." He also possessed bulging eyes which failed to improve his appearance. Not to mention that he had no personality to speak of.

"An unkind observation. Mr. Hemming is a fine man who any young lady would be pleased to have as a husband." She raised a brow. "Now, appear welcoming. Attempt to smile. Resolve to make polite conversation."

Sophia complied, stretching her lips. "I smile. Often. And I do engage others in polite conversation."

Mama looked down her nose. "There is a reason Lady Stafford's daughter no longer calls or asks you to walk in the park. Do not for a moment pretend you do not know what I speak of."

Lady Stafford's daughter, Hortensia, was an utter nitwit. Devoid of even a semblance of intelligence. She made Mara seem like an academic. Sophia could tolerate many things, but she drew the line at absolute stupidity.

"She didn't know who William Lamb is," Sophia stated, aghast. "William. Lamb. Viscount Melbourne. The Prime Minister."

"Your father's position in Her Majesty's government puts you closer to such matters. Most young ladies do not care overmuch for politics. Or William Lamb."

"I doubt Hortensia has ever picked up a book," Sophia puffed, warming to the topic. "Doesn't read at all. How on earth am I to be friends with such a girl?" She threw up her hands. "England is an island, Mama. And Hortensia *did not know*."

"Yet she has dozens of suitors." Mama's brow raised once more. "Dozens."

Sophia turned away, watching the colorful swirl of dancers before her, hating this conversation. If she could be a modest, demure, oblivious to the world around her, bit of fluff, she would be. Life would be far easier.

"I believe I'll go find a glass of lemonade," she finally said.

Probably more likely to be champagne. That would suit her. Sophia liked the bubbles.

"Don't go far." Mama, annoyed, had already turned to watch Mara, features glowing with approval at her eldest daughter. "If you see your father, ask him to attend me. And don't get into trouble, Sophia. I beg you," she cautioned over her shoulder. "Try not to…become overly amused as you did with Lord Albert."

Sophia straightened her shoulders. A young lady couldn't even watch a terrible wig slide off its owner's head and laugh so hard that lemonade comes out her nose without constantly being reminded of it.

"I wasn't the only one," Sophia protested.

"Even so. Behave. Or Mr. Hemming shall be your future. Warts and all."

Sophia strode towards the refreshment table in frustration, making sure she was far enough away from her mother and Mara that she wouldn't be seen as she snatched a glass of champagne from one of the liveried servants circling the ballroom.

She turned her head slightly to discreetly take a sip of the pale pink liquid, grinning as the bubbles tickled her nose. Quickening her steps, Sophia ducked into a nearby alcove whose only other occupant was a large fern. Draining her glass, far too quickly, she toyed with returning to Mama now that she was somewhat fortified, but caught sight of Lady Stafford heading in Mama's direction. Which meant Hortensia couldn't be far behind.

More champagne was in order. Sophia spun towards the refreshment table.

Hortensia's pink skirts appeared in the crowd, as she took Mara's hand in greeting. Her head tilted in the direction of the refreshment table and caught sight of Sophia. Her pretty features immediately soured.

"I probably shouldn't have burst into giggles when she claimed a woman gave birth through her belly button," Sophia muttered. "But I'd never heard anything so stupid."

Defiantly grabbing another glass of champagne, she turned in the opposite direction, and the breath halted in her lungs, as if all the air had been sucked out of the Perswick ballroom.

Oh. Oh. My.

She'd never thought to see *him* at a ball. He rarely attended such events, possibly because, according to the gossips, he wasn't invited. Duke or not. Libertines, especially those of such sordid reputation, were usually to be found at gambling hells or other seedy locales. Sophia had only seen him once before, falling off his horse in the park—*in an utterly ducal manner*. Because in addition to his devastating masculine beauty, the Duke of Roxboro was reputed to be a sot.

Devastating indeed. Absolutely no exaggeration.

There was no mistaking Roxboro. Not with that careless mess of coffee-colored hair, the chiseled jaw that could cut glass, and those startling eyes.

Unmistakable.

Orbs a shimmering green, shot through with threads of silver. The combination the same hue as the sky before a violent storm.

Sophia nearly dropped the champagne when Roxboro's gaze caught and held hers.

She raised the glass, fingers clutching the stem, to her lips, the sapphire bracelet clanking softly against the glass.

Roxboro raised his own goblet of wine in a silent toast, never once looking away.

Good lord, he's...magnificent.

Wealthy. A duke. Known for his exquisite and expensive manner of dressing. One could live comfortably for years on what one of Roxboro's coats cost. Reputed to have four mistresses. Prone to misadventure, most likely caused by his love of drink and propensity to haunt brothels and gambling hells. Binson's was said to be his favorite. An unapologetic libertine.

And he was...looking at *her*.

Sophia's heart fluttered about wildly. A butterfly attempting to land. She drained the flute of champagne.

Roxboro deftly slid between a small circle of guests, ignoring their bowing and scraping in a bid to gain his attention, uninterested in their efforts. The brilliant green eyes, with their gleam of gray, stayed focused on Sophia. Impossibly handsome up close, Roxboro resembled one of the statues of Apollo Mama liked to populate the Canterbell gardens with, one that had now come to life and meant to speak to Sophia.

All of which led to a lightheaded, dizzy sensation.

Or it may have been the champagne.

"Your Grace," Sophia whispered when Roxboro finally stood before her. She dipped into a wobbly curtsey, nearly toppling over. Not the fault of the champagne. Mara likened Sophia's attempts at a proper curtsey to a seizure.

"Allow me, little dove," he plucked the now empty glass of champagne from Sophia's fingers, took another from a servant, and handed it to Sophia. His fingers, large and warm, brushed along her own.

Sophia giggled, then slapped a palm over her mouth, horrified. His presence was just so overwhelming. Magnificent. Surely, the duke hadn't meant to approach her. There must be someone else he cared to speak to, possibly behind her.

Me. The rather embarrassing Canterbell daughter.

But there was no one else in the immediate vicinity. Only

Sophia.

I might swoon. She'd never done such a thing in her life but if there was ever a time, it was now.

"I've seen you walking in the park," Roxboro said, voice low and raspy, prickling over her skin. "Admiring you from afar, my dove." His shimmering gaze took her in from head to toe, "Tell me about yourself."

Admiring her? My dove?

A tingle licked along Sophia's spine, stroking along her back and ribs. She sipped at the champagne and stuttered some inadequate response.

Roxboro's lips tilted as if finding her utterly charming.

Nervous laughter burst from Sophia's lips. He'd reduced her to a giggling nitwit in mere seconds, which was terribly embarrassing, since she had long prided herself on not having anything in common with young ladies such as Hortensia.

But this was the Duke of Roxboro.

I'll be horrified tomorrow.

As Mama had so uncharitably pointed out, Sophia did read quite a bit and not all of those tomes were of an educational nature, though some might disagree. Lurid, romantic and overblown, with far too many inappropriate details. Mama didn't know about those. She thought Sophia was only immersed in the Romans. But in every one of those delicious tales, the heroine of the story was always struck dumb by the hero, who was most often a duke. Or a pirate. Sometimes a highwayman.

Roxboro's fingers trailed lightly over the bracelet on her wrist, tracing the sapphires before lingering over the top of her hand. So warm. And he wasn't wearing gloves which struck her as odd and—

"A breath of fresh air?" Words so soft, Sophia could barely hear them.

"I—" she stuttered once more. Much to her continued embarrassment.

Roxboro leaned close, the scent of wine on his breath. There was a freckle on the very tip of his nose, a small one. And an oval-shaped purple stain on his coat. He must have spilled on himself.

Well, he *was* supposed to be a sot. Sots spill on themselves.

Still, the stain gave her pause. Not the shape or the color. It was only wine. But Sophia had always heard that Roxboro was obsessed with his appearance, as only a vain, overly splendid duke could be. Dribbling wine on his coat, especially at a ball, didn't seem the sort of thing—

Lips brushed along the curve of her ear, startling Sophia from her thoughts of wine stains and producing the most profound effect on the tips of her breasts.

"I'm enamored, I confess."

With me? He's enamored with me?

She gulped her champagne. At this rate, Sophia would require another glass. Was this her second or her third?

"I intend to find your father this night and ask permission to call upon you," he murmured. "Would you like that, little dove?"

"Yes," she breathed, every fiber of her being focused on Roxboro. Not only would Papa be surprised, but Mara would be beside herself. Mama might faint and need to be carried out by the Perswick footmen.

"Let us take a stroll about the gardens so we might speak privately. I want to know everything about you, my dove."

Sophia nodded so hard, a curl fell from her careful coiffure. Never mind that this was all highly unusual. Roxboro and the champagne left her giddy. He was a duke. He wanted to court her. She ignored the whisper in the back of her mind, which sounded just like Mama, warning Sophia not to ever allow a gentleman liberties, especially in a dark garden. Duke or not.

Taking her arm, Roxboro led Sophia through the crowd and out the doors leading to the terrace, and beyond the gardens. The area was not deserted. A handful of other guests roamed about taking in the cooler night air. An older woman came forward who Sophia recognized instantly, Lady Brokeburst, who didn't bother to hide her surprise.

Lady Brokeburst liked to call upon Mama and remind her that at least she possessed one daughter who would marry well.

Sophia lifted her chin.

The older woman immediately sank low, head bowed. "Your Grace," she murmured.

Roxboro dismissed Lady Brokeburst with a flick of his wrist.

A great rush of satisfaction filled Sophia. A *duke* was guiding her about. Lord Canterbell's less admired daughter. Mara would be furious that Sophia had garnered Roxboro's attention.

He led her down the steps and onto the garden path, gravel crunching beneath their feet until they came upon a stone bench. A drooping willow tree partially hid them from view, though Sophia could clearly make out the terrace and Lady Brokeburst. The elderly woman had her head cocked at an angle attempting to eavesdrop.

Let her hear a duke declare for me.

Roses perfumed the air. Moonlight dappled the garden, allowing Sophia to see Roxboro's chiseled features so close to her own.

He's going to kiss me. Her pulse beat like a drum.

"I—we—shouldn't be out here, Your Grace."

"Nonsense. We'll be betrothed soon," he whispered. "Unless you are opposed, my dove."

Sophia shook her head, heart leaping into her throat, beating with such force, she begged it to still. This could not be happening. Roxboro couldn't truly want her, could he? And yet, Sophia couldn't seem to rush back to the safety of the terrace. His lovely eyes kept her pinned in place, even as he took her champagne glass and set it on the bench beside his empty wine goblet.

"Little dove," he said, one arm circling her waist.

Roxboro's mouth descended, claiming Sophia's. Gentle. Searching. His hand took hold of hers, thumb brushing along the sapphires of the bracelet on her wrist. Sandalwood mixed with the wine he'd been drinking caught in her nose.

This was it. A passionate kiss. One that will set me aflame.

Patiently, Sophia waited for...the fire to engulf her. Granted,

Sophia had little to no experience with gentlemen or kissing in general, but in her novels, there was a roar of passion at the mere press of the hero's lips.

But…nothing happened.

One big hand moved to glide along the slope of her breast, tracing the shape.

Still. Nothing.

Well, this is rather disappointing.

"Sophia!" The frantic call of Lord Canterbell reached Sophia beneath the willow tree. "Who is that with you?"

Roxboro immediately released her. He took a step back from Sophia.

Angry footsteps thundered down the path. "Unhand my daughter you—" A gasp filled the air as Papa caught sight of the man behind her.

"Tell him your intentions are honorable," she whispered. "He won't be angry. I promise."

A branch snapped beneath Roxboro's foot as his large form started to disappear into the darkened depths of the garden.

"Roxboro," she hissed, the realization dawning slowly, given the amount of champagne she'd consumed. "You promised to speak to my father about courting me."

There was no answer. Nothing but the slight breeze and the willow tree. Not even so much as a bloody cricket to break the awkward, embarrassing silence. The duke was… gone. If her lips weren't still tingling from his kiss, Sophia might have thought him nothing more than a champagne induced hallucination.

Every word he'd spoken had been a lie. There would be no courting. There was no admiration of her person.

Sophia's stomach pitched violently.

Oh, good lord, I'm foolish. Worse than Hortensia even if I do know who Lamb is.

"Roxboro?" Papa stomped forward, fists clenched at his sides, features contorted into absolute fury. "Flagrant rake. Debauched duke. Where is he?"

"No. I mean...yes. A gentleman was here, but not with me. Only...enjoying a cheroot." Sophia stammered. "Definitely not Roxboro." She cleared her throat. "I said I was relaxing. Here." One shaky hand trembled as she pointed out the bench. "You misunderstood me."

Oh. God. Sophia looked up to see the small cluster of guests lingering near the edge of the terrace.

"I saw the duke, though he hid in the shadows like a coward," Papa thundered. "As did Lady Brokeburst." Papa jerked his chin in the direction of the terrace. "Lying to me won't change the circumstances."

"No," Sophia shook her head so hard she wobbled and had to grasp at the trunk of the willow tree for support. She'd been...taken in by one of the biggest rakes in London. A walking vice. That's what the gossips called Roxboro. "You are wrong. Why on earth would I be here with a duke?"

Oh God. How could I have been so stupid?

Papa stared down at her with such disappointment. "You've been compromised, to my everlasting shame, by the Duke of Roxboro. What were you thinking coming out here with him?" He took her arm.

"I—" Everyone on the terrace was staring. More guests spilled through the doors. All coming to witness the ruination and abandonment of Lord Canterbell's unappealing daughter by the Duke of Roxboro.

"Don't worry," Papa's voice was gruff as he led her back towards the house. "He won't get away with this."

Sophia lowered her head. Papa was far too important for this incident to be brushed aside. Out of the corner of her eye, she caught sight of Lady Brokeburst.

"I'll fix everything," Papa said to her.

That's what I'm worried about.

Chapter Two

"Christ, my head aches. Bring me one of those powders, Timmons. And a glass of brandy to wash it down. Oakhurst was at his most outlandish last night."

Alexander Viceroy, Duke of Roxboro, sat back in his favorite chair with a deep sigh of satisfaction. Feeling poorly after a night carousing with Oakhurst wasn't unusual. His closest friend and drinking companion was an unrepentant libertine. Worse than even Alexander himself. But last night had been wild even for Oakhurst. Binson's first, for hazard and cards, of course. Then an opium den. And finally, a brothel near The Devil's Acre where the women catered to all manner of depraved sexual tastes.

"Yes, Your Grace," the butler bowed and rushed off to find something for his employer's pounding head.

Usually, Alexander enjoyed a great deal of depravity, but nearly having his throat slit by a naked prostitute who spoke nothing but French was more than even he'd bargained for. Oakhurst claimed the girl did the most interesting things with her tongue, so Alexander had followed her to a back room without a second thought, completely foxed and barely aware of his surroundings given the opium. When she'd tried to murder Alexander, for his purse he suspected, he'd fallen from the bed, hit the table beside it—*thank god he was prone to running into things, stubbing his toe and the like because it probably saved his life*—and rolled under the bed.

His would-be assailant let out a scream of frustration. Which alerted the burly gentleman standing guard at the top of the staircase. He rushed in and disarmed the murderous little trollop, hauling her away while Alexander struggled to get out from under the bed which was quite taxing given his intoxicated state. He flailed about like a fish until Oakhurst found him.

He debated on whether or not to tell the tale to his uncle. Damon Viceroy worried excessively over Alexander's well being, which, given his nephew's propensity to attract misfortune, was no surprise.

Oakhurst liked to say Alexander was the *Duke of Misadventure*.

He thought the nickname amusing, but Uncle Damon didn't care for it. Dukes were supposed to be…ducal. At any rate, Alexander's uncle didn't like Oakhurst and thought him a poor influence.

"Good lord, Timmons," Alexander said as the door opened. "I thought you'd never return. My temples ache so bad my ears might bleed."

A throat cleared. "You have callers, Your Grace."

Alexander opened one eye. "It isn't Freeman again, is it? I've signed everything he put before me yesterday."

Freeman was his secretary, a man so incredibly annoying, so lacking in humor, that Alexander often forgot he was in the room. Like a potted palm. Or a pasty colored vase. Freeman arrived, without warning, this morning, banging on the front door while Alexander was still in bed. Only Freeman would arrive before noon. Terribly uncouth. At any rate, Damon handled all of Alexander's personal affairs as well as those of the vast Viceroy empire. Estate matters and the like didn't interest Alexander one whit. Freeman should have known better.

"You refused him entry earlier. Send him away again, Timmons."

Timmons lowered his gaze to the rug. "It was not Mr. Freeman, earlier, Your Grace."

"I don't care. Pour me a brandy." Perhaps it had been his

cousin, Violet, though if it had been, she would have marched into his bedroom with absolutely no reservations at waking him.

Timmons placed a tray on the table beside Alexander with a twist of paper atop and proceeded directly to the sideboard. He poured out a snifter of brandy and carefully set it beside the headache powder.

"Timmons, what is wrong with you?" Alexander scoffed. "That's barely a thimbleful. Hardly enough to wet my tongue."

"Apologies, Your Grace." The butler returned to the sideboard and filled the snifter to the very top before returning it to Alexander.

He swallowed the headache powder, took several large gulps of brandy, and closed his eyes, waiting for the pounding in his temples to ease.

"Your Grace," Timmons said once more. "Your callers—"

"Not so loudly, Timmons. Oakhurst was in rare form last evening. I don't even recall the carriage ride home. I assume Stone put me to bed?" It wasn't the first time his valet had done so, nor would it be the last. "I seem to recall Lady Maxell. Did she come inside?"

Before Timmons could answer, the voice of Lord Damon Viceroy thundered down the hall in the direction of the drawing room.

"Where is he? Where is Timmons?"

The butler paled.

Alexander cast one bleary eye at Timmons. "Tell Uncle Damon we can speak later," he ordered. "I'm recovering."

"I think not, nephew," his uncle growled from the drawing room door. "We will speak now."

"Not so loud, I beg you." Alexander pressed a hand to his aching temple.

"Timmons, please ask Lord Canterbell to give me a moment with the duke before he comes storming in," Damon snapped.

"Yes, my lord." Timmons scurried out, shutting the door behind him.

The appearance of his uncle was usually a welcome occurrence, given the closeness of their relationship, but not when his head felt as if it were splitting open. "Good morning, uncle." Alexander attempted to sit straighter. Damon was obviously put out about something. Probably either Violet or Rose, Alexander mused. His cousins liked to cause their father no end of grief.

"What have you done, you imbecile?" Damon stomped to the sideboard. "And it is two o'clock in the afternoon."

"I had a lengthy evening." Alexander rubbed one eye. "I don't think that cause to insult me."

Damon glared at him, glancing at the still closed door of the drawing room. "I'm here about your evening, as it happens."

"Fine. I lost a large sum at Binson's but it isn't as if I can't afford to. And in my defense, Lady Hastings kept leaning over the hazard table as I threw the dice and her gown was exquisite and showed a great deal of bosom. She distracted me." Alexander chuckled. "I imagine that is why Freeman was banging on the door at an ungodly hour. Not Lady Hastings, but the rather large marker at Binson's."

Alexander was fairly certain he'd tupped Lady Hastings against the wall of the gambling hell. Discreetly, of course. But matters were somewhat blurry.

His uncle poured out a snifter of brandy. Drained it, then poured another. "Freeman is in Sussex at the moment. On business." The chiseled features, so like Alexander's own save for the eyes which were so dark they resembled onyx, hardened.

"Goodness." Alexander managed to keep himself upright. "You are in an incredibly foul mood. Did someone compromise Violet?"

Violet was bound to be ruined at some point. She sometimes accompanied Alexander to Binson's wearing a mask and a wig. If Damon ever found out, he'd marry Violet off to that dull earl who kept sniffing about her skirts. Rose wasn't much better, just more discreet. Alexander adored them both.

"No, Violet didn't ruin herself," Damon ground out. "But

someone has been ruined." Icy cold rage twisted his features as his gaze settled on Alexander. "After all my cautionary tales. Knowing how your father was trapped by your mother in much the same manner. Yet you still—" He cursed softly under his breath.

"What? I'm not sure—"

"Only widows. Courtesans. Barmaids. *Trollops*," Damon returned. "No one of importance. No virginal young ladies or you'd end up—well, now I must reconsider…" The words trailed off as Damon paced across the rug, looking at the closed drawing room door. "Matters."

"What is it you think I've done?" His head throbbed and Damon's pacing was making him dizzy. "And what matters?"

"I can't fix this, Alexander." Damon shook his head. "At least not immediately. You weren't even discreet. Good lord, of all the cliches, taking liberties with a young lady in the gardens during a ball," he snarled. "A bloody ball. And now Canterbell—"

"Canterbell? You mean the chap in Parliament you're always attempting to curry favor with?" Damon was deeply involved in politics. His ambitions were no great secret to Alexander or his daughters. Prime Minister, probably. Or a minister of some sort.

"I am Lord Damon Viceroy. I have no need to cozy up to anyone." His voice lowered. "But it is never a bad idea to have Canterbell's support. And now." He stopped before Alexander. "You've mucked things up. As if falling off that pleasure barge in the Thames wasn't bad enough—"

"That was an accident," Alexander interrupted. "I was a bit foxed."

"As you were likely last night when you took a young lady into the gardens. Now he's here, in your foyer, demanding that you be honorable." Damon snorted. "With his daughter. And not even the beautiful one."

"Who?" Alexander had no idea what his uncle was talking about. The conversation had failed to make sense since the mention of Freeman, who apparently hadn't been knocking the front door down early this morning.

"Canterbell, you *idiot*." Damon shut his eyes, as if the sight of Alexander was too much to bear. "You don't even know what you've done. Last evening—"

"I was with Oakhurst. And Lady Maxwell." Alexander frowned. "At some point."

"Stop interrupting. You compromised Lord Canterbell's daughter at the Perswick ball. A fact," his voice raised a fraction. "Of which I was apprised while attempting to enjoy my eggs at breakfast. Poached, if you must know. Perfect. But they had gone cold by the time Canterbell was done informing me of your behavior because you couldn't be roused to receive him."

Well, that explained the early morning banging on the door.

"This is easily remedied." Alexander flicked a wrist. "I wasn't at the Perswick ball. I don't even think I was invited. Lady Perswick doesn't like me." She'd tried to seduce Alexander once and when he refused, called him a debauched duke unworthy of her time. "Besides, proper young ladies hold no appeal for me. You've warned me away often enough, reciting the dangers they represent to an unwed duke and I—*oh*."

No. Impossible. I wouldn't have.

"Oh, indeed." Damon smoothed down his coat, with one hand. "Whether Lady Perswick likes you or not isn't of importance because apparently, you did attend her ball at least long enough to take Canterbell's daughter into the bloody gardens."

"But I wasn't there." He had no recollection of attending such a tepid, boring event. Alexander didn't even dance due to…his ability to attract misfortune. No point in embarrassing himself before the *ton*. Undignified for a duke unless the duke was foxed, which he often happened to be. "Pure nonsense. Wait, is this some sort of a jest? Did Oakhurst put you up to this?" Alexander shook his head. "Excellent. I shall have to find a way to get even with that rogue."

The drawing room door opened barely a crack to reveal Timmons. "I apologize, my lord, but…Lord Canterbell and Lady

Sophia wish to be admitted. Immediately. Lord Canterbell is most insistent."

Alexander's eyes widened. "You invited them here? No." He held up his palm to Timmons. "Send them away. I'm not well. Not at home."

I didn't compromise some chit.

The pounding in his temples increased.

But neither could Alexander remember…arriving home in the carriage. Or Stone putting him to bed. Not entirely unusual, though he typically had some memory of his nights with Oakhurst. But the previous evening stayed…ominously blank after the incident at the brothel.

"We will not be denied entry, Your Grace." A distinguished gentleman with a wealth of snowy white hair stepped into the room, his stance reminding Alexander of a boxer about to enter the ring. Disdain, solely directed at Alexander, pulled his lips into a sneer. "I didn't wish to cool my heels any longer, Lord Damon. This matter is most urgent. The gossip began to circulate before we even left Lady Perswick's. Now it is rampant."

"Canterbell." Damon inclined his head. "My apologies that you were kept waiting. I wished to speak to my nephew privately before our broader discussion."

Canterbell made a grunt, eyeing Alexander with dislike, not even bothering to bow. Which was quite disrespectful.

The sound of skirts caught his ear as a young woman arrived behind Lord Canterbell, a hooded cloak covering her from head to toe, giving no indication of her shape or features.

Canterbell nudged her forward. "My daughter, Lady Sophia Simmons."

Slender fingers jerked back the hood, revealing a completely ordinary young woman.

I was expecting a great beauty if I ruined her.

As if she'd heard his thoughts, Lady Sophia's chin lifted, eyes meeting his with murderous intent. She didn't look at all pleased to be here, or even triumphant at possibly bagging a duke.

If I compromised her. *Which I didn't.*
Alexander crossed his legs. *Hostile chit.*

She dropped into the most awkward curtsey he'd ever seen, like a puppet being jerked about by strings. Had he not been so utterly appalled at the situation, Alexander might have laughed.

"Your Grace," she managed to choke out, with even less respect than her father.

Damon subtly kicked Alexander's foot, urging him to stand.

The room spun a bit as he came to his feet. He fixed Lady Sophia with a dismissive look of his own.

"Every female in London tosses themselves in your direction, yet that wasn't enough, was it? You had to lure my daughter—" Canterbell clamped his mouth shut, before holding up a palm to Damon. "Apologies, my lord. I promised to hold my temper, but I am most...distressed."

"I believe we all are," Damon answered.

I don't even find her appealing, let alone worthy of compromise.

Had he seen Lady Sophia on the street, or at one of the few society events he attended, she wouldn't have attracted his notice. Hair a plain light brown. Eyes the same hue. Not too short or tall. A trifle plump. Unremarkable in every way.

Except for the mouth. That's rather nice.

Maybe her bosom was lovely. Alexander couldn't tell as it was hidden beneath the cloak.

No weeping. No quivering in shame for having been ruined. No sign of any humiliation at her situation. Only righteous indignation, as if by his mere presence, Alexander offended her.

"Your Grace." Damon sounded exhausted to the very marrow of his bones.

"I've never seen this girl before in my life," Alexander declared, *almost* certain he had not. Ducal arrogance would make it completely true. Convince Canterbell of his error. He waved his hand in dismissal at the earl and his daughter. "Obviously, this is a fabrication. Perhaps Lady Sally—"

"Sophia," she snarled back at him.

Alexander gave a roll of his shoulders, the only other movement he could manage without becoming dizzy. "My mistake." He didn't care what her name happened to be. A great many women had been kissed, fondled and seduced by him, and he had yet to forget a face, no matter his level of intoxication. This girl was unknown to him whether her pompous, overbearing father believed it or not. "I'm not sure who you were cavorting with in the Perswick gardens, only that it wasn't *me*."

She inhaled sharply.

Canterbell crossed his arms, eyes narrowing on Alexander.

"Timmons will show you out." He wanted these two opportunists out of his house so that he could lie down. Perhaps send for Oakhurst and find out if he'd drank something out of the ordinary the previous evening. Gin, perhaps? From the Rookery?

"Are you calling me a liar, Roxboro?" Canterbell regarded him blandly. "Me. The Lord Speaker of Parliament."

"My lord," Damon said hurriedly. "I'm sure that isn't what the duke is inferring."

"No, I would never accuse you of lying." He turned to Lady Whatever. "I'm accusing her. Your daughter." Alexander pressed a finger to his forehead. Would this headache ever dissipate? If Oakhurst had plied him with tainted gin, Alexander would kill him, friend or not. "You might require spectacles. Or is it only that you wish to be a duchess and saw a chance at achieving such prominence?"

"You—" the girl dared to hiss at him.

"I saw you myself." Canterbell came forward. "Lady Brokeburst watched you walk my daughter into the gardens, shortly before she decided to inform half of Lady Perswick's guests that she'd witnessed your lechery."

"Impossible. I did not attend Lady Perswick's ball," Alexander protested, glancing at Damon. "She detests me."

"I don't wonder," the savage little chit said under her breath.

"And," Alexander continued with all certainty, "as such would never have invited me. Even had I decided to attend, which I did not, Lady Perswick would have denied me entry."

That was an exaggeration. He was still a duke, though a disreputable one. Lady Perswick would have greeted him with a kiss to the cheek all the while murmuring her dislike.

"Interesting, Your Grace." Canterbell's cheeks had gone red with anger. "Lord Lacton stopped me as I led my daughter outside to our carriage while attempting to protect her from censure. Lacton had already heard the gossip spreading throughout the ballroom and confirmed he'd seen you. As did Lady Lacton. And Lady Stafford's daughter, Hortensia, as she repeated to my lady wife," he paused, "that she'd seen you lead Sophia out to the terrace."

Alexander swallowed, at a loss for words. There were witnesses? To his appearance at a ball he never would have attended? "I was—"

"In your cups? A near constant state, I understand, given your love of spirits," Canterbell interjected with disgust. "I doubt you know where you are half the time, Your Grace."

"Canterbell," Damon growled in warning.

The older man merely raised a brow at Alexander's uncle, not at all intimidated. "Rest assured, there is no one in this room less pleased with this turn of events than I. Any other gentleman in London is preferable. Even Haywood would be an improvement," he bit out.

That's rather insulting.

The Duke of Haywood was wealthy but rumored to have the pox, and resembled a withered toadstool.

"If I lured her, and I'm not saying I did," Alexander sputtered, trying to sound ducal and failing. "She allowed me to do so, did she not? Does Lady Saffron—"

"Sophia," Canterbell corrected him.

"Fine. Does she not share some of the blame?" Alexander looked at the girl standing before him. Hostility rolled off her in waves. "I'm a duke, after all. And she is—"

"How dare you," Canterbell growled. "Libertine."

"My lord." Damon pinched the bridge of his nose. "Your Grace. Please. Let us discuss things rationally without resorting to insults. Lord Canterbell, your opinion of the Duke of Roxboro is duly noted, and further disparagement is not necessary."

"My daughter smelled of champagne as I hurried her to our carriage. You likely plied her with glasses of the stuff, intent on taking liberties," Canterbell accused.

Frankly, that *did* sound like something Alexander would do. But he hadn't. Because he wasn't there.

He was...somewhat certain.

"I did not lure Lady Susan—"

"Sophia." The girl scowled back at him. "Have the courtesy to address me correctly." She paused, evidently waiting for him to notice *she* didn't bother to address *him* properly.

Alexander and Damon observed her blunt outburst with a great deal of shock.

Canterbell, with resignation.

One did not speak to a duke in such a manner. *Ever.* Her lack of manners was appalling. He would have expected better from Canterbell's daughter. Lowered eyes. Perhaps a softer manner. Good lord, where were her tears at the supposed damage to her reputation?

His fingers drummed against one thigh.

Which made her far more interesting than her appearance would suggest.

Chapter Three

Surveying the handsome sot of a duke sitting as if he didn't have a bloody care in the world when he'd destroyed her very existence filled Sophia with impotent rage. She'd never been so bloody angry in her life. Or so mortified. Suffering from an overindulgence in drink and lord knew what else, Roxboro clearly didn't recall their—

Meeting? Ruination? Tepid kiss?

—from the night before.

How absolutely humiliating.

Granted, Sophia didn't appeal to a great many gentlemen in London, not like her sister. Or Horrid Hortensia. But one man or two had found her…challenging. The kindest word used in reference to her manner. Opinionated was typically the other.

One of Mara's ardent suitors had declared Sophia…*tart*.

I am not a bloody lemon.

She'd told the gentleman as much, in possibly a less than polite way, which didn't exactly endear Sophia to anyone. Mama, as usual, had been disappointed.

At any rate, this detestable incident was entirely the fault of her sister. Had Mara not begged Lord Wilde to dance with Sophia, leaving her with no dignity whatsoever, she wouldn't have wandered off to drink champagne behind a potted fern.

Nor would she have conversed with Roxboro. She certainly wouldn't have allowed this—*dissolute libertine*—to lead her into the Perswick gardens.

Why did I call out his name? Loud enough for Papa to hear?

Sophia had not been considering the ramifications of doing so, nor anything at all beyond her foolishness in believing Roxboro's words.

Admired her in the park.

Ha!

Saw her walking.

Laughable.

Sophia had been so enamored of his attention. So enthralled with his presence, she'd failed to note that not only did he not refer to her father by name, but Roxboro never once said *her* name. This feckless sot with his head lolling about before her thought she was called Saffron. Or Susan.

Considering him now, Sophia questioned her sanity, if not her intelligence, at being so taken with Roxboro.

But the one thing Sophia was absolutely certain, besides the previously mentioned stupidity, was that it *had* been Roxboro last night. The duke was blindingly handsome in a way few other men could claim. Completely unfair given his character. And no other man in London possessed those shimmering green eyes with their streaks of silver. Sophia recalled every inch of Roxboro's appearance that night, right down to the wine stain on his coat and the sandalwood on his skin. Lady Brokeburst had *curtsied* to him. Other guests bowed when he passed and softly whispered, "Your Grace."

Vile cad.

A bit of flirtation was acceptable. Even a kiss wasn't entirely improper. Mara had kisses stolen all the time. But Roxboro leading Sophia to believe he admired and wished to court her was nothing short of cruelty. He was just another jaded rake using a stupid young girl for his own amusement, only this time, he'd been caught.

Filthy libertine.

"I swear, upon my honor—"

Sophia snorted in derision. Roxboro had no honor. Papa would insist on marriage, despite her protests. She had no desire to be wed to this...this...sot.

"I have never seen you before." Scorn flashed in those beautiful eyes. Eyes that had looked at her with such longing in the moonlight of the Perswick gardens. Whispered such lovely things in her ear. And Sophia had felt...desired. Wanted. For the first time in her life.

Now, all she felt was mortification.

Everyone in London was already whispering that the Duke of Roxboro had been so foxed, so completely intoxicated, he'd unintentionally compromised Lord Canterbell's daughter. And not the pretty one.

If I could vanish this instant, I would.

Sophia took a step towards him, the brandy fumes tickling her nostrils, thinking how Papa had grabbed Sophia's hand, pulling her through the crowd at Lady Perswick's even as dozens of eyes turned in her direction.

Good lord, but Lady Brokeburst worked quickly.

Mama, leading Mara, had appeared, her rounded features contorted into panic. "My lord," she'd whispered. "There is a rumor circulating."

"Hortensia." Mara gulped. "She said...well, it cannot be true."

Papa dragged them all, especially Sophia, in his wake. "We must leave. Now. Do not say a word until we are inside the carriage."

Mama's eyes had filled with tears. "Oh, no."

Mara had regarded Sophia with disbelief. "Sophia?"

"Hurry," Papa had said, ushering them all out. "Lady Brokeburst is a bigger gossip than I suspected. I had hoped for a modicum of discretion given I am friends with her husband. I regret to say I'm disappointed."

The escape from the Perswick ball had been filled with Mama's torrential weeping. Mara just stared at Sophia in shock;

likely put out she hadn't been ruined by a drunken duke.

Lord Damon cleared his throat, dispelling the events of the previous night from Sophia's thoughts and bringing her back to this overly lavish drawing room full of gilt and finely carved furniture. There was a hideous collection of porcelain dogs on one table and a portrait of a gentleman who vaguely resembled Roxboro above the fireplace. A relative, she assumed.

"You will address the duke politely or not at all, Lady Sophia." Lord Damon regarded her with the sort of contempt one reserves for a lesion-covered beggar in the street.

"I choose not at all," she whispered under her breath, which thankfully, no one seemed to hear.

Papa cleared his throat. He had excellent hearing.

"Lady Brokeburst," Papa started. "Has already spread the word. Frankly, I wouldn't be surprised if she hasn't mentioned the incident to enough of the other guests that an item will appear in the gossip column of the newspaper."

Sophia looked down at Roxboro's finely crafted Oriental rug beneath her feet, wishing to disappear into the swirls of blue and gold.

"That is…unfortunate," Lord Damon agreed. "Lady Brokeburst is one of the worst gossips in London." He shot a look in his nephew's direction. "You might have acted with more prudence."

"Or acted not at all," Papa huffed. "There is only one solution to the damage that has been done to my daughter's reputation, Your Grace."

Sophia bit her lip. This was entirely unfair.

Roxboro looked askance at both Lord Damon and Papa. "No."

She wholeheartedly returned the duke's sentiment, even though not wedding her would make Sophia a pariah in society. Roxboro was beyond magnificent, even reeking of brandy, but he was otherwise…*unacceptable*. Dishonest and cruel. An unscrupulous rake who'd teased her affections so that he might take advantage.

And I believed him. Every word.

An error in judgement. One Sophia did not wish to compound by marrying Roxboro.

"Your Grace," Lord Damon said to his nephew. "The situation is unfortunate."

Sophia bristled. She was the injured party. "For me, especially."

Lord Damon regarded her with thinly veiled contempt. He'd barely acknowledged her presence in the drawing room, probably faulting her for this entire situation instead of putting the blame where it was due, on Roxboro.

She returned his scathing assessment.

Damon Viceroy had political aspirations. Papa had mentioned him once or twice before now, but Sophia hadn't paid much attention. Prime Minister, that was Lord Damon's goal according to Papa, and if he wanted to achieve such an office, he could not make an enemy of Lord Canterbell. Papa was not only Lord Speaker, but he also held Her Majesty's ear. Honor had not forced Lord Damon to open the door when Papa called on him this morning, but ambition.

"We cannot allow Lady Sophia's reputation to be damaged. Or her honor," Lord Damon intoned, sounding as arrogant as his nephew. She highly doubted he gave a fig for her reputation.

Sophia wanted to scream out that she had *barely* been compromised. Dozens of other young ladies throughout the Season had a kiss stolen by an attractive gentleman. No liberties had been taken. And on the whole, Roxboro's kiss was…adequate but rather bland. Not one spark. No passion. No grand seduction. She shouldn't have to suffer marriage to him because of it. Or because Lady Brokeburst couldn't keep her mouth firmly shut. Sophia might have…been able to convince everyone—

Don't be ridiculous. He is a degenerate of the highest order. And you were in his company.

Sophia studied the rug once more.

Adding to the tragedy of last evening, Mama's sapphire bracelet had been lost. Fallen off while she was busy receiving a disappointing kiss from Roxboro. Mama would ask after it eventually, not now of course, Sophia's scandal was too great. She hadn't even noticed the loss until the entire family was in the carriage headed home last night, hiding her wrist as Mama wept and castigated her.

Which meant that the bracelet was somewhere beneath Lady Perswick's willow tree along with what was left of Sophia's reputation.

She peered at the drunken lout in distaste. The loss of the bracelet was his fault. As if *another* reason was necessary to dislike Roxboro.

"Unfortunate, indeed." Roxboro looked her up and down, like some horse he didn't wish to buy. Or a bit of spoiled pudding on his plate.

Her fingers twitched in the direction of one of the hideous porcelain dogs. A spaniel, she thought, though the artist was terrible. She could knock it to the floor, just to annoy him. Or better, toss it at his arrogant, brandy-smelling head.

"I've no desire to wed her," Roxboro drawled in his self-important manner. "I refuse. This entire scene, this display, is complete tripe. She's lying and took advantage of me while I was not clear-headed."

"Soaked in brandy," Sophia muttered.

Roxboro shot her a look before turning to his uncle. "I am the injured party in this situation."

"Your Grace," Lord Damon whispered.

"Her lover fled—or some random gentleman she was committing improprieties with—he abandoned her in the gardens and now, I am meant to pay for his—"

"Are you actually insinuating that I orchestrated this?" she seethed. In all her life, Sophia had never disliked a human being more than this overprivileged, condescending, ill-tempered sot. He was more spoiled brat than a notorious libertine.

"Yes," Roxboro said in a bored tone.

"No title." Sophia clasped her hands to keep from launching herself at him. "Not even that of duchess, is worth having to wed you." The words dripped with sarcasm.

Roxboro blinked as if she'd slapped the smug smile off his face.

"Send me away, I beg you," she pleaded with her father. "I'll go live in...Vienna, never to return. I'll tell no one who I am. Change my name. Become a paid companion." Sophia drew in a breath. "Anything would be better than to be shackled to this—this...*wastrel*."

Lord Damon's nostrils flared. He was *definitely* paying attention to her now. "Perhaps—"

"Sophia, that is quite enough." Papa interrupted her before she could say more, grabbing hold of her arm and shooting Lord Damon a pointed look. "No more of this nonsense."

The green of Roxboro's eyes clouded first in surprise and then outrage. His lovely mouth thinned until his lips disappeared. So accustomed to being worshipped, disreputable duke or not, he was struck speechless by Sophia's assessment of being wed to him.

"You do not wish to wed me," Roxboro said slowly.

"You are catching on, Your Grace. I knew you were more intelligent—" Papa stopped the rest of her sentence with a pinch to her arm.

Roxboro sat back. Rubbed his temples. "Well, there you have it. Lady Sabrina and I are in agreement—"

"Sophia," she and Father said at the same time.

"Regardless," Roxboro drawled. "This chit and I are in accord. No marriage. She's willing to go elsewhere and live a life of obscurity rather than wed me and I am in agreement. Any union between us would be an utter catastrophe. We'll say Lady Brokeburst is half-blind." His head fell back against the chair as he closed his eyes once more. "I bid you good day."

Roxboro deserved a well-placed kick to the shin.

A choking sound came from Papa, one borne of rage and disgust. One did not dismiss Lord Canterbell, as Roxboro's uncle surely knew.

Lord Damon watched his nephew, dark eyes gleaming with calculation. The duke was ignorant of what was at stake, but his uncle was not. Lord Canterbell held the ear of Her Majesty. He controlled Parliament. And he would not be denied. Roxboro would be forced to capitulate.

I would rather become a scullery maid in Paris.

"I will not allow my daughter to become a pariah because of your love of scotch. Or brandy, Your Grace." Papa lifted a brow and turned to Lord Damon. "I must insist," a thinly veiled threat laced his words. "On honor, my lord. I'm sure you can make the duke see reason." There was steel in Papa's tone.

Lord Damon dipped his chin.

Papa would make Lord Damon's life, and that of the duke, incredibly difficult. Her father's influence was highly sought after and he was powerful, with a web of connections in society and government. Roxboro, even as a duke, was no match for Lord Canterbell. Nor was his uncle. Damon Viceroy, no matter his wealth and pedigree, would not ascend any further in politics, or at all, if his nephew didn't wed Sophia.

There was no getting out of this marriage for either of them. The only person who didn't realize it was Roxboro.

"My lord," Lord Damon's tone was smooth. Conciliatory. "Might we discuss the pertinent details of this union in private? Perhaps at your solicitor's tomorrow? The duke is…under the weather at present."

"Ten o'clock," Papa grunted with satisfaction. "Wellingham and Sons. I'll have the marriage contract prepared for your review."

A tiny snore came from Roxboro. He'd nodded off. Apparently, the conversation couldn't hold his interest. The sot.

Papa and Lord Damon barely spared him a glance.

Sophia pressed a palm to her stomach at the thought of her

future with the duke. Perhaps once wed, Roxboro might...simply forget she existed, just as he was doing now. He might send her away to the country to live out her days. The idea held a great deal of promise.

Her stomach twisted again.

The butler had brought nothing in the way of refreshments. How she longed for something to assuage the pitching sensation. A scone, perhaps. Or a biscuit. She would even take a tart, though they weren't her favorite.

"Tomorrow then, Lord Canterbell. Lady Sophia." Damon politely bowed, though his eyes on Sophia remained brittle and full of condemnation.

"One more small matter, Lord Damon," Papa paused as he started to guide Sophia towards the door. "I want not a whiff of scandal attached to my Sophia. I think it best we put out some sort of explanation for the events of last evening. A secret courtship, perhaps. Her Majesty enjoys such things. She has a most romantic nature."

Lord Damon's features rippled briefly with anger at the suggestion, but his features smoothed as he nodded. "I understand, my lord. I bid you both good day."

Chapter Four

Alexander was jolted back to consciousness by the snapping of his uncle's fingers directly in front of his nose.

"Wake up. You fell asleep."

"Sorry. I'm still recovering from last evening." Alexander sat up and cracked an eye to survey the room. "Oh, they're gone. Thank goodness. The entire discussion was ridiculous. I wouldn't ruin that little harpy if you begged me. Did you hear the way she spoke to me? I hope you sent them packing and informed Canterbell that under no circumstances would I wed the shrew. I don't care what they claim."

"You missed a few pertinent points, Your Grace," Damon returned in a tired voice.

"She's lying. Anyone can see it." Alexander said, his legs only a little unsteady, as he stood and made his way to the sideboard. "Another brandy?"

Damon did not look pleased. Not at all. "Yes, thank you." The lines of his jaw grew taut. "You were at the Perswick ball, Alexander."

"I was not. I was with Oakhurst and Lady Maxwell. I distinctly recall Lady Maxwell commenting on my coat and asking when I'd had time to change it." Alexander shrugged. "I've no idea what she meant. But at any rate, I wasn't there. Lady Perswick detests Oakhurst even more than me. We would never have attended."

"Oakhurst is untrustworthy." There was an ugly glint in

Damon's eye. "And you are usually full of scotch in his company. How would you know…anything?" His uncle took the refilled glass from Alexander's hand.

"Even if I had been there, by some…miracle. I would never have touched that girl."

"Alexander."

"If she were compromised, which considering her personality I find…improbable, it would have to be a desperate man, or perhaps one that was blind. Or, someone far worse than I."

"Worse than you?"

Alexander waved a hand and nearly fell into a table. "Yes. A…tradesman perhaps. Or a footman."

"So this tradesman resembled you?" Damon scoffed. "Enough to convince Lord Canterbell and Lady Brokeburst? Do you realize how ridiculous that sounds?"

It did sound unlikely. Alexander, while he enjoyed his brandy a great deal, also dressed exceedingly well. No footman could carry off the coat he was presently wearing, for instance.

"Perhaps it is a scheme of Canterbell's to make his daughter a duchess."

"You can't possibly—does Canterbell strike you as the sort of gentleman to make false accusations? Do you sense any dishonesty in one of Her Majesty's most trusted confidants?" Damon's voice rose.

"But even had I—she's unappealing." Alexander took a swallow of brandy, letting the liquid burn a path down his throat. "I would never have engaged that chit in conversation, let alone lured her into the darkness for a kiss," he stated dramatically before falling back into his chair. "Good lord, she's terrible."

Alexander, as a rule, didn't mind terrible. Had she behaved in such a manner towards him at the Perswick ball, he might have— *No, absolutely not.* He wasn't there.

"Just because I'm accused of lechery by that old bat, Lady Brokeburst, doesn't mean I must wed Canterbell's daughter. Lady Brokeburst is nearly eighty. She has terrible eyesight and—"

"Marriage." Damon paced back and forth across the rug before pausing before the window, his back to Alexander.

"Marriage," Alexander repeated, bitterness flooding his tongue. This was a catastrophe. He didn't want to wed anyone. Honestly, he'd always assumed he'd drop dead before having to do his duty and provide Roxboro with an heir given the way he lived. Damon was still hale and not yet fifty. He'd inherit and make a much better duke than Alexander.

"I'll find a way out of this quagmire. This is only a setback to my plans," he said, turning to face Alexander. "All is not lost."

Damon's plans. His political aspirations.

A wash of regret filled Alexander. Damon's sole purpose in life was not...*him*. Or at least it shouldn't be any longer. "I—played hazard at Binson's. Tupped Lady Hastings. Stopped at the opium den."

Damon pinched the bridge of his nose. "I should hang Oakhurst from the rafters for his care of you last evening."

"The visit to the brothel after the opium den is less clear." Except for nearly having his throat slit, which he decided not to share with his uncle. Damon disapproved of Oakhurst. "There was a great deal of scotch involved. Possibly gin. Opium. Naked breasts on at least two occasions. I don't recall much after that," he admitted.

"A walking vice. You are living up to your name, nephew, and which taints Violet and Rose by association." Damon raised a brow.

"I'm not to blame for their behavior."

"Not all of it. But you set a poor example of a duke. When I encouraged you to enjoy life, take your pleasures as Charles never had a chance to—well, I didn't think you would become London's worst libertine."

The mention of Charles Viceroy never failed to dampen the mood.

Damon lived with the knowledge he hadn't been able to save the older brother he'd adored. Alexander's father, Charles, had been murdered by thugs. Dragged from his carriage and stabbed so many times the wounds couldn't even be counted properly. Damon suspected the assailants had been hired by Lord Cotswold, the lover of Alexander's mother, Marianne.

The thought of his mother had Alexander's stomach souring.

Cotswold was an adversary of Charles in Parliament as well as Marianne's lover. Damon pushed aside the gossip and his suspicions, not wanting to believe Charles was truly in danger. He blamed himself for his brother's death and as his penance, shouldered all the responsibility of Roxboro. Alexander was never given any duties. No obligations. Only told to pursue his pleasures. Live the life Charles hadn't been allowed.

"I doubt I'll be stabbed, unless I trip and fall on the blade myself." Alexander gave a short laugh to lighten the mood.

"Don't make a joke," Damon said quietly. "I live with my regret every day. Cotswold is dead and will never see justice." His shoulders sagged. "But do you see how the situation you find yourself in is similar to your father's? Marianne was an ambitious woman. One who would never have become a duchess except through dishonest means. She, too, accused Charles of ruination." His brow furrowed. "I should have demanded answers from Marianne. Made Philpot believe me."

Philpot had been the previous duke's solicitor.

"But I was barely twenty," Damon said. "Something of a rake myself." Sadness laced his words. "And I thought all marriages to be so contentious. I had no idea, until it was too late, that your mother—I failed Charles."

"You did not. You have given me everything. Raised me as your own." Alexander shut his eyes at the light streaming through the window. He really needed to lay down. "You would never fail me."

Damon gave him a sad smile. "Yet I've allowed you to fall prey to the same circumstances as your father. I do not think Canterbell capable of such deceit. But his daughter? She is another matter entirely."

"I blame Oakhurst." Alexander pressed a palm to his forehead. "I think he may have purchased some gin that wasn't—I think it must be from St. Giles given the way I feel today. And while I do not believe I was ever at the Perswick ball, I admit that I cannot account for the appearance of Lady Maxwell in our carriage." His brows drew together, sending a sharp pain through his temples.

Damon turned to face the window once more.

"Thank goodness you changed your coat, Your Grace. The wine stain was quite unlike you."

Alexander could hear Lady Maxwell's voice in his mind quite clearly. He'd been annoyed at her because not only would he not permit his clothing to be stained, but Alexander didn't drink wine. Ever. He'd had a most unpleasant experience with the stuff when a lad. The smell alone made him ill.

"But you recall the brothel you visited?" his uncle asked.

"Music. Perfume. Great loads of scotch. Oakhurst can tell us." Alexander sat up. "Timmons," he summoned the butler who stood just outside. "Send a messenger to Oakhurst immediately. Ask him to call upon me. The matter is most urgent."

Timmons bowed. "Forgive me, Your Grace. But Lord Oakhurst has left for the Continent. He was to sail this morning."

Damon turned from his perusal of the street outside. "Oakhurst has fled to the Continent?" he said in a casual tone, though his entire body grew taut. "How like him to leave you with such a debacle."

"I know you don't like him, Damon. But he's my closest friend." Alexander looked at the butler. "How do you know of Oakhurst's plans, Timmons? Were you eavesdropping again?"

"No, Your Grace. He…mentioned as much after arriving with you, though you…may not recall. Lady Maxwell waved goodbye from the carriage window. I recognized her as she…has called upon you several times in the past." The butler paused, stared at the floor, uncomfortable at the news he was forced to relate.

Bloody hell.

What Timmons meant, by his stumbling speech, was that Lady Maxwell and Alexander had been lovers for a time, and she'd stayed the night more than once. Timmons had seen her breasts in at least one instance after throwing open the door of Alexander's study upon hearing her scream while she was being tupped. Terribly embarrassing for Timmons. He was something of a prude.

Alexander and Felicia were no longer lovers and hadn't been for at least a year. They'd parted amicably. And it wouldn't have been the first time he and Oakhurst had shared lovers. So why had his friend never mentioned taking up with her?

"Did Oakhurst leave me a note? Or an address where I might reach him?"

The butler eyed him with regret. "I'm afraid not, Your Grace."

Well, this was unwelcome. Alexander had no way to reach Oakhurst. How was he to unravel the mystery of his whereabouts last night without his friend?

"Send a note to his staff. Surely, they'll know where to find him."

"Yes, Your Grace." Timmons hurried off.

"How like Oakhurst," Damon drawled. "Fleeing at a moment's notice, without regard for others."

"I don't think he fled purposefully, Damon," Alexander mused. "Nor do I think his absence is because of anything that may have happened last night. I doubt it has anything to do with me. He likes Paris a great deal. As does Lady Maxwell."

"I suppose we cannot confirm whether you were at the Perswick ball. Not from Oakhurst, at least. But given Canterbell's visit, I fear his confirmation isn't necessary. If what he says is true about Lady Brokeburst."

"I could not have been there," Alexander insisted. "I would not have forgotten an entire ball."

At least, he didn't think so.

"How can you even be sure?" his uncle thundered back at him. "You can't even recall making it to your bed last night. For all I know, you lifted Lady Sophia's skirts in the garden. Fucked her on a bench."

"No one would believe that of me." Alexander tried to sound convincing.

"Don't be an imbecile. No one will believe *you*, nephew, over Canterbell. You are an unrepentant rogue. You drink far too much. Gamble away hundreds of pounds. Throw lavish parties attended by half-naked courtesans."

"What of it? And most of them were completely unclothed. Also Oakhurst—"

"I realize you have little interest in politics," his uncle interrupted with a snarl. "Nor do you care how Parliament works."

"I do my part."

He didn't. The last time Alexander had attended Parliament and prepared to vote as his uncle requested, he'd been so bored he fell asleep.

Damon snorted. "Allow me to apprise you that Canterbell *controls* the House of Lords with an iron fist. He is the Lord Speaker. Nothing is voted on without his approval." The fingers of Damon's hands clenched and unclenched. "He dines frequently with Lamb, the Prime Minister. Do you know who that is, Alexander?"

"I'm not a complete idiot."

"Yes, you are, because compromising *his* daughter out of all the skirts in London," Damon fumed. "Was the absolute worst thing you could have done."

Alexander jerked his gaze to the door. "Timmons, you better not be listening or I'll have you sacked."

Quiet footsteps slid away from the drawing room.

"I did not intentionally muck up your grand ambitions, Damon. I would not."

Damon snorted again.

"But I do not believe I compromised that girl. Or was even at the Perswick ball. I'm sure of it."

"You've no idea what you've done."

Alexander stared down into his snifter of brandy. The guilt returned, stronger than ever. His uncle had devoted his life to the Viceroy name. Damon handled a myriad of responsibilities. Grew the Viceroy fortune and influence. He'd never once asked anything of Alexander except to follow his guidance. No well-bred, virginal young ladies who would require marriage.

He'd never once crossed that line. Until now.

I didn't touch that chit.

"I'll fix this, as I did before." Damon pressed his hand to the glass of the window; gaze fixed on the street outside. "Were she not Canterbell's daughter, I might have been able to make this entire unwelcome incident go away. Send her to the Continent with money and threats. Canterbell, however, will make sure you wed Lady Sophia." He tapped a finger on his chin, as if considering. "But you don't have to *bed* her." Damon nodded slowly as if coming to a great realization. "Yes, that's it."

"I don't think I could even if I tried. Her manner puts me off."

A complete lie. If anything, Lord Canterbell's daughter displayed a level of insolence and lack of respect for him that Alexander found oddly...arousing.

How horrifying.

"I think I need another headache powder," he said. "Timmons," he yelled for his butler.

"Canterbell's honor," Damon mused out loud though he seemed to be talking more to himself than Alexander, "Must be satisfied. The gossips silenced. He is correct that spinning a tale of the two of you, a secret courtship, will quiet everyone. And please the queen."

"No one will believe I would ever secretly court that shrew."

"Banns can be posted," his uncle ignored him. "A quick marriage, but not too quick. That will silence Lady Brokeburst. And after a time...six months, I think, but no more than a year, we'll ask to have the marriage annulled." Damon regarded him calmly.

"Failure to consummate."

"I don't feel well, uncle." Alexander looked up at him.

"Exactly. Canterbell won't disagree." Damon's mouth curved into a smile. "On the contrary, he'll thank me."

The edges of the room blurred around his uncle. He'd had at least four snifters of brandy and nothing to eat. But that was fine. Timmons would bring him something later.

"Impotence," Damon informed him. "Is valid grounds for an annulment. Given your love of spirits and opium, it should be easy to cast doubt on whether you can perform your husbandly duties. We'll say it was a recent development, given you've had…" He looked at Alexander. "Nearly every woman in London."

"Not every."

"Even Canterbell wouldn't want to doom his daughter to such a future, one without the hope for children. Lady Sophia will be pitied, but not a pariah. Her reputation will remain intact, if not a tad tarnished. It may even increase her appeal."

"Doubtful," Alexander murmured, not bothering to open his eyes as his uncle's footsteps came closer.

"But you *cannot* bed her, Alexander, under *any* circumstances. Don't even touch her hand unless it is necessary. There can be no questions of your inability to consummate the marriage."

"Don't worry, Uncle. I wouldn't bed that chit if she was the last woman in all of England."

"I'm pleased to hear it."

Alexander's mind started to drift as his uncle continued pacing about and speaking in a hushed tone to himself. Four glasses of brandy hadn't managed to blot out Lord Canterbell and that self-righteous little twit, but at least Damon had found a solution.

I never touched her.

"Maybe I won't need to worry over an annulment." Damon's voice sounded very far away. "Not with your inability to sit a horse. You've never managed it properly, no matter how I had you instructed as a child. Though now, that's more the fault of the spirits you consume. Such an excessive amount." Damon made a tsking sound with his tongue.

"I might fall into the Thames again, Uncle. Plop." Alexander made a sound while raising his hand, then dropped it. "Right into the water. You were so angry with Oakhurst."

"Yes, he apologized profusely for not…watching you closer. You nearly drowned. I was quite upset with him."

The room grew quiet save for the ticking of the clock before his uncle spoke once more. "No touching Canterbell's daughter. If you got her with child, we wouldn't be able to gain the annulment. Promise me."

"No touching. I promise, Uncle. I won't muck things up again."

"Good." The clink of the brandy glass settling on the table reached his ears. "I'll see myself out, Your Grace."

CHAPTER FIVE

"Leave your mother to me," Papa insisted as Sophia exited the carriage before the Canterbell home. "I'll explain everything to her."

Sophia didn't protest. She wanted nothing more than to go straight to her room and hide from the rest of the world while contemplating how best to avoid wedding the worst duke in London.

Avoiding Mama was in everyone's best interests.

"Yes, Papa." Pressing a kiss to his cheek, she waved as her father's carriage sped off towards Wellington and Sons to draw up the marriage contract.

Her stomach tightened once more. Tea and scones were in order.

Sophia handed her cloak to one of the footmen standing by the door, trying not to feel so completely hopeless. She'd prayed, fervently before climbing into her bed last night, that upon waking she would find that Roxboro, the Perswick ball, and most of all her own stupid behavior would be nothing more than a bad dream. A hallucination, perhaps, brought on by indulging in champagne.

Today had proven her wrong.

Cautiously, Sophia made her way in the direction of the stairs, admonishing the footman not to make a sound. If she were lucky, Mama was out…shopping.

Oh, no. She wouldn't. Not with the gossip circulating.

Or taking a nap. Strolling about the garden. Perhaps devising a more robust list of disappointments to hurl at Sophia. Her foot touched the bottom step and Sophia lifted her skirts, ready to sprint up the stairs.

"Sophia. Come here this instant."

Drat.

Maybe she could pretend she hadn't heard. She held her breath.

"Sophia."

Sighing, Sophia lifted her foot from the step.

I was so bloody close.

Approaching the drawing room doors, cracked open enough, *purposefully*, so that Lady Canterbell might hear the return of her wayward daughter, Sophia gingerly stepped inside. Clasping her hands before her, she attempted to appear subdued. Contrite.

"There you are." Mama sat perched on the damask settee, a handkerchief clutched in one hand, eyes reddened from weeping.

"Good afternoon, Mama."

"This is a catastrophe of enormous proportions. Worse than any Greek tragedy." Her bottom lip trembled. "Do you see, daughter?" Mama held up a newspaper, finger poking at the small item in what must be the gossip column. "What your careless nature has wrought?"

Oh. Dear.

There had been a chance, a very slim one, that she could somehow manage to convince Papa not to wed her to Roxboro. Sophia had even been considering that she could simply take her pin money and escape. Stow away on a ship bound for America and stay away until the scandal died down. But seeing Mama's plump finger pointing at that paragraph dashed every last hope.

Of course, Mama didn't yet know Sophia was to be a duchess or that Papa had resolved matters. "Don't be distressed, Mama. I should tell you—"

"Tainted." Mama slapped the newspaper on the settee. "The

shame of what you've brought to this family. Do you not love us at all?"

This was bound to be a lengthy diatribe. "I—"

"Poor Mara." Mama dabbed at a tear rolling down one cheek. "I imagined her a marchioness. Even a duchess. Do you know what this will do to your sister's prospects? Do you?" She lifted her eyes to the heavens, letting the words dangle in the air.

Of course, Mama's concern was for *Mara's* prospects.

Sophia took a seat across from her mother, tempted to allow Mama to go on and wear herself out. Maybe weep until she fainted, which was unkind. She loved her mother. She did. But she was nothing like Mara and never would be. Sophia caused trouble. Unintentionally.

Sometimes.

Mama was a woman who fervently believed in status, pedigree, and above all, good manners. A young lady should be demure. Modest. Have few opinions on anything other than gowns and the weather.

It wasn't her mother's fault that Sophia didn't care for any of it.

"Mama—"

"Where is your father?" She looked past Sophia and into the hall. "Leaving me to wallow in our family's shame alone, I suspect. Wait until he sees this." She thumped the newspaper. "Has he gone directly to his study? I knew Roxboro couldn't be brought to heel, no matter Lord Canterbell's influence. Oh," she wailed. "How will your father ever hold his head up in Parliament again? Her Majesty will be most distressed. We will have to retire to the country. Perhaps permanently." She raised a handkerchief to dab at her eyes. "Roxboro laughed, did he not? The rogue. No one would ever believe he would—well, I can hardly merit it myself. Even this column." She pointed to the paper. "Claims he was likely so deep in his cups he confused you with someone else." Placing a palm on her forehead, she wailed, "I hope no one saw the duke tossing you both out."

"That isn't at all what happened." Sophia proceeded to demolish the tea tray, the usual reaction to Mama and her dramatics. There were tiny ham and cucumber sandwiches. Scones. Biscuits. Strawberries. "Father went—"

"I can barely look at you, Sophia," Mama interrupted again, not allowing Sophia to say one word in her own defense. Very rarely were you given the opportunity to present your side of things with Lady Canterbell, *especially* if you were Sophia.

"Lady Brokeburst," Mama trilled. "Called upon me shortly after you departed this morning. Far too early in my opinion. It was she who brought me this." The newspaper was raised once more like a flag before battle. "Under the auspices of sympathy, which was patently false, because Lady Brokeburst lacks concern for anyone else which is apparent by the way she whispers everyone's secrets. She came to gloat, and gloat she did." Mama dabbed at her eyes. "You are soon to be a pariah. Cast out from society. Young ladies will cross the street when they see you. Not even in the country will you be free of censure given the way gossip travels. You'll be snubbed by the villagers. Is that what you want, Sophia? To be snubbed by the cheesemonger?"

Sophia munched on a ham sandwich, waiting for Mama to be finished.

"Have you nothing to say in your defense? We had to flee the Perswick ball. *Flee.*"

She plucked the newssheet from her mother's fingers. Surely, it could not be that terrible. Sophia was hardly newsworthy. Her eyes widened in horror at the small item. A handful of sentences which sealed her fate.

The Duke of Roxboro is known for all manner of questionable behavior; the only surprise is that he engaged in a lack of decorum with Lord C's daughter. The one known for her blunt opinions more than her appeal. No doubt a great deal of brandy was involved on Roxboro's part to cause such a lack of judgement. London is aghast. But there is no end to what a young lady will do to become a duchess.

Sophia tossed the paper aside with a grimace.

One paragraph and she'd been reduced to a scheming, ambitious young lady who had taken advantage of an intoxicated libertine.

How flattering.

Mama fell back against the cushions as a flood of tears cascaded down her cheeks. A small pile of used handkerchiefs were piled beside her. "Roxboro has discarded you before all of London."

"No, Mama. He—"

Her mother collapsed, face first on the settee, holding up a hand to silence Sophia. "Not another word. I am prostrate with grief over the loss of Mara's future." Then she added as an afterthought. "And your own."

How does my father tolerate such nonsense?

Thankfully, at that moment, Lord Canterbell appeared at the entrance of the drawing room, took one look at his wife weeping into the cushions, and exchanged a resigned look with Sophia. Taking a seat on the settee, Papa pulled Mama upright and pressed a kiss to her cheek.

"Stop your weeping, dear. It isn't good for your fragile constitution."

Fragile? Mama?

"I do apologize I didn't come to you directly upon my return, but—"

"A pariah," Mama screeched. "That's what will become of Sophia, my lord. Roxboro has refused and now we must make other plans. We must go to France." Mama nodded. "Mara would make a fine comtesse and Sophia might wed a…titled gentleman of some import."

Sophia took a large bite of a scone, chewing as loudly as possible.

"None of that will be necessary." Father patted Mama's hand in a soothing manner. "Sophia will not become a pariah. She'll be a duchess."

Mama stopped weeping and dabbed at her eyes. "You

mean—"

"That's right, darling. We won't have to send her to a convent. Roxboro will be honorable."

"A convent," Sophia choked, looking between her parents. "Had that been considered?"

"Now, I apologize, my lady, for not coming to you sooner with the news," Papa continued, ignoring Sophia. "But I thought it best to visit the solicitor immediately so that the marriage contract can be prepared for Lord Damon's perusal tomorrow."

"You're serious—you were going to send me to a *convent?*" Sophia demanded. "Force me to become a nun?"

"Well, yes, Sophia," Mama regarded her shrewdly. "We were considering our options. Running away to France. Or...Brussels. A convent, perhaps." She threw up her hands. "You should have told me Roxboro capitulated the very second you arrived home. Cruel of you to allow me to believe otherwise."

"But I tried—"

"Let your father speak." A gloved palm appeared before Sophia's face. "Allowing me to believe the duke had refused. How *could* you?"

Sophia opened her mouth, then just as quickly pressed her lips together. She would not win this battle. Not with Mama.

"The duke was...not receiving when Sophia and I first arrived at his home, therefore, we went to Lord Damon Viceroy, his uncle. Once I explained matters to him," that note of steel entered Papa's voice. "He and I were in complete agreement." He looked down at the newspaper, eyes moving as he scanned the article. "I see Lady Brokeburst wasted no time at all."

"She called upon me, my lord. Brought me the newspaper. I'm sure she whisked it off the press herself, barely waiting for the ink to dry. Couldn't wait to show it to me."

"It matters not. Roxboro will be honorable. The marriage contract is being drafted. Lady Brokeburst will look like the unwelcome gossip she is once word gets out that Roxboro and Sophia have been courting in secret."

Mama gasped. Her hands clapped together. "Truly? A welcome alternative to intoxicated ruination."

"The banns will be posted. The marriage within the month. There will be no one to gainsay our tale of a courtship."

The scone nearly fell from Sophia's mouth. "The end of the month?"

"Lady Brokeburst will look like a great fool." Papa squeezed her mother's hand. "Lord Damon knows what is at stake." Papa's eyes gleamed with absolute authority. Conviction. This was the Lord Canterbell so many feared. Damon Viceroy had been threatened in the most polite, subtle way in order to ensure Roxboro would wed Sophia and agree to the ridiculous tale of a secret betrothal.

"Roxboro had the audacity to claim he didn't attend the Perswick ball, probably in a bid to ignore taking liberties with our daughter." Papa growled. "The sot."

"It was only a kiss," Sophia whispered to no one in particular. A less than inspiring one.

"But I saw him myself," Mama gasped to her father. "There isn't any mistaking Roxboro, though, he did seem…less well turned out than usual. I've never seen him appear so slovenly. His formal attire left much to be desired. Far too handsome for his own good with that goblet of wine dangling from his hand. Despite his reputation, I suppose that is why you went into the gardens with him."

Sophia flinched under her mother's disappointed, unwavering stare. "As I said in the carriage last night, Roxboro expressed admiration for me. He'd seen me walking in the park." Even to her own ears the excuse sounded weak.

"Goodness, Sophia." Mama raised a brow. "He was under the influence of an excessive amount of spirits. Wasn't it obvious?"

That stings.

"Roxboro did not give the impression of intoxication." Sophia wasn't about to admit that she'd drunk three glasses of champagne before following him outside and was likely foxed herself.

The stupidity of her actions was appalling. "After expressing his admiration, Roxboro...asked if he could call upon me." She didn't bother to add that he'd said he would speak to Papa about courting her. Every word he'd spoken had been a lie.

"Oh, Sophia," Mama's tone was laced with pity. "Roxboro is a rake of the highest order, and not a trustworthy man. And you claim Mara is a pea-hen." Mama shook her head. "She would never have followed the duke out into the gardens."

Sophia could say nothing. Believing Roxboro, following him into the dark of the gardens, *had* been stupid. She had little defense for it. All she'd been thinking was how...pleased Mama would be if a duke called upon her. Finally. How she would finally have triumphed over Mara and the Hortensias of the world.

"Well, I suppose it no longer matters." Mama's eyes were now dry. "I'm not pleased, mind you, given the gossip, but your father has matters well in hand. And although I am pleased you'll be a duchess." Mama preened for a moment. "I do wish you weren't going to be *Roxboro's*, no matter his looks and wealth. His character is questionable." She shrugged. "No matter. I daresay you'll be a widow within a few years at any rate, given his love of spirits not to mention his other habits."

"Mama. That is a terrible thing to say." Sophia didn't want to marry Roxboro, or even like him, but she didn't wish him dead.

"Your mother is correct." Papa frowned as he examined the tea tray. "What happened to all the ham sandwiches? The truth is, Sophia, that Roxboro slips off his horse with great regularity, mostly due to his love of drink." He smiled at finding a ham sandwich hidden beneath a pile of the watercress. "Tripping about and such. Falling off that pleasure barge into the Thames. I am surprised Roxboro has lasted this long. Oddly clumsy for a libertine. You would expect him to be a bit more graceful in his movements."

"The Thames?" Which was filthy and full of diseased things. Not to mention the smell. She had heard mention of Roxboro going for a swim in that disgusting body of water but she'd thought it a jest.

"Fished out while singing a bawdy tune. Had an eel caught on the buttons of his coat. Lucky he didn't drown. Thought it all a great lark. So foxed he barely knew his own name."

Good lord. Why hadn't she just…stayed hidden behind that blasted potted fern at Lady Perswick's ball?

"And." Mama leaned forward. "Roxboro was nearly decapitated by a thresher after passing out in the wheat at The Pillory. The ducal seat."

"Decapitated?" Roxboro became less appealing by the moment. "And his estate is called The Pillory?" Pillories were used to confine a person for punishment.

"Yes. Can you imagine? Slicing off a duke's head? I had it firsthand from Lady Witsworth whose estate is a half day's ride from The Pillory. Roxboro fell into a stack of hay after a night of carousing at some tavern with Lord Oakhurst. No one knew he was in the hay, including Oakhurst. The servants had been searching for him for hours. Lord Damon was beside himself."

"How horrifying," Sophia whispered. "But you want me to wed him? Despite all these tales?"

Both her parents stared at her, agog.

"Well, of course," Mama insisted, her tone leaving no doubt she thought Sophia to be an idiot. "He's compromised you. Rather publicly. No matter how disreputable, Roxboro is still a duke, Sophia. A young, attractive one, despite his numerous flaws. There isn't another duke this Season save Hayward. Yes, Roxboro will gamble, keep a mistress, and drink far too much. Eventually, he'll drown in a barrel of whisky or choke on a fish bone. But you'll be a duchess."

"You're joking." Sophia reached for another biscuit.

"You must give him an heir as soon as possible," Mama instructed, eyeing the biscuit in Sophia's hand. "Not another. You've had at least six. A young lady should not be a glutton. As I was saying, a child will solidify your position in society as a duchess and mother of a duke. Think of the influence you'll wield."

Sophia didn't care for wielding influence, especially now that she must consider *bedding* Roxboro. She was still trying to come to terms with the fact that she must marry him. Or that she might never again have a taste for champagne. But of course she must provide him an heir.

An unexpected curl of heat unwound inside her.

No. Despite Roxboro's physical attractiveness, he was a terrible, awful, human being. She wouldn't look forward to sharing a bed with him at all. In fact, she would spend the rest of the day imagining all the ways to avoid marital relations with that unrepentant sot.

"I don't care about being a duchess," she finally said.

Mama fell back against the settee once more, lips pursed. "I do. I plan to call upon Lady Brokeburst tomorrow and relay to her just how incorrect her assumptions were. You and Roxboro developed an affection for each other. A secret one. Your father knew, of course." She beamed at Papa. "But I was kept in the dark, thus her waving about the newspaper shocked me." She thought for a moment. "Your father didn't want it to take attention away from Mara's Season. But the fact remains, you and Roxboro did nothing wrong. Not really. And once I was apprised of the situation, I was thrilled beyond measure."

"I don't know why there isn't more ham." Father took up a watercress sandwich. "A month is long enough, I think, for the banns and the wedding, given you've been courting."

"But we haven't been." Panic swept through Sophia.

"Tomorrow, you'll be officially betrothed." He finished the tiny sandwich.

"I don't like him," she insisted. "Not in the least."

"Perhaps you should have disliked him sooner," Mama said firmly. "Before allowing him to compromise you. I can't wait to inform Lady Brokeburst that she's made a complete cake of herself by spreading such gossip. She won't be invited to the wedding."

"I don't want to marry him. Surely, there is something you can do, Papa." Roxboro was magnificent on the outside, but he was a sot. Possibly an opium addict. Certainly, a debauched libertine. Which made the disappointing kiss he'd bestowed upon her, that had caused this entire debacle, that much worse.

You'd think a libertine could kiss well.

"Do you want to be sent to a convent, Sophia?" Mama lifted a brow. "Become a nun?"

"Well, no, but—"

Mama stood with a clap of her hands. "Well, I'm off. There is much to do and little time to do it. There's a wedding to plan. I must write to Lord Damon immediately." She rushed out of the room in a flurry of skirts, no doubt intent on spreading the news to every matron in the *ton*. "I'm to be the mother of a duchess."

"Papa," Sophia pleaded, once her mother was gone. "Won't you reconsider?" She was desperate to escape her fate. "Nothing happened. It was merely a kiss. Barely a peck on the lips. He doesn't even remember me."

Father munched on a biscuit. "The convent is in Scotland, near a bog, so it is cold and dreary the entire year. Oh, and the nuns take a vow of silence." He regarded her with little sympathy.

She looked down at her lap, pulling at a bit of lace on her skirt.

"Make the best of this match, Sophia. Don't embarrass your family." Papa's voice was gruff. "Do your duty. As the daughter of Lord Canterbell should."

CHAPTER SIX

ALEXANDER WAS USHERED into the Canterbell drawing room by their butler, who introduced himself as Powell. He fervently wished, as he was waved forward, that he could be anywhere but here, preferably between the thighs of his latest mistress. Florenza was a soprano from Milan. Not a very good one, grant you, but she did have other talents.

Paying calls and sipping tea wasn't an enjoyable activity. Alexander had paid only a handful of calls in his life and didn't intend to make it a habit. But at the insistence of his uncle, Alexander was forced to call upon his new betrothed and sip tea in this overly feminine drawing room decorated in pale yellow and cream. Given the story circulating that he and Lady Sophia had been courting in secret for some time, and had been "discovered" in Lady Perswick's garden, it would seem strange if Alexander *didn't* call upon Lady Sophia and her mother, Lady Canterbell.

Perhaps, Alexander mused as he observed his surroundings, was that Canterbell's drawing room was empty.

The audacity.

Powell, the stern looking little troll of a butler, eyed Alexander with dislike, before gesturing to one of the chairs decorated with a motif of butterflies across the back cushion. "Lady Canterbell and Lady Sophia will be along in a moment, Your Grace."

Dukes, Alexander wanted to remind Canterbell's snide little butler, did not wait upon others; they waited upon *him*. But he merely inclined his head and settled into the chair, repulsed by the pattern of monarch butterflies.

His eyes caught on the settee—*a horrid thing of green velvet the exact hue of mashed peas*—where an embroidery hoop had been discarded on one of the cushions. An uninteresting design of a basket of flowers, partially finished, decorated the linen. Dull. Alexander had to keep from flinching at the sight.

Boredom loomed and its name was Lady Sophia.

Alexander had every intention of tolerating Canterbell's daughter for the duration of this "betrothal" and the eventual moment the vicar addressed them as man and wife. He'd promised Damon to be on his best behavior. But once wed, Alexander had every intention of ignoring Lady Sophia. His London home was large. She could have an entire wing to herself. Go about town and pay calls as the Duchess of Roxboro. Damon warned Alexander to have as little contact as possible with his new wife, nor make any attempt to bed her. Eventually, the silly little chit would complain to her parents and Alexander would reluctantly admit his inability to consummate the marriage.

It was all part of Damon's plan to secure the eventual annulment, though Alexander couldn't fathom anyone believing his cock didn't work. He countered that he could claim marriage under false pretenses, after all, Alexander was certain he hadn't been at that bloody ball. But Damon reminded him there had been too many witnesses attesting to Alexander's appearance there that night. All confirmed by his uncle.

Alexander's next suggestion was to claim Lady Sophia suffered from some physical ailment that precluded sexual activity. Improperly formed lady parts, for instance. But Damon rejected that notion. Easily disproved and it would only serve to anger Canterbell.

So, impotence it was.

Alexander was known for any manner of sexual proclivities, some of which were, unfortunately, true. Not the bit about the sheep. That was completely false. But being bathed by six women in the middle of Madame Forand's establishment was...not an exaggeration. And while Florenza was his only mistress at present, he usually kept more than one. He couldn't fathom anyone believing that his cock wouldn't rise to the occasion...but Damon insisted it was the best way to dissolve the marriage to Lady Sophia.

That also meant Alexander had to say goodbye to Florenza. If his cock didn't work for Lady Sophia, it couldn't work for his mistress either.

Not one soul in London dared to refute the tale that Alexander had been courting Lady Sophia in secret, though he doubted anyone believed it. Most assumed he'd had far too much brandy, stumbled upon her in the Perswick gardens, then had the misfortune to be seen by Lady Brokeburst.

Old bat.

Alexander had sent word to Oakhurst's staff asking for his friend's location, but was surprised to have the messenger return, claiming Lord Oakhurst's home was closed. Only the housekeeper, Mrs. Launton and a groom remained to oversee the stable, which meant Oakhurst had no plans on returning any time soon.

He questioned Timmons again, but outside of knowing that Oakhurst was leaving and apparently with Lady Maxwell, Alexander's butler knew little else. Entirely frustrating because only Oakhurst knew what really happened that night. He was forced to wait for his friend to make contact, which Oakhurst would undoubtedly do at some point. Alexander recalled absolutely nothing of that night after leaving the brothel and couldn't imagine why he'd gone to a ball, especially one he hadn't been invited to.

Women. Dancing. The smell of perfume. And...nothing else.

Alexander gritted his teeth.

I can't remember.

His gaze landed on a decanter of brandy sitting on Canterbell's sideboard, resisting the urge to pour himself a small glass. The inability to recall the night with Oakhurst bothered Alexander a great deal. Yes, he drank far too much, but...he'd never not remembered his whereabouts or whether he'd kissed a woman, let alone an entire bloody ball. And while he likely needed that entire decanter of brandy to get through the next hour, Alexander had vowed earlier to keep a clear head. He didn't trust Canterbell or his twit of a daughter.

I'll drink myself senseless later.

Canterbell's dislikable butler reappeared, waving forward a maid carrying a tray. A steaming pot of tea. Biscuits. Tiny finger sandwiches. Scones. Jam.

None of it appealed to Alexander.

An older woman clothed entirely in fuchsia, paused at the entrance to the drawing room, before following in the wake of the tea tray. The bright color of her gown had him blinking, as did the array of small bits of brilliants glittering among the folds of her skirts.

Good lord.

He came to his feet.

"Your Grace." Beringed fingers were extended in his direction. "We're so pleased you've called."

"Lady Canterbell." He took her hand. "A pleasure. And your gown is exquisite," he said smoothly. "The hue in particular is one of my favorites."

A blush crested over her cheeks. "I've been warned of your charm, Your Grace."

"I'm only being truthful. Lord Canterbell is lucky indeed."

A soft, girlish sound of pleasure left her lips. "You flatter me."

"I only speak the truth." He released her hand, giving her the half-smile that had ladies all over England swooning. Alexander was not ignorant of his effect on the opposite sex, after all, there was a reason for his reputation.

A disgusted sound reached his ears.

Oh, yes. Almost forgot.

Lady Sophia, Alexander's unwanted bride, strolled into the room, fingers clenched in her skirts, dark eyes glowing with barely controlled hostility.

The little twit had no reason to be hostile and her manner greatly annoyed Alexander. Why should she be so antagonistic? She'd taken advantage of him. The girl before him was either a clever liar or so bloody blind she couldn't tell him apart from her butler. Or merely an ambitious schemer.

Alexander shot her a bland, bored look.

Her shoulders stiffened. She seemed about to hurl herself at him.

Why wasn't she more thankful Alexander was so bloody honorable? Or that Uncle Damon had political aspirations? Lady Sophia was going to be a duchess, albeit for a brief time. You'd think she could at least…be polite.

Ungrateful chit.

If Alexander had had his way, this contentious little shrew would be left to twist in the wind. He didn't give a fig for her reputation. Even now, there was nothing about her he recognized. Nothing familiar. Not her scent. Nor the sound of her voice.

Absolutely nothing.

Outside of the shape of her mouth which he appreciated.

Alexander was something of an expert, after all, in female mouths.

Lower lip full and plush, like a small pillow. The upper, curved into a bow. Sinful. Decadent. Likely capable of a great many…misdeeds. Could those lips have been enough to lead Alexander to stupidly take her into Lady Perswick's gardens?

I'd remember that mouth.

A finger flicked against one thigh in annoyance. Alexander didn't want to appreciate anything about her. Her unwanted presence would be gone within a year.

There wasn't any way to disprove Lord Canterbell or his

daughter, not with so many witnesses at the ball claiming to have seen him. Alexander had finally come to the unwelcome conclusion that...maybe he *could* have been there. How or why, he'd no idea. It did explain why Lady Maxwell hadn't been at the gambling hell or brothel, but he recalled conversing with her. The only explanation was that he and Oakhurst must have retrieved her from the Perswick ball.

Lady Maxwell's face swam before him. She'd been smiling. Patted his coat. Asking him when he'd changed. The memory faded as quickly as it came.

The delicate scent of roses hovered in the air as she dipped into yet another awkward curtsey, almost as if her legs didn't bend properly.

"Lady Sophia. How lovely to see you today."

Roses. A soft, feminine scent. Completely unwelcome on this termagant. She should smell of...rotted plums.

"Bravo," she ground out in a whisper. "For recalling my name."

"Scheming liar," his lips said along her knuckles.

"Feckless sot," she returned under her breath while straightening.

But his being at the ball didn't mean he'd touched Canterbell's daughter. Had she mistaken someone else for him? That seemed the most likely. Or possibly Lord Canterbell wanted a duke in his pocket. Hayward would have been a better target. He had far more influence in political circles no matter how ancient.

In any case, mutual dislike didn't bode well for their impending union, no matter how short he intended it to be.

Lady Sophia's fingers curled away from his, trying to escape.

Alexander tightened his grip, refusing to release her. She was getting what she wanted. Marriage. To him. No matter how unpleasant she would find the experience to be.

Squeezing her fingers once more, he released her. She immediately drifted to the horrid green settee directly across from Alexander, looking for all the world as if she were floating in a bowl of pea soup.

Alexander detested pea soup.

Lady Canterbell's lips curved into a polite smile as she regarded him through the steam rising from the pot of tea on the table. "Tea, Your Grace?"

"Yes, thank you."

He didn't like tea. Copious amounts of milk or sugar didn't improve the taste. Nor honey. Brandy was what he wanted. The thirst for it or scotch grew by leaps and bounds with every moment he spent in the Canterbell drawing room. The cut crystal decanter on the sideboard mocked him. But Alexander didn't care to be called a feckless sot. Especially not by this scheming little chit.

A cup was placed before him.

Alexander stared at his tea for a time but did not touch it. Nor the plate of biscuits he was handed.

"I am pleased we have this opportunity to become better acquainted, Your Grace," Lady Canterbell said. "I realize the circumstances are somewhat…irregular, but I hope we can look forward to a splendid and fruitful union."

Lady Sophia fairly cringed at the word "fruitful," which even though Alexander had no desire to bed her, it was rather off-putting to realize she didn't want to bed him either. He'd never in his life had a woman not wish for his attention. Usually, Alexander had to swat them away.

He sat back in the butterfly chair. If he repulsed Lady Sophia, it would make attaining an annulment that much easier. Alexander should be thrilled he disgusted her to such a degree.

Yet, he was not.

"That is my hope as well." Alexander cleared his throat, unable to stop his eyes from drifting to the sideboard once more where the brandy glittered back at him like some jewel.

Lady Sophia, damn her, followed the direction of his gaze and…snickered.

His fingers curled along the arms of the chair.

Lady Canterbell poured two more steaming cups of tea, one for her and one for her awful daughter, still prattling away, filling the room with gossip about nearly everyone in London. Tedious stuff. Who had been riding in the park. Some lord's new carriage drawn by four perfectly matched bays. All the bits of life in society for which Alexander cared little. Lady Canterbell was so consumed by the sound of her own voice, she never paused in her recitation, which gave Alexander no opportunity to reply or comment as she spoke.

Which was fine as he had nothing to contribute.

His unwanted bride said nary a word during the entirety of the soul-stifling hour, though she made her opinion of Alexander clear with a series of derisive snorts, dramatic eye-rolling, and a disgusted puff here and there whenever she chanced to look his way.

Lady Canterbell pointedly ignored her daughter.

Glancing at the clock, Alexander was satisfied he'd been tortured long enough and could finally take his leave. Damon expected him to take Lady Sophia on a carriage ride next week through the park so that they could be seen in each other's company, but stopped short of forcing Alexander to escort her to a ball.

He'd be expected to dance with her, which even Damon agreed was a poor idea. Alexander had two left feet.

Just as he was about to excuse himself, that troll of a butler appeared at the door.

"My lady," Powell bowed. "I apologize for the intrusion, but there is a problem with the linens which require your immediate attention."

A linen emergency. How subtle.

Lady Sophia's face held the briefest flash of panic at having to be left alone in his company. She seemed to shrink back into the ghastly settee, which had the benefit of…making her bosom move and catch his eye.

If Alexander wasn't mistaken, Lady Sophia's breasts were

spectacular. Pity he'd never see them.

"Please excuse me for a moment, Your Grace." Lady Canterbell gave her daughter a warning look. "I'll return momentarily." She departed, making sure to leave the drawing room door open to avoid any impropriety. Which was rather ridiculous given the circumstances.

The room went silent except for the clock ticking away every interminable minute.

Abruptly, Lady Sophia reached out and snatched another biscuit off the tray. Those plush lips widened as she bit into the pink icing, crunching loudly and obnoxiously.

"Well," Alexander started, stretching out his legs beneath the table and crossing them at the ankle. Close enough to Lady Sophia she made a point of pulling her skirts back.

"Well," she snapped back, chewing on the biscuit like some cow in the field.

The desire for the brandy, sitting so innocently on the sideboard, increased.

"Your tea is getting cold," she pointed out.

"I'm not in the mood for tea."

She leaned in, giving him a better glimpse of her bosom. Or at least some of it. "I suppose you aren't. It doesn't contain any brandy."

Alexander was rapidly regretting his decision to stay clear headed. Surely, this girl was more tolerable when he was in his cups. She made his temples ache. Once he left this hellish place, with his temples pounding, he planned to visit his club and spend the remainder of the day, and possibly most of the night, getting completely foxed.

The sound of her teeth grinding together had the hairs on the back of his neck standing up. Every crunch felt like a hammer against his skull. "Can you please stop?" Alexander flicked his wrist at her. "Chewing so loudly?"

"Why, Your Grace? Do you find it offensive?" She deliberately took up another biscuit and gnawed at the edges.

"You resemble a feral squirrel." He tried not to glance in the direction of the brandy and failed.

Her response was to slurp her tea.

Good lord, I need...something. Even sherry would do.

"Let us speak plainly, Lady Sophia," he croaked, forcing his gaze from the sideboard.

"I thought we were, Your Grace. Speaking plainly." Another biscuit was pressed to her lips. Good god, she'd eat the entire tea tray.

Crunch. Crunch.

"You don't wish to wed me," Alexander stated plainly.

"No. I do not. I would say it isn't personal, except that it is." She licked a crumb from her entirely sinful top lip. "I would rather be sent to a convent than endure you for a lifetime. Though given your habits, I doubt it won't take that long."

I yearn for the annulment and I haven't even wed her yet. Entirely worth confessing my cock doesn't work.

"I may have...been at the Perswick ball." Alexander could no longer make a compelling argument for denying his absence, though that didn't mean he'd done anything else. "But I did not lead you into the gardens. Nor did I compromise you. Given our mutual dislike, I find it to be an impossibility." He tossed the word out, expecting her to immediately become defensive. "I was likely only taking in the night air."

"You are correct on the dislike, Your Grace. However, we conversed at the refreshment table." There was a flicker of vulnerability in her features before it vanished. "You kissed me, though it was little more than a peck." The luscious mouth pursed into a rosette. "Certainly not worthy of marriage. My father, and most of London, however, disagree."

Alexander watched the movement of her lips, which was on the whole, rather enticing. He could...possibly *imagine* being drawn to such a mouth, were he intoxicated.

"I was foxed."

"While that is your usual state, Your Grace, you did not appear to be in your cups at the Perswick ball."

"Don't you find that odd? If that is my natural state."

Termagant.

"Exceedingly. I imagine if you were to cut yourself, brandy would pour from the wound instead of blood."

Good lord, she was annoying.

And…somewhat arousing.

Alexander shifted in the chair, eyes roaming over the pale yellow of her dress, noting the way the silk seemed to cling to the curves of her generous form. The cut was incredibly modest, which was what made her all the more…enticing.

I could have kissed her. With that mouth and that bosom. That venom.

Her rounded features pinched at his perusal. Dark lashes swept over her cheeks. "And not a very good one."

He hadn't been listening, far too immersed in his perusal of this girl who claimed Alexander had ruined her. "What wasn't very good?"

"The kiss. Don't tell me that in addition to all your other faults, you are also hard of hearing. Will I need to string one of those horns around your neck?" She bit her lip to keep from laughing aloud. "So that you may hold it up to your ear?"

Never in the entirety of his life had anyone spoken to him with such a lack of respect and he was starting to like her for it, against his better judgement.

"You haven't an ounce of decorum. No tact. Obnoxious in your bluntness. Disrespectful."

"Well, you're a sot." She shrugged. "I was speaking of the press of your lips at the Perswick ball. I say *press* because I refuse to keep calling it a kiss. There was little to recommend the action and the execution…sloppy."

"Sloppy." Alexander jerked back, so astonished he momentarily forgot his craving for the brandy.

"A great disappointment given your reputation." She set down her tea. "Frankly, I expected something more spectacular.

The moon to become that much brighter. The earth to move beneath my feet. But alas, the kiss lacked any magnificence."

He deliberately knocked the table with one foot, making her cup rattle against the saucer so that she had to jump to catch the tea before it spilled. "Untrue. And I've far more experience than you, Lady Sara."

A small growl came from her. "Sophia, you sot. And I disagree. Dukes go about imagining themselves to be superior, and they are not. People tend to tell a duke whatever it is they want to hear."

"No one has ever lodged a complaint but you," Alexander snarled back. "Perhaps I wasn't properly motivated. In fact," he flicked a finger in her direction. "I'm sure I was not."

A soft hiss came from her.

"Any kiss bestowed by me has always been lauded as nothing short of intoxicating," he growled. "There's dozens of women who I've kissed into a state of euphoria."

Good lord, why was he defending himself to this...*harridan*? More importantly, why was he...aroused...by *her*?

"Nonsense," she stated.

"You've just proved my point, Lady Saffron."

A sound came from her, she picked up the spoon from her saucer, perhaps thinking to toss it at him, then set it back down just as quickly.

"If the kiss was sloppy, it simply could not have been bestowed by me. It's an impossibility."

"Goodness, but you are arrogant."

"I'm not sure what you hoped to accomplish with your accusations, but I suspect it is because you wanted to be a duchess. Even mine will command respect, Sarafina."

The dark eyes flashed at him with murderous intent. Her cheeks reddened. "You—"

"Or were you trying to hide the identity of your lover? Some poor gentleman," he drawled. "Who didn't want to be stuck with you either?"

She cocked her head, not the least put out by his insults. "Your rebuttal is based solely on the fact that you are incapable of kissing poorly. Is that your only defense?" A bark of laughter came from her. "Lady Brokeburst—"

"Is elderly. Addled, possibly."

"What about my father? Is he addled as well?"

"I do not kiss in a sloppy manner. I'm not a bloody puppy." He ran a hand through his hair. "Perhaps," he deliberately softened his tone, trying to reason with her. "It was an honest mistake. It was another gentleman that you only *thought* was me. After a glass or two of champagne..."

The color left her cheeks.

I knew it.

"The garden was dark," Alexander continued. "At least admit as much to me. So we may move forward in honesty."

"There was moonlight."

"We can explain to your father and my uncle together," he coaxed. "Break the betrothal. Happens all the time. Simply admit it wasn't me. I promise to offer my support."

"You are loathsome." Her hand hovered over the teapot and for a moment, Alexander thought he might be doused with hot tea.

"Then tell me this. Given your disgust, why would you go into the gardens with me? What could I possibly have said to entice you to do so?"

Her lips pressed shut.

"Answer the question."

She fidgeted. Looked away. Her cheeks pinked once more. "We—conversed. You were interesting. Charming. Flirtatious." Her eyes fell to her lap. "Excessively so."

Alexander studied her closely. She was *embarrassed*. He'd wounded her...pride.

Her fingers tugged at the silk of her skirts in agitation. "What did we discuss? The latest fashions? The ball?"

Eyes raised, she glared at him.

"It doesn't matter. Not a bit of it was true." Hostility emanated from her once more. "And I won't go to my father and recant because it *was* you. My father recognized you." There was a slight tremble in her words. "As did Lady Brokeburst and dozens of others. You may deny it all you like, Your Grace."

"I will continue to do so." The banns had been posted. The date set. Canterbell would never allow a broken betrothal now, even if she did recant. Alexander must bide his time. Wed her. Declare himself unable to perform his husbandly duties. It would be humiliating, but worth it to be rid of this little nuisance.

They regarded each other over the tea. He and Lady Sophia were at an impasse.

"Can we at least agree to blame Lady Brokeburst?" he murmured.

Lady Sophia jerked her chin. "Yes." She looked so miserable, so desolate at her circumstances, Alexander had the sudden urge to offer comfort to his future wife.

I really need a glass of brandy. Or scotch. Maybe gin.

"I hope I wasn't gone too long." Lady Canterbell sailed back into the room and noting the tension filling the air, looked between them.

"Not at all, my lady." Alexander came to his feet and bowed. "Lady Sophia and I were just discussing puppies."

Lady Sophia stiffened, but said nothing else.

"I fear I must take my leave, my lady." He took Lady Canterbell's hand. "A prior appointment and I dare not be late. With your permission, I shall take Lady Sophia to Gunter's next week after a ride through the park." Both could be accomplished without a chaperone, especially given their betrothal, and Alexander wouldn't have to tolerate Lady Canterbell during the outing. She gave him a headache.

"Oh, my. Well, of course," Lady Canterbell cooed. "Sophia would be delighted."

"Splendid."

"I can hardly wait," his bride murmured, so low only he could hear as Alexander took her hand. "I shan't sleep a wink."

CHAPTER SEVEN

THE ONLY GOOD thing about this entire day would be that it would end with an ice from Gunter's.

Sophia liked ices. Lemon. Lavender. Pistachio. Really, any flavor but parmesan. She'd have to suffer Roxboro's company in order to have her ice, but nothing good was gained without a bit of suffering.

Roxboro's carriage, as one would expect, was lavish and well-sprung. The vehicle glided through Hyde Park with barely a jolt. The day was cloudy, but warm and Roxboro had instructed that the carriage top be rolled down. Better to be seen by all of London, which was the entire purpose of this outing.

Lady Brokeburst could barely show her face after trumpeting Sophia's non-ruination. She looked foolish. Just as Mama had said she would.

Sophia turned from the passing view of the Serpentine to take in Roxboro, who was more glorious than the bloody flowers dotting the trail. How could a man be so bereft of character but blessed with such masculine beauty? He should resemble something more in line with his personality. A toadstool, perhaps. Or a rotted potato.

Instead, his hair, the color of coffee, batted against the shimmering green of his eyes with their slashes of dark silver gray, making him appear more than ever like the hero of Sophia's last beloved romantic novel, *The Lord of the Castle*. She was aware that, given her personality, it seemed odd that she gravitated to such literature, but truthfully, she possessed a romantic heart. Perhaps if she hadn't, Sophia wouldn't have been so taken with Roxboro at the Perswick ball.

He'd said little as they rolled through the park, only doffing his hat as they passed an acquaintance, though Roxboro didn't have his driver stop. No introductions were made, which wasn't surprising. Every so often, his hand would sneak into the pocket of his coat, withdraw a small flask, and take a sip.

Brandy, Sophia surmised. The scent, mixing with his bergamot shaving soap, permeated the carriage. He wasn't foxed, or at least he didn't appear to be. Roxboro didn't slur his words or stutter. He had tripped getting into the carriage, but from the blush crawling up his neck below his ears, Sophia didn't think his clumsiness was a result of the brandy.

Being known as something of a sot was probably vastly preferable than having society mock a blundering duke.

"It's rude to stare, Lady Sally."

"You are aware of my name," Sophia replied crisply. "Start using it."

"Your Grace." The side of his mouth twitched. "Address me properly, Lady Sabrina."

Thus far today he'd called her Sadie, Sage, Sable, and Samantha. He'd tried Cerebellum, but then Sophia pointed out that it was not spelled with an S but a C, though secretly, she gave Roxboro points for his creativity.

He deliberately avoided using her name, just as she'd decided, sometime during their last encounter, to be intentionally disrespectful of his lofty title. A battle of sorts, likely the first of many, given neither wanted to wed the other. Today though, their little war had felt more like…teasing.

"You aren't even trying," she said lightly. "You've already used Sabrina. Perhaps consult Debrett's for a broader assortment of names, Your Grace."

Elegant fingers drummed on one knee, causing Sophia to

lower her gaze.

Roxboro might have a propensity for tumbling from a horse, but it certainly wasn't due to a lack of muscle in his thighs, all of which was outlined to perfection given the cut of his trousers was incredibly...sharp.

Scowling at her, he said, "I suppose it is time to end this torture and retire to Gunter's." He rapped on the side of the carriage, instructing the driver to leave the park. "I think enough of the *ton* has seen us."

Torture? Sophia wouldn't have said they were having a lovely time, but her presence could hardly be called torture. It wasn't as if she were having him disemboweled.

"Do they have brandy flavored ice at Gunter's, Your Grace?" Sophia asked politely. "I can't imagine you'd want to visit otherwise. Or will you simply dabble your flask over the top of your ice?"

"Shrew," he tossed at her.

"Feckless sot."

"It wasn't me at Lady Perswick's," he bit out. "You should...admit your mistake. Acknowledge you are in the wrong."

Why did he continue to debate this point? Sophia wasn't blind. Neither was Lady Brokeburst. Lord Lacton. Her own father. Roxboro's stubborn refusal to admit he'd just been so intoxicated he couldn't recall anything, including her—*especially her*—bordered on absurdity.

A small, awkward pinch dug into her chest, as it often did in knowing that simple truth. Roxboro wasn't even the first to find Sophia so disinteresting. But his disregard bothered her the most. "I realize I am forgettable, Your Grace."

He smacked the leather seat, the bits of gray in his eyes darkening. "That isn't what I am inferring."

"Yes, it is," she shot back. "I am so unremarkable that according to society, you had to be nearly *blind* with brandy to want to lead me into the Perswick gardens. Lord Canterbell's intolerable daughter. Did you mistake me for my sister? She is the willowy, beautiful one."

"I've only seen your sister once." Roxboro's gaze dropped to her mouth. "It was not me because I do not lure well-bred misses into ruination."

"I suppose you made an exception for me."

"Or perhaps, you merely saw an opportunity. Lord Canterbell would enjoy having a duke in his pocket, wouldn't he? At least I'm doing the honorable thing, which is more than I can say for a young lady who refuses to admit her mistake."

"A duke in his pocket? You? A stumbling drunk who is known for his lack of character more than anything else?" An ugly laugh came from her. "Poor Roxboro. London's finest libertine brought low by the plain and opinionated daughter of Lord Canterbell. And your honor at best is questionable. I think it more your uncle's political aspirations."

Roxboro sucked in a breath, the line of his perfectly sculpted jaw grew taut.

"If it is easier for you to believe I orchestrated this entire incident, fabricated the tale and then somehow coerced Lady Brokeburst and the guests at Lady Perswick's ball, then by all means, continue. You are a sot, Your Grace. You fell off a pleasure barge and into the Thames and came out singing a bawdy tune, like some gin swilling mermaid. Your degenerate behavior is fodder for the gossips. Did Binson's charge you for breaking their faro table when you tupped Lady Winston atop it? Or did they merely add it to your other markers, which I'm told could fund the Royal Navy. The most ducal thing you could possibly do would be to sit a horse properly, yet you cannot even claim that much."

"Stop the carriage," he growled, practically swatting his driver. "Immediately." Roxboro's chest rose and fell as he took ragged, furious breaths.

"You've doubtless debauched dozens of women. Only now—"

He immediately hopped to the ground as the carriage rolled

to a stop, landing on his feet with not so much as a wobble.

"Only now," he snarled back at her. "I've been caught, by the most undesirable," he accentuated every syllable, "of young ladies. Lady Scathing. A woman so devoid of anything remotely likeable in either manner or her appearance, that she must wait for a man to be numbed in both mind and spirit to entertain any thought of her company."

Sophia fell back against the leather seats.

"If you'll excuse me, my darling bride to be, I've decided not to enjoy an ice with you. Your presence would only ruin the taste. My driver will see you home." Roxboro stalked off, back in the direction of the park.

"Good day, Your Grace," she felt the need to say to his retreating back.

The broad shoulders did not turn back to her. Roxboro didn't even care to return a parting shot.

As the carriage started towards the Canterbell home, Sophia blinked back the tears she refused to allow to fall.

"TERMAGANT," ALEXANDER SPIT out as he walked away from his carriage and that…that viper…as quickly as possible. He'd never been so bloody furious in his life.

The Duke of Roxboro was known for drunken behavior. His lechery, capable of seducing anything in skirts. His love of amusements, mostly sexual in nature. But *never* his temper. There was never any reason to become angry when the world bowed and scraped for you. When you are a wealthy, attractive duke, your place of privilege secure in the world, you simply…floated along the surface of life. Indulged yourself.

What a bloody selfish existence I lead.

He was angry at Sophia—*yes, I know her damn name, but I enjoy annoying her*—Alexander was far angrier with himself.

He reached into his pocket and drained every drop of brandy

in the flask.

Today, he had wanted to rail at Sophia, and Alexander had never yelled at a woman in his entire life. Women were soft, lovely creatures. Worthy of protection. Great care. He adored them.

Yet, Sophia, his unwanted future duchess, made him want to—strangle her.

Or…fuck her senseless.

Alexander was rather torn on that point.

Bad enough he had to wed her, but his attraction to such an aggravating, shrewish, not even beautiful, woman was… infuriating. Smelling of roses when she was nothing but thorns. Her complete disregard for his title. A duke was nearly royalty. Her opinion of his character. None of which he should have cared about, but yet he did.

He was back in the park, staring at the twist of the Serpentine once more.

I want to strip her naked. Thrust into all that antagonistic, plump flesh. Make her moan my name.

"Good lord," he whispered. "What an unsettling thought. Lady Sophia is nothing more than a schemer. A liar."

He reached for his flask again, remembered it was empty, then turned and walked out of the park once more to hail a hack.

"I don't even like her," he hissed. "Not at all."

Chapter Eight

"Scotland is lovely this time of year, I understand. The solitude would be good for me." Sophia would even make a go at the vow of silence, though doubted that would last. "I can tend sheep. Or bees. Churn butter." She tried to picture herself doing so in a serene country setting. "Maybe learn to weave."

Mama pinched the bridge of her nose.

"And after a few years, I can leave and retire to the country. Forever. I vow to never return to London." She'd never cared overmuch for society or the Season. Paying calls and attending balls was fine but monotonous. Only the bookstores and museums held her interest. "In a year or so, no one will remember you had a younger daughter. Mara's reputation won't be infringed upon in the least. Roxboro would be relieved. As would Lord Damon." She gestured towards her sister as she walked into the drawing room. "Mara's prospects would remain forever untainted."

Her sister glided into the drawing room, skirts belling out about her trim ankles as if she were floating. Sailing directly to the settee, Mara fluffed out her skirts in a fetching manner as she settled against the pillows. Back straight. Chin tilted at exactly the correct angle. An entire stack of books could be placed atop Mara's head, and the tomes would be in no danger of falling.

She really is absolute perfection.

"Don't be absurd," Mama replied. "You'd make a terrible

nun. You've not an ounce of humility, Sophia. Now, do something with your gown." She waved a finger. "Emulate Mara. See how she places the folds of her skirts about her to make it seem as if she's sitting in a flower?"

Sophia half-heartedly waved the silk folds of her gown about her, trying to imitate Mara, but failed miserably.

Mama sighed. "Stop. You look like a floundering fish."

"I could learn humility. I can be pious. I've always liked livestock."

"We are not sending you to a convent. Or the country. Goodness, the banns have been read. The church reserved. Invitations to the event have already gone out. You are to be a duchess, which I find more unbelievable than anyone else."

"I could end the betrothal," Sophia offered, her desperation apparent. "I would put no blame on Roxboro. Things merely didn't work out."

"*Roxboro* could end the betrothal and if he did, the shame would fall upon you as a discarded young lady. He would survive because he's a duke, but not you, Sophia."

Absolutely unfair.

"Mama's right," Mara chirped. "You must wed Roxboro, or else things will go poorly for you, Sophia. Just yesterday as I walked in the park, I came across Miss Newsome." Her sister made a face. "Who made a rather impolite comment about you and Roxboro."

"What was it?" Sophia had a general idea. The talk hadn't been complimentary towards her. Also, the park brought to mind the ill-fated carriage ride with Roxboro. A painful outing which was nothing more than an indication of the future that awaited her. She and Roxboro had said terrible things to each other that day, all of which, Roxboro deserved. He blamed her for this entire mess, insisting he hadn't been at the Perswick ball, and that even if he had, Sophia took advantage of the situation because he was foxed.

Good god, he's always foxed.

"Well," Mara fluffed the pillow beside her. "All of London knows Roxboro drinks overmuch. You weren't oblivious—it doesn't matter," Mara hurriedly added after a pointed look from Mama.

"You think I orchestrated my own ruination to become a duchess?" Sophia nearly choked on the words. "Because he drinks too much?"

"Of course not, dear," Mama said in a soothing tone.

"I would never," Sophia insisted. "You truly believe I would deliberately lead him out, completely intoxicated, for the sole purpose of ruination? Because I want to be his duchess?" She threw up her hands. "I've been begging for weeks to be released from this betrothal. For goodness sakes, I'm begging to become a nun."

"It isn't what I think, Sophia," Mara said, in a condescending tone. "*I* believe you, of course."

No she didn't.

"Miss Newsome is only jealous," Mara continued. "She's had her eyes on Roxboro for some time, despite his reputation. Always crowing about how a good woman could set him to rights and that reformed rakes make the best husbands. I gave her a brilliant set-down by insulting her bonnet."

"You're such a dear to defend your sister." Mama nodded in approval.

Insulting her bonnet. What was next? Disdaining her shawl?

"I would have blackened her eye," Sophia fumed. She had never cared for Miss Newsome. Turning her gaze to the window where a large elm sat directly outside, she tried to calm her raging thoughts. The branches swayed in the wind, leaves fluttering about.

"Oh, Sophia." Mama took her hand. "You've done nothing your entire life but thumb your nose at the rest of the world. Perhaps it is time to try a different tactic. I don't know what compels you to behave in such an obstinate manner. You will have a distant, if amicable marriage to Roxboro, which frankly, is how most marriages in society are conducted. You'll find your own interests. Have a great deal of freedom as a duchess. Besides, he's bound to tumble down the stairs after too much brandy or scotch one night."

"I wish you would stop saying such things, Mama." It was rather disturbing how often her mother claimed Roxboro would meet an early demise.

"I only want you to see that there are distinct advantages to the situation. A politician's wife learns to be pragmatic about such things. And you should thank your sister for putting that horrible Miss Newsome in her place."

"Thank you, Mara," Sophia dutifully repeated.

Mama could crow all she wanted about becoming the mother of a duchess and enjoy her elevated status, but Sophia did not share her opinion of a positive future. If Mama knew of Sophia's heated, ugly discussion with Roxboro during the carriage ride, and that it was likely the reason he hadn't called upon her since, she wouldn't be so pleased.

Truthfully, Sophia shouldn't have lost her temper. Nor insulted him. That wasn't the way to move forward. But his continued insistence that he did not recall her, not even vaguely, reminded Sophia of how *utterly forgettable* she'd felt her entire life. Which resulted in blunt, somewhat scathing observations spilling from her lips, or thinly veiled insults.

I really am terrible. I deserve to be wed to a libertine.

"I couldn't allow her to disparage you." Mara clasped her hands in her lap, turning her head so that her gorgeous profile was on display. "You are my sister."

Ugh. Mara must have been practicing before the mirror. She resembled a bloody cameo.

"Lord Damon and the duke will arrive at any moment," Mama said, gazing with approval at her eldest daughter. "We'll have a lovely dinner. Unfortunately, Lady Violet and Lady Rose will not be able to join us as they are with Lady Falworth. A house party in the country to which they were committed. But,"

Mama clapped her hands. "They'll return to London in time for the wedding. I expect you four will become fast friends."

Doubtful. Sophia had even less in common with Violet and Rose Viceroy than she did with Miss Newsome.

"A house party?" Mara raised her brows. "Oh, Lady Dunkirk's." She narrowed her eyes on Sophia. "The one Mama and I had to decline due to...your impending nuptials, Sophia."

Sophia had also somewhat reluctantly, she suspected, been invited, but would have feigned sickness not to attend. The only thing worse than a ball, in her opinion, was a house party.

"The Marquess of Caster isn't even in attendance at Lady Dunkirk's," Mama reassured Mara. "I have it on good authority. So there's no worry he might be snatched up. And," she winked. "Lady Falworth is close friends with the Caster's mother, the Dowager Marchioness, which is rather lucky. Once we are family, I'll receive an introduction."

Good lord. Mama *was* a mercenary.

Lady Falworth was her mother's newest future conquest in society, though the poor woman was completely unaware. She was the sister of Lord Damon's late wife, May, and had assisted in Violet and Rose's upbringing since their mother's death. Mama knew a great deal about the three women, as she did Lord Damon and Roxboro. At this point, she could probably rattle off the entire lineage of the Viceroys, their estates and the names of their servants.

Mama was very thorough.

The previous duke and duchess, Roxboro's parents, had met tragic ends. Roxboro's father was murdered. His mother died giving birth to him. Lord Damon, who was barely twenty and newly wed to Lady May, raised Roxboro as their own. Rose and Violet were born a few years later. Perfect young ladies, that is what Mama said of Lord Damon's daughters, if a bit snobbish.

Sophia had only met them once and was more than happy to wait on furthering the acquaintance as she'd found both young women a tad arrogant, which given they were Viceroys, made a great deal of sense. Neither had seemed inclined to speak to Sophia outside of a polite introduction, though Mara flitted around them like a moth around a torch for as long as possible.

Well, I suppose they won't be able to avoid me now, given I'll outrank them.

The knowledge brought Sophia little comfort. She didn't want to be Roxboro's duchess. Or anyone's actually. Society had strict expectations of a duchess, none of which Sophia could hope to meet. Ducal behavior. Snootiness. Absolute commanding presence. Splendid clothing. Constant calls paid upon her. Sounded absolutely…. exhausting.

Sophia had always assumed she would wed some moderately attractive gentleman, with wealth and name to match. A scholarly viscount, perhaps, who if he didn't set her aflame with any great passion—*the books she loved always claimed searing fire and flame between the hero and heroine*—there would be companionship. A liking for each other.

Not a duke known for his debauchery who couldn't even recall compromising her.

"Rose and Violet are so elegant," Mara enthused. "Their gowns are the envy of every lady in the *ton*. Lord Damon brings a modiste from Paris who designs for them exclusively. They are always dressed in the latest fashions well before anyone else in London." Mara nodded. "Can you imagine?"

"No," Sophia said. "I cannot."

"Rose speaks five languages. Violet only three but she is a renowned equestrian." Mara leaned in. "She sits a horse far better than her cousin."

I mocked him for that. Which was unkind.

"Pinch your cheeks," Mara shook her head. "You look like a corpse. It is rather unbecoming."

Sophia ignored her. As soon as Mara turned to say something to Mama, she picked up the embroidery her sister had left tucked behind a cushion, discreetly pulling out two rows of stitches. The basket of roses depicted on the cloth was now ruined. She tossed the hoop behind one of the chairs, feeling much better.

"Perhaps a bit of sun on your cheeks prior to the ceremony would not be remiss." Mama turned to study her. "You *are* much too pale. Sit in the sun for a bit tomorrow. Just enough for a hint of color. We don't want anyone to think you've taken ill. The wedding is in two days, after all."

I should be so fortunate as to contract the plague.

This family dinner was the only event leading up to her ill-fated nuptials. Mama had wanted to host a lavish ball and an even more extravagant dinner party leading up to the wedding. There had also been plans for a wedding breakfast with no less than fifty guests directly after the ceremony.

Roxboro had politely, but firmly, declined Mama's suggestions as had Lord Damon. Papa, in a shocking display of defiance, agreed.

Sophia and the duke would be wed at St. Paul's in front of a large assortment of important personages, and leave the church in an open carriage, so that all of London might share in their joyous occasion, but that was all Roxboro had agreed to.

Sophia was vastly relieved.

The ice blue gown, created out of a silk so sheer the fabric shimmered in the light, hung upstairs. Mama always insisted Sophia dress in blue, claiming the color highlighted her hair. She would carry a nosegay of lilies and Mama *insisted* on the sapphire bracelet. The same bracelet lost the night of the Perswick ball. A tense discussion followed when she'd had to admit to misplacing the bracelet.

Mama was not pleased.

What followed was a scouring of the house by the staff who of course, did not find the bracelet, possibly because Sophia was certain it was in hiding in the grass of Lady Perswick's garden.

I'll send a note once I'm…the Duchess of Roxboro. When Lady Perswick would be less likely to ignore her.

Papa walked into the room, pausing to look at the three of them with a pleased smile. "My lovely girls. Has ever a man been so blessed?" He came forward to kiss Mama's cheek. "And you the fairest of them all."

Mama playfully swatted him. "My lord, the things you say."

Papa gave Mara a kiss before lightly touching the top of Sophia's head. "It will all work out, moppet," he whispered to her. "I'll make sure of it."

That was what she feared.

Powell, the Canterbell butler, appeared a few moments later. "My lord. His Grace, the Duke of Roxboro and Lord Damon Viceroy." He stood aside, ushering the two men in.

Roxboro entered first, so bloody beautiful and elegant in appearance that it hurt Sophia's eyes. Her heart flapped about inside her chest at the sight of him, watching as all that controlled sensuality stalked towards the three Canterbell women. When they'd driven through the park together, ladies walking together had halted to stare at him. Even their maids grew flustered. There was a reason he was known as one of the worst rogues London had ever produced.

Perhaps that was why Roxboro had chosen to amuse himself with Sophia on that fateful night. She'd been something of a lark for a jaded libertine. But even a reminder that he'd been so cruel to her did nothing to dispel Roxboro's allure. Watching him now, Sophia didn't wonder she'd followed him so blindly into the garden without a care for her reputation or whether he was deliberately leading her astray.

There wasn't a woman in London who would object to his attentions.

Mara made a sound. One of appreciation. Her entire body bowed in Roxboro's direction.

Oh, good grief.

The magnificent picture Roxboro presented ended a second later, however, when he stumbled, hit the edge of a table and nearly upended a vase of flowers.

There's the Roxboro I know. Sot.

Sophia observed the tips of his ears, pink like the underside of a seashell, a sign he was embarrassed by his clumsiness. She'd observed the same reaction before and in neither instance, had she thought him foxed.

Was it more acceptable to stumble about as a duke in his cups than one who was merely...awkward at times? She thought it might be.

I will not feel sorry for him.

"Apologies, Lady Canterbell. Lord Canterbell." Roxboro righted himself, grabbing the vase before it could fall to the floor. "My toe caught on the edge of the rug, which I must say, is uniquely lovely."

Papa merely gave a small shake of his head, assuming Roxboro already full of brandy. "Your Grace."

Mama rushed towards him. "I've never cared for that vase at any rate, Your Grace. Had it broken, no one would mourn its loss. Powell," she said to the butler. "There is a loose bit of fringe on the rug. Make sure it is corrected before someone else harms themselves." She presented her hand for Roxboro to take and dipped. "We are so pleased you could dine with us, Your Grace."

"I understand you set a fine table, my lady," Roxboro returned. "I would never miss such an invitation." A half-smile tilted his lips. A lovely one.

Mama fluttered her lashes, already taken in by his charm, just as she'd been when he'd called a few weeks ago at the beginning of this farce.

"My eldest daughter, Lady Mara," Papa introduced Sophia's sister.

Mara's curtsey, as usual, was nothing short of spectacular. Skirts pluming out around her like the unfurling of a rose bud. Not a hair out of place, the golden strands sparkling in the light of the drawing room, giving the impression she glowed. Or wore a halo. As she lowered her chin, one curl artfully glanced off her shoulder.

In short, Mara was utterly flawless in both appearance and manner.

Disgusting, really.

"Lord Damon Viceroy." Roxboro's uncle came forward to take Mama's hand, lips grazing her knuckles. "Lady Canterbell." The dark eyes lingered on Mara a tad too long. "Lady Mara." Damon drew out each letter as if Mara's name was the rarest of treasures. Which, of course, had the desired effect.

Mara swayed slightly as Lord Damon took her hand with a smile, nearly falling into a swoon.

Sophia didn't even blame her sister or mother. Roxboro was glorious, there wasn't any doubt, as was his uncle. The Viceroy looks were the stuff of legend. Rose and Violet Viceroy were lauded for their beauty. And Lord Damon, though far older, was widely regarded as one of the most handsome men in London, second only to his nephew. The day at Roxboro's home, when this entire arrangement had come about, Sophia hadn't noticed how breathtaking they both were, standing side by side, like a pair of stunning bookends.

Pity, Roxboro is so devoid of any redeemable qualities.

Mama had some stupid theory that Lord Damon, a confirmed bachelor since the death of his wife, would be overjoyed to welcome Sophia into the family, no matter the circumstances. Because he was his nephew's heir and the only male Viceroy left. Sophia would be saving Lord Damon from having to remarry, something, much to the dismay of a great many females in London, he showed little inclination to do.

Lord Damon's smile faltered, finally disappearing entirely as his dark, brittle gaze landed on Sophia. Ice coated her immediately at that look.

No, he does not see me as beneficial, Mama.

Roxboro regarded Sophia with a great deal of wariness hovering in those shimmering eyes. As if she meant to attack him, here in the Canterbell drawing room.

Would that stop the marriage if she flew at him like an enraged hedgehog?

Did hedgehogs become enraged?

Perhaps a beaver, then. They seem vicious.

Anger towards Roxboro was justified, Sophia reminded herself. It had been entirely unnecessary to lead her to believe he admired her at the ball, when he clearly did not. Sophia had castigated herself dozens of times for believing Roxboro's lecherous drivel. She couldn't seem to force the words away, no matter how she tried. It was one thing to be compromised publicly—

Damn Lady Brokeburst.

—quite another to have the gentleman in question to be so drunk as to assume he was merely kissing a shrub. Or insisting he'd not been present at all.

It was humiliating. And cruel.

Roxboro's gloved fingers curled around her own, warming the skin beneath her gloves. "My lady," he said in a clipped tone.

Sophia dropped into the best curtsey she could muster under the circumstances, which wasn't saying much. She not so discreetly sniffed the air between them for a hint of spirits.

He squeezed her fingers tighter, pulling Sophia forward. "I'm not foxed," he murmured under his breath.

"I don't care," she whispered back. "Be a sot."

Roxboro peered down at her from his far greater height, completely composed and supremely ducal. But she caught the small twitch at the corner of one of those sea storm eyes. It annoyed her future husband when she referred to him as a sot. He regarded her with pained tolerance, still holding her fingers as Sophia's family and Lord Damon made their way to take a seat while Powell offered refreshments.

"Not at all memorable," Roxboro drawled quietly. "Because it was not me. Lady Seraphina."

This again. Sophia's annoyance flared to life. "Stop doing that. And it is not my fault that your love of drink and opium—"

He blinked at her with all innocence. "Only a little opium."

"—cause you to have a faulty memory. Mine, however, is intact. Your lips," she whispered. "Are akin to the skin of a toad.

Fleshy and wet as *I* recall."

Roxboro released her hand, a lazy smile pulling at his lips. "You're a combative little chit, aren't you? But I am going to wed you, much as I'd like to avoid doing so. You might consider, that you'll be *my* wife, under *my* thumb, and be more careful with your words, my lady."

A not-so-subtle threat.

Vile cad.

"The longer I spend in your company, Roxboro, the more I regret knowing you."

"Your Grace," he gritted his teeth.

"I do not desire to become your wife, contrary to what your inflated ego likes to believe." Sophia glanced at the settee where Mama observed them, her brows drawn together. "I thought I'd made my feelings clear during our carriage ride. I've begged for my father to send me to a convent rather than wed you."

The green of Roxboro's eyes deepened. "You? A nun?" A soft chuckle came from him. "God help us."

The tense set of Mama's shoulders relaxed. She sat back against the cushions assuming, incorrectly, that Sophia and Roxboro were having a pleasant conversation.

"I think I'd be rather good at it," she hissed back. "Please refrain from your continued assumption that I concocted some scheme to become your duchess—"

"I thought," he interrupted her calmly. "We'd agreed to blame Lady Brokeburst. At any rate, I do hope we are seated beside each other at dinner so that I may enjoy more of your wit, my lady. I cannot wait for a lifetime of it."

"A much briefer length than my own, I'm certain. Given the misfortune you attract and the spirits you indulge in."

"Bloodthirsty as well as annoying and hostile." His nostrils flared. "What a joy our union will be. I count the minutes until our wedding day," he said with barely a hint of sarcasm. Without looking away from her, he said to their butler, "Powell. A glass of scotch, if you have it." Roxboro leaned forward once more and whispered, "I like it almost as much as brandy. And if I hadn't a reason to become foxed tonight, I believe I've found one."

HE HADN'T MEANT to lose his temper.
Nor...feel such a rush of feeling at the sight of his unwanted bride to be. Annoyance, of course. Anger. But also...the unexpected need to cover that scathing, but completely decadent mouth with his own.

Alexander instructed his butler, Timmons, to pull out a copy of Debrett's from a dusty shelf in the library—*because, God knows, he'd never actually looked at the bible of society himself*—and write out all the names for women beginning with the letter S. He had an entire collection now, ready to be hurled at his future duchess.

Alexander didn't bother to acknowledge why he needed such a list.

Nor why, since the day of the carriage ride through the park with his little shrew, he had not ventured to Binson's. He put it down to the absence of Oakhurst, but there were dozens of acquaintances Alexander might have joined there. Nor did he visit Florenza, his mistress, not even to say goodbye. Instead, he'd sent her an overly expensive diamond necklace with his regrets.

Oakhurst would be so disappointed. Alexander was a poor excuse for a libertine.

Her fault. All of it.

Powell handed him a glass of scotch which smelled heavenly.

Alexander took two large swallows, enough to ask for the glass to be refilled. As discreetly as possible, he gestured the butler to his side.

"Make sure," he said in a low tone. "That my scotch is served well-watered during the meal. I have plans later." Alexander didn't have anywhere to be, but he also didn't want Powell gossiping with the servants that the Duke of Roxboro had asked to have his scotch watered. Nor did he want his uncle to question why he was doing so.

Alexander had no intention of giving up any of his vices, no matter how...unappealing they'd become as of late. Not yet. But the urge to...tamp them down had appeared the last week and refused to go away.

Also, her fault.

A temporary pause, only. When Oakhurst returned, things in Alexander's life would return to normal. But in the meantime, he meant to keep his wits about him, especially in dealing with Canterbell and his daughter. Neither of whom he trusted.

He observed Sophia from across the room, pleased when she twitched at his pointed perusal. She was not...beautiful, not like Lady Mara who was frankly, nothing short of exquisite. But Sophia had claws. Claws that dug firmly into Alexander's chest. He'd taken himself in hand at least twice since that carriage ride with her in the park, imagining how it would feel to—dominate Sophia. Hear her moan his name. Beg him.

Which was rather unseemly. There wasn't any reason for Alexander to stroke his own cock. Florenza was a perfectly good mistress. Or had been.

Most definitely Sophia's fault.

Scowling at her, Alexander drummed his fingers along the edge of the chair he'd settled in, wondering at the odd turn his life had taken. He couldn't even ask Oakhurst's advice because he still had no idea where his friend had gone. Inquiries to the residence of Lady Maxwell proved just as fruitless. Uncle Damon was equally mystified over Oakhurst's disappearance, and suggested gambling debts. But Alexander had only laughed. Oakhurst had never once mentioned any pending impoverishment or debts of any kind.

Although his friend had also never mentioned bedding Lady Maxwell.

Powell returned with another glass of scotch.

Alexander took a sip and nodded. There was enough scotch to make the taste palatable and ease his thirst, but little else.

"Perfect, Powell. I will expect the same all during dinner."
"Yes, Your Grace."

Chapter Nine

Roxboro was intoxicated.
 He had to be.

Sophia cocked her head, studying her unwanted betrothed and the half glass of scotch at his elbow that Powell kept filled without Roxboro asking.

Under the circumstances, Sophia didn't blame him for drinking endless amounts of scotch during this dinner; had she been able, she would have waved away the few glasses of wine Mama allotted her and gone right to something a bit stronger. Fortitude and courage was required for this evening. What did it matter if Sophia found it in a bottle?

But despite the amount of scotch Roxboro consumed while enjoying the roasted duck, he never once appeared drunk. His hands, with their long, elegant fingers, never wavered. Not a bit of sloppiness. No slurred word. Didn't miss his mouth and poke his eye out with a fork. Cut his meat without slicing off a finger. Both of which would have made things interesting.

Impressive.

Roxboro's eyes, those glorious orbs that sent young ladies for the smelling salts, were the exact color of lichen where it clung to a rock in the forest, the striations of gray deepening as they passed over Sophia.

It would be impossible to mistake him for anyone else.

"He's exceptionally handsome," Mara pinched Sophia's thigh.

"I can see why Mercy Eldridge wrote a poem about his eyes."

"That hurt. And Mercy is an idiot."

"True," her sister agreed. "Though she does have a way with words. There was much sighing and pressing a palm to her heart as she recited the poem to me."

Ugh.

"His tolerance for drink is quite remarkable."

Would Mara never shut up? "I don't think that's a compliment. Given his pursuits and the company the duke keeps, one would expect he enjoys spirits."

"Not to mention," Mara continued, undeterred. "His legion of conquests." Her voice lowered further. "Of which you, dear sister, are the most recent."

"Yes, I believe that has been established." Sophia lowered her fork and pressed it into Mara's knee.

Her sister's leg jolted. "Poor Mama. Torn between disappointment at the scandal you created, utter disbelief it was Roxboro who conquered you and the thrill that she'll soon be a duchess."

"I was not *conquered*," Sophia whispered back. "Nor am I a castle to be stormed. There was no grand seduction as you well know. It was *barely* a kiss. I've told you so repeatedly. Lord Wilde has taken more liberties. With you."

Mara's lips rippled. She smoothed her hair though not one strand was out of place. Two signs she was about to tell a lie.

"An exaggeration. Even so, at least I was wise enough to make sure Lady Brokeburst was nowhere in the vicinity. I heard her tell Mama, before Roxboro decided to be honorable, that you were clasped in a torrid embrace. Bent over his arm passionately." Mara glanced at Roxboro. "How…stimulating."

"Lady Brokeburst saw nothing of the kind, because it never happened. She's beastly. I blame her for this entire affair. And then Papa with his ridiculous tale of Roxboro and I courting in secret. I think I would rather be a pariah."

"You should thank Lady Brokeburst for making you a duchess." Mara nodded. "And as for Papa's little tale, parroted by Lord Damon and even Roxboro himself, not one soul believes it, as my set down of Miss Newsome proves. Most believe the duke was so in his cups he might have thought you one of his paramours and followed you to the gardens. You, in a burst of ruthlessness because you are Lord Canterbell's daughter, took advantage." Mara looked up to make sure Mama wasn't listening. "I don't blame you," she continued in a low tone. "Nor do any of the ladies I've encountered, though they drip with jealousy. He's dreadfully good looking, a duke and wealthy. The rumors of his...debauched nature have only titillated, not put off anyone." Mara turned to spear a piece of the duck. "You saw an opportunity. Given your prospects on the marriage mart..." the words trailed off with a shrug of her sister's shoulders.

"I did not." Sophia sputtered, horrified that even Mara thought her capable of such treachery. "He's a sot and an overindulged, arrogant cad. Hardly the catch of the Season."

"There are many who would disagree. Not on the first part of your statement, but the last."

Mama cleared her throat subtly, a signal that she'd seen their heads bent together and didn't care for it.

"Even I would be tempted," Mara picked at the duck. "Just look at him. Or," she turned her sights on Roxboro's uncle. "Lord Damon."

"Mara." Mama cautioned from her place at the table.

"I must confess," Lord Damon drawled as he sat back in his chair. "This is the finest meal I've had in some time, Lady Canterbell. The duck was nothing short of extraordinary. I don't suppose I could steal your cook?" he teased.

"My lord. You flatter me," Mama stated humbly, but her cheeks pinked at his attention.

Damon Viceroy knew how to compliment a woman. Mama had giggled like a schoolgirl at nearly everything he said during the meal, lowering her lashes with a soft, rosy flush creeping up her neck. There was also the mild stammering when Lord

Damon looked directly at her, as if Mama might call for smelling salts at any moment.

Papa wasn't fooled. He laughed at every jest or humorous tale, but the calculating look directed at Roxboro's uncle never wavered. Lord Canterbell wielded a great deal of influence in Parliament because he wasn't stupid.

Lord Damon reminded Sophia of a crocodile, especially when he smiled. The flat, flinty gaze. The perfect row of teeth ready to sink into his prey. Not that she'd ever seen a crocodile, only an artist's rendering in a book. *Lord Black and the Pirates of Ruin*, one of her favorites. She'd read it three times. The heroine is saved from a crocodile whose resemblance to Lord Damon was uncanny.

"I'll relay your compliments to our cook, Mrs. Cotton," Mama said, ever the ideal hostess. "She is responsible for the duck, my lord, not I." Pressing a palm to the base of her throat, she said, "I merely wrote out the menu."

"Then you are responsible for pairing such delicious potatoes with this exquisite sauce. I think you far too modest, my lady. You contributed as much to the meal as Mrs. Cotton."

Sophia struggled keep from making a face.

"It is a shame that Lady Violet and Lady Rose could not join us this evening," Mama said, so unsettled by Lord Damon's compliments, she nearly dropped her fork. "And of course, Lady Falworth."

"A pity. But Lady Falworth was most insistent that their plans could not be altered. I understand doing so would have played havoc with the seating charts at the Dunkirk house party."

"I can well understand," Mama agreed.

"But Lady Falworth promises to return well before the wedding. Tomorrow evening, as it happens." Lord Damon dabbed at his lips with a napkin, dark eyes glittering like black ice as they passed over Sophia.

"How delightful. We shall look forward to becoming better acquainted after, won't we?" She nodded at both Sophia and Mara.

"Indeed," Lord Damon said. "I hope you don't mind I did add two last minute guests to the wedding, my lady. The widow of a dear friend and her son who I hadn't thought would be in London. Lord Caster and Roxboro grew up together, and I've known the Dowager Marchioness for ages. She's close friends with Lady Falworth."

"The Marquess of Caster?" Mama beamed at him. "Of course not."

Mama had set her sights on Caster some time ago for Mara, deeming him eminently suitable for her daughter. Honestly, if Lord Damon had asked Mama to toss Papa in the Thames right now to gain more influence with Caster, she would have.

"You are too kind, my lady." Lord Damon said. "And I am deeply," he stressed the word, making Mama blush even further. "Appreciative. Especially on such short notice."

"It would be our great pleasure," Mama glanced at Papa. "And they must join us for the wedding breakfast as well, given that His Grace and Caster are so close."

The wedding breakfast had been deemed for family only.

Papa made a grunt and took a sip of his wine. "Yes, we insist."

Roxboro said nothing, neither confirming nor denying whether he and Caster were even acquainted, let alone great friends. Her future husband was most usually mentioned in the gossip columns in conjunction with Lord Oakhurst, along with a string of titled ladies. But never Caster.

Clever Lord Damon. He'd found a way to put Mama in his debt.

I find I dislike Roxboro's uncle even more, though I admire his strategy.

"Lady Falworth will be so pleased," Lord Damon continued. "As will Violet and Rose. I do wish my May was here to celebrate the occasion with us, but I think," a mournful look crossed his features. "She will be there, watching over us all."

"I met her once, my lord." Mama's features were contorted in sympathy. "A lovely woman of great modesty. Well-regarded by everyone in London."

"Here, here, Uncle." Roxboro lifted his glass. "To Aunt May."

"She spoiled you." The side of Damon's mouth lifted to a half-smile as he addressed Roxboro. "May was a rare gem. Impossible to replace."

"You're still young, uncle." Roxboro sipped from his glass.

"Indeed, my lord," Papa intoned from the head of the table. "Given your aspirations, an astute woman versed in politics would be a great asset. I agree with the duke. I would never have gotten far without Lady Canterbell at my side."

Mama *glowed*. As if lit from within by the sun. She'd been complimented by Lord Damon and Papa, then given the immense opportunity of ingratiating herself with not only Lady Falmouth, but also Lady Caster, whose son she wanted for Mara. She wouldn't sleep a wink tonight.

"The idea has merit, my lord," Damon murmured. "Perhaps when the time is right, Lady Canterbell might introduce me to a lady who matches her own skill and capabilities. I would accept nothing less." Those dark, calculating eyes lingered over Mara.

Mama nearly melted into the table.

Mara lowered her gaze, a tiny smile on her lips, a bit of color flooding her cheeks.

Ugh. Could no one else see what Roxboro's uncle had just done?

Sophia raised her chin a fraction to see the duke watching her. There was a tiny, almost imperceptible roll of his shoulders directed at her.

He knew what his uncle was up to.

Lord Damon snapped his fingers at Powell. "Another glass for His Grace."

Papa didn't flinch at Lord Damon's audacity at ordering the staff about because given the previous conversation, it would do no good, not with Mama salivating over the possibility of Caster *and* Lord Damon for Mara.

Sophia gaining a duke by accident barely signified.

Roxboro toyed with the glass Powell set before him, motioning for the butler to lean over. He exchanged quiet words with the butler, who nodded in agreement.

"Yes, Your Grace." Powell faded away into the background of the dining room once more.

Roxboro tilted his chin in Sophia's direction, pinning her in place with those unusual eyes, sculpted features composed and somewhat bland. No charming smile for her. Only what appeared to be polite disinterest.

Not exactly an auspicious start for a marriage. The only thing she and the duke agreed upon was that neither wanted to wed the other. Oh, and Lady Brokeburst's needless meddling.

Once Sophia became a duchess, the very first thing she meant to do was give that old gossiping harpy the cut direct. The second, a demand that Sophia be sent to the country. Anywhere really, her only request was that it be far from London. Roxboro must have a distant estate somewhere, a place Sophia might build a life of her own. She'd no desire to spend her days paying calls or dangling off Roxboro's arm at society events in town. Nor did she want to endure further speculation on how Lord Canterbell's troublesome daughter managed to wed the stunning Duke of Roxboro, particularly when she didn't care to be a duchess. Also, she would be out of Mama's orbit. She could enjoy her books in peace. Roxboro couldn't possibly object to living as far apart as possible.

The problem was, of course, begetting an heir.

Roxboro had made his feelings clear on Sophia's desirability. A bit of a sting, but she returned them tenfold. Unfortunately, the marriage would have to be consummated at some point.

An heir must be produced. And given Roxboro might trip into the Thames again or drunkenly fall off his horse, there might be more than one...bout of marital relations.

A flutter took up residence in her chest at the thought.

Mama spoke of little else but Sophia's 'duty'. One she'd no interest in performing.

Oh, come now, Sophia.

Traitorous thoughts. Of those beautiful features so near her own. Those elegant fingers touching Sophia in a manner that would leave her breathless. She didn't want to think of it, tried not to find it appealing but...for goodness sakes, he resembled a statue of Apollo. Or more appropriately, Hades.

Hopefully she could...enjoy matters at least from that perspective.

Stop it, Sophia. This instant.

Sophia met Roxboro's look, stabbing at him with one of her own.

Magnificent or not, he lacked a great deal of character. There was no shortage of tales related to his escapades, many of which she'd heard well before meeting him at Lady Perswick's. Some were so horrifying, so wicked in nature, she couldn't imagine they were true. That story about the sheep, for instance...

Yet, I still...went into the gardens with him.

"Your Grace." Mara addressed Roxboro, perhaps sensing the tension hovering over the dining room table. "I understand you enjoy the opera."

The duke's attention flicked to Mara briefly before returning to Sophia. His fingers drew over his drink lazily, which would have any woman wishing fervently to be that glass of scotch.

Oh, for goodness sakes, Sophia.

"I like opera singers, Lady Mara," he said slowly while continuing to study Sophia. "Italian sopranos, in particular."

"You favor their arias?"

Sophia wanted to swat Mara. Only an idiot would fail to recognize that Roxboro was making an impolite innuendo. His comment had nothing to do with an Italian soprano's singing ability.

"In a manner of speaking, my lady," Roxboro answered, earning him a displeased sound from Papa.

"Your Grace," Lord Damon ground out in warning.

"Do *you* enjoy the opera, Lady Sophia?" Roxboro murmured

sardonically, ignoring his uncle. "I confess, I'm curious as to your opinion on…sopranos."

Horrible wretch.

"The opera is not to my taste." Sophia intentionally neglected to address him properly, gratified when his brows drew together in irritation. "I couldn't tell a soprano from a tenor, I fear. It all sounds the same to me. Like goats screaming to each other in the countryside."

Mama's eyes fluttered shut in shame at Sophia's response.

"I expected that to be the case. I, however, find opera to be rather stimulating which is why I have a box. You'll accompany me as often as possible to help broaden your appreciation."

"It is unlikely I will." Sophia returned as politely as humanly possible, mostly to keep her mother from having a fit of apoplexy. "I am hoping to retire to the country which I'm sure is something we can agree upon."

A horrified sound came from Mama. As if she were choking on the duck.

"I believe we can," Roxboro stated plainly, not looking away.

The entire table went silent. Mama started fanning herself. Even Sophia's father eyed her with disappointment. Roxboro was the only one who didn't seem surprised she wanted to be sent to the country and away from him. Lord Damon seemed…almost giddy at the news.

He doesn't care for me in the least.

"I'm sure it is only the Italian that puts my sister off," Mara interjected, voice a bit higher than usual, attempting to return to the original subject, which no one gave a fig about. "She doesn't speak Italian. When you know the language, or at least have a general understanding, opera becomes that much more enjoyable. My Italian is barely passable, but I am fluent in French."

Roxboro leveled a sensuous smile on her. "Comme c'est delicieux," he said in perfectly accented French, ignoring Papa who did not care for the duke's response nor the way in which he gave it.

Mama choked into her napkin. She was fluent, as befitting a politician's wife. Doubtless, Lord Damon spoke French. Powell might even know the language.

But Sophia did not, leaving her at a distinct disadvantage.

Hours of tutelage in French had only managed to annoy Monsieur Frank. He left Lord Canterbell's employ, stating that Sophia was incapable of speaking anything other than English. Or behaving with any modesty.

I only said it sounds as if he's speaking through his nose.

"Oui, Monsieur le duc." Mara fluttered her lashes at Roxboro in a fetching manner.

Intolerable. Roxboro is my betrothed whether I want him or not.

Sophia kicked her sister beneath the table, but when Mara didn't flinch, she opted to grind her heel into the top of Mara's slipper.

A tiny sound left her sister. A painful one.

"Your accent," Lord Damon said. "Is impeccable, Lady Mara." The gleaming black ice of his eyes dropped to Sophia. "A shame…you don't speak French, Lady Sophia. Luckily, I know an excellent tutor."

CHAPTER TEN

*Y*ES, A PITY *his bride didn't speak French.*
But given Sophia's extreme stubbornness, Alexander didn't find that to be terribly unusual. Tutors likely fled the Canterbell house as if the devil were at their heels rather than instruct her. But the real pity was that Alexander hadn't ruined the stunning, far more accomplished Lady Mara. She would have made an adequate duchess. But a bland one.

She wasn't nearly as entertaining as her terrible sister.

Who, Alexander was, unexpectedly and unfortunately... *lusting* after. Why, he had no idea. He still didn't recall her at all. Nor the kiss Lady Brokeburst allegedly witnessed. A kiss Sophia had compared to the slobbering tongue of a puppy.

Alexander was skilled in the art of seduction. He enjoyed women a great deal. And he had never, not since bedding his first at the age of fifteen, bestowed an inadequate kiss. Or an insufficient *anything*.

Now, because of Sophia, he would endure the added humiliation of having to confess his cock didn't work as a means to rid himself of her. Damon's argument was to blame Alexander's use of opium, which admittedly, was a valid excuse. If a gentleman smoked a great deal of opium, one couldn't do much of anything, let alone bed a woman.

She's nothing more than an inconvenience.

He peered at Sophia over the rim of his much-watered down

scotch. Every word Alexander spoke during the meal elicited a scowl, a grimace or some odd sound from her, very much like a feral squirrel. An unending stream of disdain contorted her features, all directed at him, during the entirety of the meal.

Alexander sighed in frustration.

He hadn't attended the Perswick ball, but had no explanation for why others claimed he'd been there. Nor did he have any explanation for the comments on his mussed clothing. Cravat improperly tied. No stickpin. A stain on his coat. More than one acquaintance had expressed concern to Damon directly over Alexander's general state of dishevelment at the ball.

I would never arrive at a ball in such a condition.

All of which left him greatly concerned for the state of his mind.

And while Alexander was sure he hadn't compromised her…if Sophia didn't confess she'd made a mistake, he'd be forced to admit…

He sipped at his barely scotch.

Not that any of it mattered at this late date. Nothing would stop this marriage. Canterbell would never allow it. Nor Damon. Which meant Alexander would wed a girl he didn't even like, in two days.

I do like her hostility. Quite a bit.

The lower half of his body tightened like a knot. Given the cut of his trousers, which was unforgiving, Alexander was endlessly grateful for the length of his coat. He'd had the same reaction to her that day of the carriage ride through the park. And if he were being truthful, the sensation struck Alexander the minute she declared him a sot in his own drawing room.

He ran a hand through his hair, pushing it back from his forehead and once more studied his unwanted—*but oddly desirable as his cock assured him*—bride.

Sophia wiggled about like a worm stabbed by a hook at his regard.

She cut her duck so viciously during the meal, Alexander was sure she imagined him beneath the knife. But her blatant animosity would work in his favor to secure the annulment. Alexander might be able to claim Sophia was so hostile to his attentions, he feared she might attack him. Better than declaring impotence, though it would make him look like a milksop.

Lady Canterbell laughed uproariously at something his uncle said.

Good god. Hadn't Damon charmed that woman enough for tonight? Going on about Caster knowing full well that Lady Canterbell had set her sights on the marquess as a potential suitor for Lady Mara. The truth was, Alexander hadn't seen Caster in years, though Lady Caster was a close acquaintance of Lady Falmouth. Damon would take full credit for the introduction to Caster and his mother and use it to gain Lady Canterbell's support when the time came to secure the annulment.

Clever of his uncle.

But when Damon expressed what a splendid job Lady Canterbell had done in raising her two daughters, Alexander nearly spit out his drink. She'd only managed half the job. Just look at Sophia.

Sophia stopped chewing for a moment, eyes narrowing on Alexander as if reading his thoughts. Her fingers wrapped tighter around the fork she held as she lowered her eyes to his neck.

His trousers pulled tight between his thighs.

She wants to be sent to the country.

He understood his future bride's desire to depart London. Now that Oakhurst wasn't here to amuse him and Alexander had taken to watering down his spirits, town was far less amusing. Grayer. Contrary to what most would assume, Alexander liked the countryside. There was something peaceful and calming about the smell of grass and wildflowers. The scent of farm animals and dirt. His estate, The Pillory, was lovely and warm, more comfortable than the Duke of Roxboro's ostentatious London residence. The Pillory had the added benefit of seclusion. No curious eyes to watch him fall off a horse, save Barstow, his butler. A duke who couldn't ride well was a disgrace, according to Damon. Even Hayward, that shriveled up old toad, never so much as slid off his saddle.

Easier for the *ton* to think Alexander too full of drink to keep his seat. Less of an indignity.

At any rate, The Pillory was a wonderful, bucolic spot. If Sophia liked the country, she would adore his estate. Alexander could easily imagine her traipsing about with a basket on her arm, snarling at a patch of wildflowers that dared to offend her. Or terrifying the wildlife.

Her mouth pulled into a scowl at the sudden twitch between his thighs.

Damn it. Stand down.

"You are an utter delight," he murmured softly, knowing Sophia could read his lips if not hear the sarcasm in his words.

"*Sot,*" she mouthed back.

Sophia was utterly terrible, yet something in his chest stirred as he took her in. Damon complained of her scathing tongue and unpleasant manner, declaring how unfit she was to be a duchess. Not that Sophia would be one for very long.

"Your Grace?" Damon stood behind his chair. "Shall we join Lord Canterbell for a brandy?"

Alexander looked up to see the entire table had come to their feet, the ladies ready to withdraw, all eyes turned in his direction. He barely recalled dessert he'd been so lost in his thoughts. It may have been toffee cake.

"Absolutely," he took a final sip from his glass. "You know how I enjoy a brandy."

CHAPTER ELEVEN

ONCE THE INTOLERABLE dinner was finally over, Papa escorted Roxboro and Lord Damon to his study to partake in a brandy and a cheroot, while the Canterbell ladies made their way to the drawing room to await them.

Sophia thought it a stupid custom, to separate the sexes after a meal. She didn't care if a cheroot was smoked before her, in truth, she'd tried a cheroot herself. Sneaking one from her father's study, Sophia had run to the very back of the gardens behind a flowering wisteria when Mama and Mara left to go shopping one day. After a great deal of coughing, and having made so much noise Powell found her, she came to the conclusion that puffing on a cheroot wasn't something she'd enjoy again in the future.

But one should always try new things.

Sophia had wanted to point out to the others in the dining room as they all came to their feet, that Roxboro didn't require a brandy after imbibing so heavily of Father's favorite scotch throughout the meal. She'd counted eight glasses while he enjoyed the duck.

Eight.

But she restrained herself.

"Stop frowning, Sophia. You'll give yourself wrinkles," Mama cautioned, taking a seat with a sigh. "I don't understand why you continue to be so averse to your future. Things did not start well, that much is true, but the path has been set forward. It does you no good to antagonize Roxboro or Lord Damon. Why you continue to make things harder for yourself, I do not understand."

"I would embrace my marriage, Mama." Sophia's sister settled perfectly on the settee.

Like a bloody swan.

"Of course you would, dear." Mama patted Mara's hand before both regarded Sophia with twin looks of exasperation.

She expelled the air in her lungs slowly, primarily to keep from screaming at them both. The assumption that she was always difficult, stubborn and more a challenge than was warranted wasn't an incorrect one. She'd been born that way. Perhaps something had happened to Mama when she carried Sophia, to account for her unpleasing personality. The idea was worth considering.

"Were you inordinately frightened or did you fall down the stairs before my birth, Mama? Or eat something far too spicy, that might have given you indigestion? Or were you cursed by a gypsy, perhaps, when—"

"Cursed by a gypsy? Good lord but you are fanciful. No, nothing untoward at all occurred when I was with child." She looked between Mara and Sophia and raised one plucked brow. Taking the glass of ratafia offered by Powell, she said, "But you *were* combative even in the womb. Kicking and moving about. As an infant, you had colic for months. Always fussy. Red-faced. Angry at all of us for having been born."

"Oh." Well, that explained a great deal.

"Sophia, if you cannot smile, at the very least, try not to appear as if you've something bitter in your mouth. Attempt to be pleasant. I beg you. The duke behaved wonderfully at dinner despite drinking half the contents of the sideboard and dodging your insults. Roxboro was lovely when he called upon you. He took you for a carriage ride through the park and then to Gunter's." She lifted the ratafia to her lips once more and paused. "Roxboro is doing everything to make something of this…misstep. I do not understand why you cannot do the same."

"I find him charming," Mara piped up.

"As do I," Mama said. "Despite his unwelcome reputation which I am inclined to believe might be exaggerated given what I've seen thus far."

Sophia's lips parted. Aghast. "You said yourself he was disgraceful, Mama. A terrible libertine. Goodness, you informed me I'd be a young widow as he'd likely trip and break his neck due to his love of drink."

"I said no such thing," her mother insisted.

Sophia's fingers clasped together and twisted. "You did. You said—"

"I agree that the situation is unwelcome," Mama interrupted, as usual. "I am not fond of scandal, nor your father. But I do not understand how you found yourself in the Perswick gardens if you dislike Roxboro to such a degree. If he is so disagreeable, why converse with him at all?"

Sophia looked down at her lap. Studied her fingers as they laced and locked.

Mama would never understand. She'd been a great beauty once, just like Mara. Lauded for her modesty and ladylike manners. Mara was very like her. How could Mama possibly comprehend how Sophia had to go through the world, always being compared to not only Mara, but the great Lady Canterbell? Having Roxboro, arguably the most spectacular man in London, a jaded rake who could have any woman he wished, seek out Lady Sophia, the other Canterbell daughter had been…intoxicating. Vindicating. Proof that possibly she wasn't so unappealing. For the first time in her life, Sophia had felt…seen.

Until Roxboro abandoned her in the garden and Sophia realized she wasn't special. Or desirable. Only a source of amusement for a libertine who'd had too much wine. Any girl would've done just as well in his drunken state. He didn't even have the decency to remember her.

"We mustn't blame Sophia, Mama. What young lady in her

position when encountering a gentleman like Roxboro," Mara paused to position herself so that when Roxboro and Lord Damon came through the door, she would be the first thing they'd see. Perfect. Modest. Lovely. "Wouldn't be tempted to lure him out to the gardens to steal a kiss?"

"I did not *lure* him." Sophia threw a pillow at her sister.

Mara caught it with one hand before it could hit her in the head.

"Girls." Mama clapped her hands. "You are young ladies, not children. Sophia and Roxboro have been courting in secret," she ground out. "Nothing improper occurred. They were only indiscreet and it is a splendid match. That is the truth." She took another sip of ratafia. "I do not wish to hear anything to the contrary."

Sophia snorted and flopped into a chair.

"Things could be worse. Look who Miss Walton had to wed. Lord Dram has that unsightly mole on his cheek and a corpulent form."

"Lord Dram is a lovely man." Mama made a chuffing sound, trying not to hold back her amusement. "But I quite agree on the mole. Your sister makes an excellent point."

"Roxboro lacks moral turpitude," Sophia insisted, though the argument was pointless. "His character is corrupt. His wit is as practiced as is his charm and fueled by a great deal of spirits."

"Perhaps your father and I should have sent you to that dreary convent in Scotland instead of allowing you to wed a handsome duke. What punishment," Mama snapped back at her. "We are all aware that your opinion of this match is not favorable, but have you given one thought to what our family has suffered? The scandal? If I must tolerate the whispers of Lady Stafford and Hortensia, I would rather do so as the mother of a duchess." She took a deep breath. "Frankly, Sophia, we are all exhausted with hearing of how terrible this must be for *you*."

"It is quite awful. Because—"

"Because *you* went into the gardens with him willingly. According to Lady Brokeburst, you were practically skipping. Grinning like some deranged inmate of Bedlam. He did not drag you screaming out to the terrace." Mama's features hardened. "You *desired* his attention. *Allowed* him to take liberties." She let out a puff of frustration. "Stop behaving as if he's wronged you. You are to blame as well."

Sophia fell back against the cushions with a small gasp. She turned away from her mother and sister as they proceeded to dissect the merits of tulle over damask. Biting back a sob, one filled with a great deal of misery and self-realization, Sophia stared at a portrait of a bluebird on the wall without truly seeing it.

Mama was right, no matter how much Sophia didn't want her to be.

STOP BEHAVING AS *if he's wronged you.*

Alexander halted at the entrance to the drawing room, waving aside Powell who appeared like a shadow beside him. "No need to announce me. I thank you for your attention to my requests through dinner, Powell. And your discretion."

Lady Canterbell's little speech, no matter how correct, struck a sour note with him. Alexander had ascertained that his future wife was not only annoyed that he didn't recognize her, but believed a far graver injustice had been visited upon her. Other than being compromised. That much was clear from the conversation he'd managed to overhear.

Well, that certainly explains the hostility.

What else had been done or said to her that night—*and Alexander still wasn't completely ready to admit it had been him*—to distress Sophia to such a degree. Did he insult Lord Canterbell? Invite her to join he and another woman—no, they were in the gardens. Alexander preferred a bed for such activities. What could possibly have transpired?

Curious.

Damon was still in Canterbell's study, crowing over some ancient map of Rome hanging on the wall. But Alexander had wanted a private word with Lady Sophia, so he made an excuse to join the ladies in the drawing room. He might have to accept he had been at the Perswick ball, because he couldn't prove otherwise. But not a bit of Sophia's story made sense. Besides the absolute dislike of Lady Perswick—*he'd had Timmons find every invitation Alexander had received in the last two months and not one was from her*—Alexander had never once attempted to seduce a young lady of good family. Not even when they tossed themselves at him, which happened with great regularity. Damon had warned him away from such women his entire life. He would never have stepped out of...bounds, given what had happened to his father.

You don't wish to end up like Charles, do you? Trapped and unhappily wed to a scheming skirt.

Lady Marianne, Alexander's mother, had been a spoiled, wellbred young lady who set her sights on becoming a duchess from the moment she'd spied Charles across a ballroom. Impropriety followed. Her ambitions and lack of any desire for her husband became clear in the first year of their marriage, with Marianne declaring that the moment she birthed an heir she would leave for the Continent.

But conceiving Alexander had not come easy. Marianne hadn't wanted to ruin her lovely form, according to Damon. Her earlier pregnancies ended...rather abruptly. Charles found out she had an account at the local apothecary. And a lover. His greatest rival in Parliament. Cotswold.

Alexander longed to confront Cotswold. But he had died shortly after Marianne.

All of which was to say that he would never, under any circumstances, seduce some well-bred virgin. He was intimately aware of what could transpire. Nor did he want to end up like Charles. The young ladies of the *ton* were to a fault, ruthless and calculating, especially if you were a duke. The fact that he was prone to every wicked excess in England didn't put any of them off.

Especially not this young lady, who was far more intelligent than most.

And terrible.

"Lady Sophia," Alexander said from the door, watching as she jumped at the sound of his voice, likely shocked he'd used her name. "I would love to see the gardens. Perhaps you could show them to me." He made a quick bow to Lady Canterbell. "With your permission, my lady."

"There are flying…insects," Sophia grumbled. "And it is dark. You won't see anything." She turned from him. "And I'm rather full of duck."

Good lord, she was sour.

"The servants have lit the torches along the path, and it is a perfectly lovely evening for a stroll," Lady Canterbell said pointedly to her daughter. "I feel certain it will help the duck to settle. Please enjoy the night air, Your Grace."

"But—" the little twit protested. "Fine." Her lips pulled tight as she stood and waltzed past Alexander and into the hall without so much as taking his arm. "Come along."

Alexander had to shrug off the sudden spike of arousal. What was *wrong* with him?

Lady Canterbell shot him a look of apology. "Your Grace—"

Alexander smiled. "I see Lady Sophia is impatient for our walk, my lady. I promise to return her shortly."

CHAPTER TWELVE

SOPHIA FLOUNCED OUT the terrace doors, coming to a halt at the start of the path to take in the Canterbell gardens. There wasn't a great deal to see as the area was rather small. A twisted maple at the only bend in the path. Some peonies. A burst of roses.

Her heart thumped hard in her chest, irritated that he'd forced her out here. Why couldn't Roxboro merely bid them all good night, and she'd see him the day after next before the vicar? There was no reason to pretend, at least for her family, that they had any great liking for each other.

Strolling about in the moonlight. Of all the ridiculous ideas.

"Ah," his footsteps sounded behind her. "Doesn't this bring back memories, Lady Saffron?"

"Not fond ones, Roxboro."

"I must have been excessively charming that night because I didn't force you outside. Nor tug you along like some villain in a novel, else Lady Brokeburst would have included that in her recitation of events. Which means you went with me of your own accord. Thus, I must have enticed you, no matter how displeasing you find me now."

Roxboro took her arm, the scent of bergamot shaving soap drifting in the air between them. A hint of brandy. Possibly scotch, after all, he'd had multiple glasses at dinner. "Remind me of our meeting at the Perswick ball."

The sarcastic note in his low, rumbling voice was gone. There was no anger. No annoyance.

"Unbelievable," she scoffed, pulling away, not caring to be reminded of her stupidity yet again. Mama's speech had been distressing. And true. "I have given you a complete accounting of the tale, more than once."

"You had champagne. A glass or two."

"I see you remember that much." Sophia stiffened. "But I wasn't foxed." She'd been lightheaded. Dizzy with awareness of Roxboro. "The room was warm. We retired to the garden for fresh air. I received a pathetic kiss." Lord, but this was…embarrassing.

"Continue."

Sophia plucked absently at her skirts. Why must they repeat this exercise again?

"My father arrived on the terrace," she threw at him, recalling her shock. Her pained disappointment that she was no better than Hortensia or any of those other pea-hens. "You had slid into the shadows, like the coward you are."

"Had I kissed you yet?"

"Yes. When my father arrived, I called out to you because," she pulled away from him and walked towards the maple tree. "I was shocked you would leave," she managed to say with as little emotion as possible. "With little notice."

Roxboro truly didn't recall a moment of their encounter.

He trailed behind her, the gravel crunching beneath his feet. "I—think you *imagine* it was me," he said carefully. "Enough so that when you called out *Roxboro*, Lord Canterbell assumed the same. Did he see me clearly or only—"

"Dear God." Sophia threw up her hands in anger. "This again."

"I am often intoxicated." His brows drew together. "I do not think that is in debate. But I have never forgotten my whereabouts. Or if I attended a ball. Nor do I seek out young ladies of your ilk for obvious reasons."

"My ilk?" Sophia crossed her arms.

"Virginal, modest, well-bred young ladies," he replied bluntly. "You hold no interest for me, not to seduce or engage in any way. I don't attend balls as a rule because I do not dance."

"I imagine you dance as well as you sit a horse." Sophia swatted away a moth.

Roxboro made a sound.

"Is there a point to this inane conversation?"

"That while drunken behavior and lechery are part of my nature, taking a young lady, such as yourself, into a dark garden without caring whether we were seen, is *not* how I behave. Ever. I simply would not have done so. I wouldn't find it appealing."

Sophia stopped, digging her heels into the gravel. "And I am just as certain that it was you, Your Grace."

"You don't strike me as unintelligent. Nor easily led about. If I am accused, shouldn't I know my crime? What did I say for you to throw caution to the wind and follow me outside?"

Sophia clenched her fists. Fine. Roxboro would hear it all, even though it made her seem pathetic and something of an imbecile.

"You—told me that you had admired me from afar," the words came out in a halting manner. "After seeing me in the park. You were taken with me. Ridiculous, of course. I can see that now. You claimed—you wished to court me and meant to speak to my father."

Roxboro went completely still.

She turned and took several steps away from him, unwilling to allow him to see her after such a confession. "I should have known better, given your reputation. You see, I am not as intelligent as you imagine. Lady Brokeburst and her eyesight are not entirely to blame."

Roxboro took her arm once more, gently pulling her beneath the tree.

"No wonder you are so angry, Lady Salmon." The words were soft.

Sophia bit her lip. "Now you're just making names up."

"I am guilty of a great many misdeeds," he breathed into the night air. "You've heard the stories, no doubt. But there is not one in which I debauch a girl of good family? Never. I avoid—"

"Ladies of my ilk." Sophia looked down at her slippers. The gossips were clear on Roxboro and his pursuits. Drinking. Gambling. Deviant behaviors. Women too numerous to count. But he was correct. There were no tales of him pursuing a girl such as herself. "Perhaps I was the exception."

"It wasn't me," he murmured. "I can prove it."

"This is madness, Your Grace. There simply is no one else it could have been, no matter how you protest. You are...unique in your looks. Difficult to mistake." She raised her chin. "But very well, how do you intend to prove that it was not you?"

"Like this."

Roxboro grabbed her around the waist with one arm, the fingers of his other hand sinking into her hip until she was secured against the long muscular lines of his torso. Bergamot, stronger now, filled her nostrils.

I didn't realize he was so tall.

That was her last coherent thought before his mouth descended on hers, warm and full of so much heat Sophia's knees buckled. A wave of—*dear God, I may faint*—pure fire lit along her skin. An ache filled her, the sort they only spoke of in romantic novels.

Now this...her mind whispered. *Is a kiss.*

Damnable troublesome twit.

The scent of roses came from her hair, mixing with the aroma of the flowers in the garden. Delicious and full of thorns.

I don't mind thorns.

A sound left her. A delicate whimper before her lips parted beneath his. He pulled her closer, running the tip of his tongue along the bottom of her mouth just as he had longed to do every time she hurled an insult, or called him a sot. Sophia tasted of wine. Innocence. Blistering irritation.

Alexander swallowed all of it. Begged for more.

She gave a brief, fruitless struggle, all the while her fingers curled into the edges of his coat, so that all Sophia succeeded in doing was to rub that generous form along the already hard ridge of his cock. Each one of her curves softened against him, molding until they fit perfectly together.

A soft groan, whether from him or her, filled the air beneath the tree.

This...*this* was the sensation he chased in every glass of brandy or scotch. At a game of hazard. Or the women he bedded. A sense of pure, unadulterated bliss that left room for little else. A complete emptying of Alexander's thoughts so that nothing else mattered but the physical ache of awareness. The prickle of his skin. Arousal and unadulterated lust pulsed between his thighs, threatening to strangle his cock.

Christ, I might swoon.

Sophia returned his kiss, enthusiastically if not with a great deal of experience. She followed the movements of his tongue, making soft, feminine sounds that sent another wave of longing down his body. Each breath urged him for more. Tiny teeth nipped at his bottom lip. Alexander pushed her back to the trunk of the tree, pinning her to the bark.

"Sophia," he said against her mouth, pressing the hardened length of his cock directly between her thighs.

"Oh," she softly panted before arching more firmly into his chest.

Alexander's hand slid from her hip, cupping Sophia's backside, squeezing at one luscious, plump—

Dear God.

He pulled away so abruptly that Sophia stumbled, grabbing on to the tree trunk to keep from falling. Taking a lungful of air, demanding his heart stop the crazy tumbling inside his chest,

Alexander stepped back from his terrible, annoying twit of a bride. His cock throbbed. *Ached*. His entire body burned.

For her.

Eyes wide, hands trembling against her skirts, Sophia stared at him in shock.

It had *not* been him at the Perswick ball. He would never have forgotten.... *Her*.

"That," she sputtered, the mounds of her breasts rocking with every halting breath. "That," Sophia shook her head, fingers brushing along her lips, "It wasn't—"

"Me," Alexander whispered, daring to look at her mouth once more.

She spun about and took a few halting steps in the direction of the house, pausing just outside a circle of torchlight. Took two deep, gulping breaths. Fingers clutched in agitation at her sides, the fingers jerking ever so slightly. But Sophia did not turn. Did not face him.

"I bid you good evening, Your Grace." Her words were sharp. Like knives. "The duck did not agree with me and our walk did not help matters. Please apologize to Lord Damon for not bidding him good evening. I will see you at the church, Your Grace."

Alexander nodded, though he doubted she could see him. If nothing else, he'd proved to himself, if not Sophia, that he hadn't ruined her.

Though now, he dearly wanted to.

She sprinted up the steps to the terrace, not sparing him another glance and disappeared into the depths of the Canterbell home.

Alexander waited a moment or two before reaching into his coat pocket. His fingers closed around the small flask filled with scotch, one he continued to carry though he hadn't taken a sip in weeks. Lifting the flask, the scotch fell down his throat, making his belly burn.

He had his truth, though Alexander wasn't sure what he would do with the information.

CHAPTER THIRTEEN

I DON'T THINK—BUT *it had to be—but it couldn't—*
The gnawing, insistent whisper gnawed at the fringes of her mind as she looked up the length of the aisle, each pew decorated with sprays of roses and baby's breath. The path that would bring her to Roxboro. His handsome features were calm. Composed. Save for the tiny smirk he made no attempt to hide.

The lilies in her bridal bouquet quivered as she took a step. Then another.

The kiss Roxboro bestowed upon her only two nights ago had shaken Sophia to the core. As Roxboro surely knew it would. He hadn't lied. Roxboro did not kiss like a slobbering puppy. Nor without pronounced sensuality. Sophia's senses, her very soul, had left her body during that kiss. Not at all like...before. Even his mouth felt different...like another pair of lips—

Don't think it, Sophia. Don't even consider it.

The green of Roxboro's eyes, bits of silver glittering in the morning light streaming through the windows of the church, trailed over Sophia. Impudently, though his features remained perfectly smooth. She struggled to keep her gaze on the vicar as Papa walked her forward, not daring to look at the guests filling the pews. Mama wanted a grand wedding for her daughter, no matter the reason behind it. Half of London was in St. Paul's, the rest outside awaiting their exit. Everyone wanted to see the infamous Duke of Roxboro brought up to snuff by Lord

Canterbell's daughter.

Sophia grew dizzy just thinking about it. She pitched to the left, but Papa caught her elbow.

"Buck up now, moppet," his breath crested over her ear. "I'll make sure you are treated well."

Yes, because having Papa constantly tossing threats at the Viceroy family was a brilliant way to begin her marriage. A union Sophia now considered was being made under false pretenses.

That kiss.

If the claiming of her mouth was any indication of how Roxboro might stake his claim on her body, Sophia would be reduced to nothing more than a pliable mound of flesh as they consummated their marriage. Mama had given her a version of what to expect, none of which made a great deal of sense. Each body part was given a charming euphemism, namely the 'gentleman's length'.

My God. What a stupid name for the male anatomy.

The lilies in Sophia's hands shook so hard as Papa left her beside Roxboro, a petal fell from the bouquet and drifted to the floor.

She should flee. Run out of the church and into the street. If she were lucky, a carriage might run her over. Mama would be horrified at the scandal, but Sophia would be dead, so it was unlikely to matter and—

"Ow," she hissed as her forearm was pinched, somewhat viciously and would probably leave a bruise.

Roxboro was staring at her in irritation, the vicar with expectation.

"I'm…sorry. I didn't—" she choked.

Another pinch.

"Stop that," she said under her breath, causing the vicar to raise his brows in question.

"Try to pay attention," Roxboro murmured. "This is somewhat important."

"I do. To all of it," Sophia said, gripping the bouquet to her chest, a shield against what was happening. The vicar droned on about the sanctity of marriage, while she took in the chiseled line of Roxboro's jaw, the shape of his brows, the patrician nose and—

Sophia inhaled softly, the breath halting in her lungs.

There's no freckle at the end of his nose.

Her mouth went dry.

There had to be. Possibly she couldn't see it from this angle. Leaning forward slightly, twisting as she tried to get a good look at the end of his nose.

A soft growl came from Roxboro. "Are you having a seizure of some kind?"

Her heart beat furiously, like a bloody drum in her chest. Panic, the sort which heralds impending doom, sank into every inch of her body.

Why hadn't she noticed before? Why—

"Do not faint. It's unseemly at a wedding," Roxboro said in a bored tone.

"I'm not going to faint." She turned back to the vicar who looked more annoyed than the duke.

"Your Grace," the vicar intoned, inclining his head in Sophia's direction.

Roxboro dipped his chin, the green of his eyes so brilliant as he brushed his mouth rather seductively along Sophia's own. Not a kiss. More an imitation of one.

A soft sound came from her chest. Pin pricks drew along her arms and down between her thighs. And then it was over.

Applause erupted from the pews as the guests stood and Roxboro turned Sophia, to guide her out of the church. Dozens of eyes, accusatory, she imagined, drew over her as she walked at Roxboro's side.

No freckle.

Mama was weeping, dabbing at her eyes with a handkerchief. Papa was at her side, patting her shoulder in a soothing manner. Mara sat to their right, her gaze fixed not on Sophia but the Marquess of Caster who sat across the aisle directly opposite her.

Lord Damon's features were schooled into chilly politeness, that dark, flinty gaze stabbing at Sophia with dislike. Lady Violet tilted her head as Sophia passed, eyeing her with a great deal of curiosity and not the good kind. Lady Rose's features reflected nothing but absolute boredom. Only Lady Falmouth regarded her with welcome.

Stepping outside, Sophia blinked at the sudden burst of light after the dimly lit church. Her feet dug in as she noted the crowd assembled. Roxboro's grip on her arm remained firm as he coaxed her forward, forcing her slippered feet to move.

"We're almost finished, Lady Salamander. You can faint once we get to the carriage."

"I'm not going to faint. Also, I am not a reptile."

Roxboro shrugged.

A crowd outside St. Paul's gathered to congratulate the duke and his new duchess, jostled about, trying to get closer. Someone grabbed at the train of Sophia's gown. Others yelled out to Roxboro. But he never stopped, nor waved. He led her straight down the steps to his waiting carriage, stumbled at the bottom step and righted himself, turning to face Sophia as he did so.

No freckle.

The night of the Perswick ball, Roxboro had a bloody freckle, just on the end of his nose. Tiny. Barely noticeable. Sophia recalled thinking at the time how attractive she thought that freckle happened to be. Like a dimple.

Roxboro unceremoniously shoved her inside the carriage, pushing aside her skirts and kicking his leg when the fabric wrapped stubbornly around one ankle. "I'm not sure what is wrong with you, Lady Sesame," Roxboro gritted his teeth. "But please stop behaving as if I'm about to have you drawn and quartered. Smile, if you know how. Wave." He picked up Sophia's arm and flapped her wrist. "Like this."

She didn't argue. Couldn't. Instead, for the first time in her life, Sophia obeyed. She waved and nodded politely as if their marriage were the most wonderful thing that had ever happened.

The carriage pulled away from the church, slowly rolling down the street in the direction of the Duke of Roxboro's home where a lavish wedding breakfast awaited them, the very thought of which made Sophia's stomach pitch violently.

I do not believe a scone will fix this.

Her new husband leaned back against the luxurious cushions with a grunt. Tugged on his cravat to loosen the pristine white folds. Reaching inside his coat, one that fit the breadth of his shoulders like a second skin, he pulled out his flask. "Here."

"No, thank you," Sophia managed to say, still staring at his nose.

"Suit yourself. I thought it might put some color in your cheeks." He took several swallows, filling the carriage with the scent of scotch. "Better." Roxboro cocked a brow at her and leaned forward. "What? You're staring at me as if I've grown a second head."

It could have been a drop of wine, not a freckle.

Sophia nodded slowly. Yes. A drop of wine.

"My god, have you hit your head?"

"No, Roxboro," she snapped. "You're more the one that stumbles about."

He sat back, looking somewhat pleased. "Oh good. I didn't want you fainting during the upcoming blissful celebration," he drawled, ensuring that Sophia knew the breakfast would be anything but. "Or sliding under the table." Roxboro's gaze locked on her mouth for a moment before he looked away.

Sophia paid him no mind. She was too overwhelmed with relief. There was no cause for alarm. None at all. Roxboro had tasted of wine in the Perswick gardens. As they stood conversing by the refreshment table, he'd had a glass of something jewel toned dangling from one hand.

Merely a drop of wine. *Not* a freckle. Never a freckle.

Lady Brokeburst curtsied. Lord Lacton bowed. She repeated the words like a prayer before taking a deep breath of reassurance to steady herself. Sophia hadn't been mistaken. There was only one

Duke of Roxboro. It wasn't as if he had a twin roaming about. Now as to the magnificent kiss after dinner at the Canterbell home, there was an explanation, she only hadn't thought of it yet.

"I am merely wondering if you'll stumble up the stairs of your own home."

Roxboro let out a bark of laughter. "I'm not foxed, my lady. Not yet, at any rate. Last night was another matter." He took another swallow before placing the flask once more into his coat pocket. "I was rejoicing at our upcoming nuptials."

"Splendid."

He shifted in the seat across from her, eyes lingering over her mouth once more until the air between them grew thick, buffeting along Sophia's limbs. He'd pinned her against the tree trunk and kissed Sophia as if he…hungered for her. Warm bergamot surrounded her, just as it did now, drowning out any hint of spirits.

Bergamot. But he hadn't smelled of—

Sophia pushed the unwanted thought aside because…well, it was impossible. She was only suffering from nerves as any woman forced to wed a feckless sot of a duke might be.

"Well, here we are," Roxboro said as the carriage rolled to a stop before an enormous brick home. She'd barely noticed when Papa dragged her here to confront the duke, but now she took in the duke's residence with fresh eyes. The house, more mansion, stretched nearly the length of the street and was surrounded by a wrought iron fence. Blooms spilled from boxes situated beneath every window. Two towering Italian cypress, not a leaf out of place, guarded either side of the massive black door.

"What is wrong with you?" Roxboro said as he stepped carefully out of the carriage.

A footman came forward and bowed to Sophia. "Your Grace, welcome home."

Chapter Fourteen

Sophia's uncertainty over Roxboro, the freckle that might have not been a freckle, the bloody bergamot scent that seemed infused into his skin now, but hadn't been the night of at the Perswick ball and that...kiss, persisted during the entirety of the wedding breakfast.

The panic would grow by leaps and bounds, then dissipate, only to return more forcefully moments later. The sense that something was...*wrong* persisted. Sophia stared at Roxboro's nose for so long while toying with her poached chicken, he finally leaned towards her and asked if *she* was foxed.

"That is more your area of expertise, Your Grace," she said, trying to avoid looking at his nose.

"Just so," Roxboro gave her a roguish wink. "A rather pleasant state of being. I'm well on my way." His mood was...friendly today, which left Sophia even more unsettled. She'd expected Roxboro might ignore her. Or be unkind.

A glass of scotch remained at her husband's elbow the entire meal, never once allowed to go empty. Whenever the amber liquid dipped, even slightly, Lord Damon would wave for one of the footmen to refill his nephew's glass.

That unsettled Sophia nearly as much as Roxboro's mood. Did Lord Damon want his nephew stumbling about, mind fogged by spirits all the time?

Laughter came from the other side of the table where Mara

sat beside Lord Caster. Lady Rose was on Caster's other side, while Violet sat directly across from Sophia. In a mild breach of conduct, Roxboro had insisted Sophia take the chair to his right instead of the opposite side of the table.

Every so often, Violet would leave the conversation between Caster and the other two women, so that her shrewd gaze could linger on Sophia. Given the circumstances, it was hard to blame her. Clearly, Violet didn't believe the tale her cousin and Sophia had been courting in secret, and had questions. But the most interesting thing about Violet, outside of the throaty way she laughed, was the way she kept her distance from Damon Viceroy.

Violet was polite, of course. Courteous. But she did not engage her father in conversation. Nor once after offering a greeting, look in his direction.

She doesn't like Damon. Something we have in common.

"I regret our first meeting is over aspic and an overly large fruitcake, Your Grace," Violet said to Sophia. There was no malice in her dark eyes, so like her father's, though Violet's were far less calculating.

She didn't respond immediately, not realizing that Violet was addressing *her*.

Roxboro kicked her under the table.

"Stop doing that," Sophia said under her breath, before kicking him back. "I too am chagrined we could not be acquainted earlier."

Violet watched the exchange between Sophia and Roxboro, lips twisting upward just slightly. "Poor of you, Xander, not to introduce us sooner, given you were…courting."

"I'm poor at a great many things, Vi."

"Not everything, Xander." A fleeting emotion crossed her features. "You do have some talents."

Roxboro snorted. "Hear, hear."

Violet took in Sophia for another moment. "Tell me, Your Grace, do you have hobbies?"

Roxboro nudged her thigh. "She's speaking to you."

Sophia grabbed her knife. "I'm aware." She gave him a cutting look before turning to Violet. "I like to read," she replied to Violet. "A great deal as it happens. I might be something of a bluestocking according to Lady Canterbell. Museums interest me."

"Do you ride?" Violet's lips twitched once more.

"Far too bouncy," Sophia answered without thinking.

"That's probably for the best," she glanced at Roxboro once more. "Needlework?"

"No, I'm afraid not. I kept pricking my finger. Blood everywhere. Nor gardening, I'm afraid. I've tried with violets, but they often end up dead. I was once advised to start a collection of seaweed by a group of academics I met at the museum."

"Seaweed?" Violet's eyes widened. "Really?"

"Apparently it is nearly as popular as the collecting of ferns. The ladies had formed a club to discuss the techniques of collecting seaweed. They found the task to be...stimulating." Sophia took a sip of her wine. Champagne had been offered, but she'd declined. "But alas, I found seaweed collection to be boring. I'm entirely unexceptional, I fear," she smiled at Violet.

Sophia could hurl a good insult. Punch decently as Mara could attest. Throw books, hairbrushes, rocks and the occasional slipper with varying degrees of accuracy, but those were all useless skills for a young lady.

"Oh, I disagree, Your Grace." Violet cast one more look at Roxboro and then returned to the conversation with Lord Caster, who Mara was questioning about the Dunkirk house party.

"You're a bluestocking. I should have guessed," Roxboro drawled in that silky, bored tone.

"You might try a book instead of spirits," Sophia retorted. "They are the rectangle shaped things covered in leather and full of words."

Violet, across the table, placed a hand over her mouth as if to stifle a laugh.

"God," Roxboro, her husband—*a strange, wildly terrifying*

thought—rumbled in a low tone. "You *are* terrible. With a tendency to fall into melancholy."

"I will agree to terrible. Nor do I suffer from melancholia. I am merely considering whether I should drown myself in the white wine sauce covering the turbot." Sophia was suddenly, intimately aware that she would not be leaving with her parents and Mara once the meal was over. The same sensation had struck her earlier, when she and Roxboro arrived, as she looked up at this magnificent house. This was now Sophia's home. Even now, Ann, her maid, was upstairs unpacking her things.

"I did offer you my flask on the way. You declined."

"It is still quite early in the day, Your Grace." She turned to her parents. Mama was engaged in conversation with the Dowager Marchioness of Caster and Papa was speaking to Damon and Lady Falmouth. Neither were overly concerned with Sophia. Or that she'd possibly wed Roxboro under false—

It is impossible, Sophia. Stop thinking of it.

"Time." Roxboro flicked his wrist. "A social construct. Scotch tastes the same no matter when you have a glass, my unwanted wife." The hint of a smile on his lips took the sting out of his words. Teasing her again.

"Tell me about your cousins, my sot of a duke," she returned, nodding just slightly to Rose and Violet. "And Lady Falmouth."

"Lady Falmouth," Roxboro said, "isn't related to me. She is the sister of Damon's late wife, May. She and my uncle have never really got on." He tilted his head towards her. "She begged May not to wed him."

"Hmm."

"Lady Falmouth feels, strongly, that it is her duty to take Rose and Violet under her wing in the absence of their mother. A direct reflection on her feelings that Damon lacks the skills to parent his daughters. May died," he closed his eyes in thought. "Eight years ago. I adored her." He looked down into his glass of scotch and took a slow breath.

Roxboro had *loved* May Viceroy.

"In any case, Lady Falmouth faces quite a challenge given the temperaments of my cousins."

Sophia mulled that over. There were rumors, of course, about the Viceroys, but outside of Roxboro, Rose and Violet had done nothing that was considered reputation damaging. Not yet. But Sophia could see the arrogance in them both, much like their cousin. Bred into them. A confidence that the world would simply do as they asked.

Given their looks and pedigree, it likely would.

"My uncle has received numerous offers for them both but has refused them all, though that earl is still mooning over Violet." Roxboro snapped his fingers. "Woodstone? Woodberry?" He shrugged. "The name escapes me, only the image of a rather timid gentleman resembling a parrot."

"A parrot?"

"Tuft of hair." He pointed to the top of his head. "Sprouting out like feathers. Wouldn't survive a week with Violet. She'd have him thrown in a sack and tossed onto a ship bound for India. Damon's most fervent desire is that Lady Falmouth cease being a widow and remarry, but she is not inclined to do so probably out of spite."

"Why would it matter to him?" Sophia wondered.

"She's always underfoot and as I said, she and my uncle are amicable, but little else. Rose," Roxboro nodded to the dark-haired girl laughing at something Mara imparted. "Is my uncle's favorite of my cousins, though he would never admit it. I suppose because she is the most like him." He didn't elaborate what it meant to be like Damon Viceroy. "Violet, however, is...less agreeable. Scathing temper, which she loses as frequently as she does at whist."

Violet had been listening to their conversation, as evidenced by her turning to give Roxboro a pained look. *I'm bored*; she mouthed.

He lifted his glass to her. "Too bad."

Violet turned away.

"She'll likely come to a bad end one day," he murmured. "She's quite terrible. Much like you, Your Grace."

"I'm not terrible. Nor will I come to a bad end. Though I'm certain marriage to you won't help my prospects."

Roxboro chuckled into his glass of scotch. "A matter of opinion. I happen to like terrible." He watched Sophia for a moment, the silver bits in his eyes glowing against the green. "Then there is Uncle Damon."

"He doesn't like me," Sophia blurted out.

"You have a blunt way of speaking, after all, why need to overthink things. But you aren't wrong. Damon doesn't care for you at all."

"That's rather impolite." It was one thing to think it, another to hear Damon's opinion of her voiced aloud.

"To be fair, Your Grace." An odd look crossed Roxboro's features. "There are times I don't think he likes me much either. But do not fear. You won't see him often. Damon hates the country, so he won't be coming to The Pillory."

"The Pillory?" Oh, yes. The somewhat alarming name of Roxboro's ducal seat.

"It's a lovely estate, despite the name. The Romans once had a fort near there and a general, whose name escapes me at the moment, built a series of stone towers. The towers still stand. None of my ancestors had the desire to tear them down. The house was built around them. The general kept his wife captive in the largest of the three towers."

"Captive?"

"He was gone often, commanding his troops. She was flirtatious and quite beautiful, according to the tale. The tower he locked her in has no windows, only holes large enough to stick one's head out or perhaps your hands or feet. Originally, I believe the holes were for defensive reasons. I'm not sure. But when he took off on one of his campaigns and shut her inside, the only contact with the outside world were those holes. A prior Duke of Roxboro decided the tower reminded him of a pillory, the sort you use for punishment. Which is fitting, because being locked in a tower for weeks on end couldn't have been pleasant. Up until then, The Pillory was known as Roxboro Woods which isn't intriguing at all." He leaned over, smelling of warm bergamot with a hint of scotch.

Sophia's pulse instantly quickened. Why must he be so...alluring? She had the urge to push her nose into his chest.

"Good grief," she choked out loud.

"Don't worry, Lady Serpent. The tower isn't habitable." Roxboro wiggled his brows at her before draining his glass as another was immediately placed at his elbow. "But renovations could be made."

Sophia looked down at her plate, deciding how to answer. But her husband had already turned away to strike up a conversation with Lord Caster. He ignored her for the remainder of the meal.

CHAPTER FIFTEEN

Hours later, Sophia walked the length of her elegant new suite of rooms, admiring the delicate lines of damask covered chairs grouped around a small delicate table of mahogany. The walls were painted the hue of creamy butter. Vases of fresh flowers dotted the room. The space was elegant and charming. Far more lovely than she'd imagined.

Her maid, Ann, had been installed while the wedding breakfast was enjoyed, just as Sophia had hoped, but she'd only unpacked one of the trunks along with Sophia's hairbrush, a jar of pins, and a small pot of cream Sophia used on her face before bed. Her beloved books remained in their crates and not lining the bookcase at the other end of the room.

When Sophia questioned why all her things hadn't been unpacked, Ann replied, somewhat apologetically, that the books, along with the remaining trunks, had already been sent ahead to The Pillory.

Sophia and Roxboro were to follow in two days.

Well, I suppose I don't need to worry over making calls.

Roxboro's estate was tucked away on the northeast side of Essex, not a great distance from London, but far enough to stow an unwanted wife. Which Sophia most definitely happened to be. He hadn't wasted any time in expelling her from London, though he thoughtfully planned to accompany her to The Pillory.

"I did request to live in the country," she said under her

breath. "He took me at my word."

"My lady?" Ann looked up from the trunk she was unpacking. "I mean, Your Grace."

"Nothing, Ann. Continue."

Roxboro was only doing as Sophia had asked by hiding her away at his estate, where he and Damon could forget she even existed. Just as well. Because unlike Mara, who had great dreams of becoming a leading matron of society, Sophia's desires were much more moderate and less ambitious in nature. Goodness, she didn't want to spend her days having calls paid upon her, or listening to endless gossip all while sipping tea. Solitude appealed to her. She didn't mind her own company. Sophia would have her books. Walking down country paths. Villagers to converse with as she enjoyed hearty fare at a local tavern.

Good lord, I'm boring. Just as well to be sent to the country.

After a round of sherry and Mama's practiced conversation in the drawing room, Lady Falmouth had pushed Violet and Rose out the door, bidding her a safe journey and promising to call upon Sophia's return to London. Rose murmured a polite goodbye, barely taking Sophia's hand. Violet, surprisingly, pressed a kiss to Sophia's cheek.

You've the courage. Patience and comfort are required.

She'd no idea what Violet meant by those words, only that they must pertain to Roxboro in some way. But he would be here, in London, and Sophia would be at The Pillory.

Lord Caster and his mother, Lady Caster departed behind Lady Falmouth. If Roxboro and Caster had grown up together, whatever closeness they'd shared was long gone. Caster was not an unrepentant rake or a sot and thus had little in common with Roxboro. They bid each other a polite goodbye.

And finally, Lord and Lady Canterbell, with Mara in tow, still mooning over Caster. Her sister appeared so starry-eyed it was a wonder she could make her way to the carriage. Caster was…attractive, Sophia supposed. But not in the same way as Roxboro.

Mama kissed Sophia's cheek, reminding her to be obedient and dutiful.

Roxboro overheard and gave a drunken snort. He was well and truly foxed, glass never once going empty as it was continuously refilled by the attentive butler, Timmons.

Once Timmons shut the door behind their guests, Roxboro motioned for the butler to come to his side. The two held a whispered conversation before Timmons approached Sophia. "Allow me to show you up, Your Grace."

Sophia glanced out the window. It was only mid-afternoon, but the day had been lengthy. A respite would be welcome before the evening meal.

Lord Damon continued to hover about in the foyer, watching Sophia with eyes like hardened bits of coal. He'd arrived in his own carriage, not with his daughters or Lady Falmouth.

"I bid you good evening, Your Grace," he said, regarding Sophia as if she were a fly he'd found floating in his morning tea.

Roxboro followed behind his uncle, only pausing to bow in Sophia's direction.

She had been dismissed. On her wedding day.

Standing at the base of the stairs, Sophia listened to their footsteps fade away. Loneliness struck her. She was an unwanted bride in a house that might never feel like her own. Even Mara's company would be welcome. Thank goodness Ann had agreed to come with Sophia.

"Your Grace?"

Sophia gave her a weak smile. "I was just thinking how pleased Lady Canterbell appeared."

Ann draped some diaphanous, nearly sheer, bit of silk over her shoulders.

"Where did this come from?" Sophia would never have chosen something so…. ghastly.

"Lady Canterbell, Your Grace. I believe she wanted to surprise you."

"She's succeeded." There was a great deal of lace. A great

mound of it. Ribbons tied and placed in specific places to draw the eye. A spray of fabric roses fell over one shoulder.

Sophia stopped in front of the mirror, frowning. "I look ridiculous. Like the cake we were served earlier. All tiers of icing and bits of fruit."

"I'm sure His Grace will appreciate the overall effect." Ann bit her lip. "If not Lady Canterbell's taste." She cleared her throat. "Forgive me, Your Grace, but you do know what to expect, do you not?"

This is why she had chosen Ann as her maid when she turned sixteen. No nonsense and as blunt as Sophia herself. "Lady Canterbell informed me of my duty." She turned to regard the maid. "Would you care to elaborate?"

"Would you like me to elaborate, Your Grace?"

Sophia took a seat and gestured to the chair beside her. She wasn't even sure that Roxboro would visit her this evening given his intoxicated state. She'd merely assumed...it *was* their wedding night. Consummation was required at some point, was it not? "I would. As you can imagine, Lady Canterbell was more focused on my being obedient than anything specific."

"The duke is," Ann's features took on a mildly rapturous glow. "Likely well versed in such matters. He's quite a reputation, if you'll forgive me for saying."

"Yes, he's glorious. A complete reprobate. Skilled in wickedness. But I don't do well with obedience. I'd prefer some knowledge before..." She plucked at the silk and lace covering her. "I doubt this overly large doily is going to induce Roxboro to great heights of passion."

Thinking of passion and Roxboro led to the contemplation of his mouth, his lips and kissing. Which, in turn, had her considering, once more, the absence of the freckle on his nose.

It was a drop of wine.

Sophia pushed aside those troubling thoughts. "Enlighten me, Ann. I insist."

AN HOUR OR so later, she contemplated the bottle of wine Ann had brought up. Looked appropriate and of a decent vintage, though Sophia knew nothing about wine. Halfway through Ann's rather informative educational discussion of physical relations, Sophia had grown flustered and tasked her maid with retrieving a bottle of…something. Brandy. Gin. Scotch. Rum. Wine. Just not ratafia which she detested. Roxboro was bound to have the best stocked sideboard in all of London and if ever she needed a drop of courage, it was tonight.

Goodness, there was so much to consider.

The first, was that under no circumstances was Sophia going to refer to Roxboro's male anatomy as his 'gentleman's length'. At the mention of the term Mama used, Ann had laughed so hard she'd nearly fallen out of her chair. Nor was she going to call it a 'shaft of delight' or a 'middle leg' which had Sophia imagining a stool. Prick was fine, she supposed, although that might be more a comment on Roxboro's personality, given the word had multiple uses.

Ann liked the word 'cock'. Short. Succinct. Brought to mind a rooster, but it seemed the best of the lot.

According to Ann, whose descriptions were far more detailed than Mama's, Roxboro was going to insert his *cock* into her quim—or as an alternative, Ann suggested, *lady parts*—and thrust vigorously. Sophia had already surmised as much, given her taste in lurid, romantic literature which alluded to such matters. Her maid assured Sophia that if the gentleman knew what he was doing, and they both agreed, given Roxboro's reputation, it was likely he did, Sophia would be well pleased and pleasured.

Ann's features grew blissful as she tried to describe 'well-pleasured'. She went on about one of the Canterbell footmen and the size of his…cock, but Sophia had heard enough to become…tingly thinking of Roxboro. So she asked for spirits. Wine. Anything.

Ann brought up not only the wine, but a tray of small sandwiches, grapes and cheese. It had been hours since Timmons had shown Sophia upstairs, yet Lord Damon's carriage still sat outside. She'd no idea when or if Roxboro might arrive and open the closed door between their rooms. Or if he meant to dine with her.

Her stomach rumbled. She snatched a bit of cheese and popped it in her mouth. Ann had already poured the wine. Sophia brought the glass to her lips and took a large swallow, swishing it around in her mouth.

"That's delightful," she said as Ann declared the unpacking finished, at least for now.

"I'm so pleased, Your Grace. I know you said you'd entertain any sort of spirits but I thought wine would be best, though it took some searching to find a bottle. There was not a drop left over from the meal today. I found that." She nodded. "Tucked away in the kitchens. I've no idea where the wine cellar happens to be and didn't want to ask Timmons."

"He's rather somber. Reminds me of Powell," she said of the Canterbell butler. "Did you speak to any of the other staff while preparing this lovely repast?" She popped a grape in her mouth. "Which I appreciate since I've no idea if the duke means us to dine together. Gossip, Ann. I want to hear it."

"I shouldn't, Your Grace."

"You most certainly should."

Ann was the closest thing Sophia had to a real friend. She loved Mara, but Sophia and her sister were more competitors than anything else. There weren't any other young ladies who she could call more than acquaintances. Most were like Hortensia. Or Miss Newsome.

"I want to know everything. I certainly can't ask Timmons. And Roxboro is not forthcoming." She glanced out the window. "We have time. Lord Damon still lingers downstairs."

Like the plague.

Rude to stay, given it was Roxboro's wedding night. His

uncle should have departed with the others. Or at least after one last celebratory brandy.

"The staff adores the duke but worries over his well-being given his...pursuits. Especially," her brow wrinkled. "If he is on horseback. Apparently, the duke has never sat a horse terribly well even before...." The words hovered in the air.

"He became a sot?"

Ann nodded.

Sophia had already assumed as much. Roxboro, for all that he moved elegantly and was stunning to look at, happened to be clumsy. Which was oddly endearing considering he was a duke. And a libertine.

"So why not simply take a carriage?"

"Lord Damon insists he ride as a duke should."

Sophia took another sip of the wine. Roxboro's uncle seemed far too involved in his nephew's life, in her opinion, though it was hardly any of her affair. This marriage had been made to satisfy her father's honor and preserve Sophia's reputation. The less she knew about Roxboro, the better off she would be.

"That's all I overheard, Your Grace. But I'll endeavor to learn more. I have already met Stone, the duke's valet. He is not so...reserved as Timmons. Stone worries greatly for His Grace."

Implying that Timmons did not.

"I'm sure I'll make Stone's acquaintance at some point." Manners dictated that she be presented to the entire staff, which should have occurred immediately upon arriving for the wedding breakfast, but that hadn't happened. Nor before she'd gone up to her new rooms. But given Roxboro was sending her to live in the country, maybe he'd decided she didn't need to become familiar with the staff here or run the household.

Still, rather strange.

"I'll take my leave, Your Grace, unless there is anything else. If there is a light supper to be served, I'll bring up a tray or," her eyes ran up and down Sophia's lace covered form. "Come dress you."

"That won't be necessary. This," she waved a hand over the tray Ann had prepared. "Will suffice. I won't need you again, Ann. Thank you for coming with me. I assume Timmons has given you quarters?"

"He has." The maid bobbed. "And it is my pleasure to continue in your service, Your Grace." Ann headed out the door, shutting it behind her with a soft click.

Sophia sat in the silence and sipped her wine. Picked at the food on the tray. Stared at Damon's carriage outside. Listened for Roxboro.

Her husband was a strange paradox. Duke. Debauched libertine. Beautiful in a way few men were. A bit of a clumsy oaf and prone to accidents. Not *exactly* the wicked rogue she'd first imagined.

A laugh bubbled out of her.

But also…she suspected, firmly wedged beneath the thumb of Damon Viceroy. Whether because of Roxboro's unapologetic lifestyle which made him unfit for many of his ducal duties or because Damon refused to release his grip on the Roxboro estate, Sophia wasn't sure. But neither reason sat well with her.

Closing her eyes, Sophia's mind drifted over the day's events. If Roxboro appeared, she would submit as was her duty. Consummate the marriage. Hopefully, produce an heir so that there would be no further reason to submit to his attentions. He was free to go about his business. She had an entire speech planned, reciting the words in her head as she enjoyed her wine.

More time passed. The sun dipped low in the sky before disappearing completely. The front door finally opened and shut. Low voices drifted up the stairs along with the sound of Damon's carriage finally rolling away.

She glanced at the clock. Later than she'd thought. Roxboro was certain to appear any moment, if for no other reason than to bid her good night. Sophia chewed another grape. Listened for Roxboro's tread to come up the stairs, but the house remained quiet and the connecting door stayed firmly shut.

Sophia fluffed out the folds of her nightgown. And waited.

Another hour passed. Noises came from the hall.

Deciding to be courageous, thanks to the half bottle of wine she'd consumed, Sophia marched across the room, determined confront her husband. Unsteadily, she came to her feet and went to the door connecting their rooms and turned the knob.

The door didn't budge.

Locked. Roxboro had locked her out.

Spinning about, the atrocious night rail spilling about her ankles, Sophia flung open her own door to find...Timmons?

"Your Grace," the butler bowed, averting his eyes as if he hadn't seen far worse at Roxboro's butler.

Sophia made to pass him and enter Roxboro's rooms, but the butler stayed in place before the door.

"I wish to speak to Roxboro."

"The duke is not...here at present." Timmons surveyed her with a look of pity. "His Grace has gone out for the evening in the company of Lord Damon."

The words, heavy and more hurtful than she wished them to be, sank into her skin.

How utterly humiliating.

Roxboro couldn't even be bothered to tell Sophia he planned to avoid her on their wedding night. While she stood here, with his bloody butler, in this stupid confection of silk and lace. Abandoned. Like an ill-fitting shoe. Given his past behavior, Sophia should have expected as much, but he'd been so kind at their breakfast and—

"I see," Sophia said as imperiously as she could. "Good night, Timmons."

"Your Grace."

She hurried back to her own door and shut the heavy wood firmly behind her. Roxboro didn't find her desirable and never had. Yes, he'd been cordial earlier today, but he'd only been putting on a show for her family and Caster. If he didn't care to bed her, consummate their marriage, who was Sophia to question her good fortune. She and Roxboro would lead separate lives.

Her eyes landed on the bottle of wine.

"Well, if he isn't going to remain sober on our wedding night, I see no reason for me to. I'm relieved, nay *gratified* that I won't have to suffer his attentions."

Which was only partially a lie.

Flopping into the chair, Sophia decided not to bother with the glass.

Chapter Sixteen

Sophia swallowed down what remained of the wine, lifting the bottle to her lips until not a drop was left.

Drat.

She'd done nothing since her discussion with Timmons but drink wine, scribble out a list of character flaws for Roxboro until she ran out of paper, and stew at yet another humiliation she was suffering at his hands. Sophia glanced down at her list, blinking away the blurriness from her vision.

Drinks far too much.

Excessive arrogance.

Compromises young ladies and doesn't recall doing so.

Annoying wit.

Sophia thought for a moment.

Far too handsome.

"I need more wine." Sophia came to her feet, nearly fell over but grabbed the arm of her chair. Ann said she hadn't been able to find the wine cellar, but obviously, there must be one in this brick monstrosity of a house. Likely near the kitchens. A footman might help her if one was about.

Or, God forbid, Timmons.

She stumbled out of the room, whipping the lace and ribbons behind her, carefully to hold up the edges lest she trip. Clinging to the banister, Sophia made her way carefully down the stairs. "Can you imagine what the gossips would say?" she said out loud. "The Duke and Duchess of Roxboro," she snorted. "Both taken far too young by drunken mishaps." She snorted. "Well, I must say, I can see why my husband enjoys an excess of spirits. It's quite euphoric."

No Timmons lurking about. Nor a footman, which was unfortunate. There was a light flickering at the end of the hall, which meant the kitchen must be in that direction. She hoped.

Sophia started towards the light, trailing her fingers along the wall to keep her balance.

Goodness.

"Is that you, Timmons?" Came the low, scotch-soaked rumble from behind a partially open door. "Can you find me another bottle if you please. Scotch or brandy. I don't care which."

Roxboro.

Her fingers pressed into the wall, quite furious through the haze of the wine. Sophia straightened. Fluffed the stupid silk rose on her shoulder. She had much to say and Roxboro was going to hear all of it. One does not...abandon their bride on the wedding night. It's impolite even if you have no intention of bedding her. She glanced towards the stairs. She'd left her list of Roxboro's faults in her room.

Drat.

Taking two steps forward, still clinging to the wall, Sophia entered Roxboro's study. Her toes dug into the plush carpet at her feet.

Oh, I've forgotten my slippers.

A fire, flames dancing merrily in the hearth, cast a golden glow across the room, but gave off little light, not enough to make out the shadows along the walls.

"Oh, it's you," Roxboro's rumbling, sardonic tone came from the darkness. A lump, which she'd mistaken for a chair, moved. "Why aren't you asleep?"

She held up the bottle in her hand. "Where might I find more of this? Also, I've a list of your character deficits that I'd like to review, but I left them upstairs."

The dark outline moved. Lit a lamp. Plopped back down on a

leather sofa. "I have no idea. Timmons handles such matters. I don't care for wine. Reminds me of rotten fruit."

There was something in that statement that nagged at Sophia, but her head was too muddled at present. "Pity. I happen to enjoy it."

"Well, there isn't any in here. You made a list?"

"I did. There was little else to occupy my time other than this," she held up the bottle again. "And writing out your flaws. I ran out of paper."

"Good lord," his voice softened to a warm rasp. "Why do you look like an enormous snowflake? Are there…roses on your shoulder?"

Sophia sat down on the sofa, mere inches from Roxboro, the leather cool beneath her thighs. The wine made her annoyance towards Roxboro seem less important than it had earlier. Not with all that bergamot scented heat wafting so near her, along with scotch and…*she sniffed the air*, possibly a cheroot.

"Yes, these are roses, Roxboro." She swatted at a silk petal. "But I did not order this hideous creation, the blame falls squarely on Lady Canterbell."

"That makes much more sense. You resemble a bit of lace now that you are closer. Tatted by a blind, elderly matron."

"You are too kind." Sophia closed her eyes. "As usual."

Roxboro made a sound. Leaned closer and nudged her shoulder. "You're upset with me."

Sophia didn't open her eyes. "I am. This is our wedding night. Given your abandonment of me, I will assume you've no interest in…."

"The doily," he let out a small laugh. "Was meant to entice me."

"Again, Lady Canterbell is to blame. If you'll merely hand me a bottle of…something," she waved her hand in the direction of the sideboard and opened her eyes. Sophia's head felt quite heavy and unsteady on her neck, which made it difficult to lift her chin and stare Roxboro down. "My spray of silk roses and I will be on our way."

"You don't require the doily," he said in a soft tone that sent a shiver along her arms. "Nor did you deserve...abandonment. What is my biggest flaw?"

"Drinking to excess and arrogance. But I realize both are required in a duke and a rake."

"That's two flaws, but I take your point." Roxboro took a swallow from his glass and nudged her shoulder again before nuzzling along the edge of her neck with his nose. "You've some yourself, Lady Sausage."

Sophia couldn't help it. She giggled. "You barely know me, Your Grace." Her nose wrinkled. "And you smell like the inside of a bottle of scotch."

"You are terrible, Sophie. But I like terrible. Makes things interesting. That is the first thing I know about you." Roxboro's mouth lingered along the slope of her neck, lips skating over her skin until he found a sensitive spot beneath her ear.

A soft breath left her. Her entire body flared to life at the light touch. Rather marvelous.

"You smell of roses." Teeth nipped at the lobe of her ear. "The scent is in your hair and skin, which I've always found odd."

"Odd?" she shivered as he found another spot that had the skin prickling along her arms.

"In consideration of your caustic wit and personality." His breath feathered her hair. "Which others mistake for mere rudeness and lack of decorum. That is the second thing I know. Your blunt manner is used to shock others so you will be...*seen*."

Sophia tilted her head. Roxboro's mouth was very near her own.

"Your hostility towards me is," he whispered with only a fraction of air separating their lips. "Is because you think *I* don't see you, Sophia, Duchess of Roxboro. But I do." His mouth caressed hers. "I only pretend that I do not."

"Oh," she sighed. Warmth bloomed along her chest.

"I will not admit to it tomorrow." Roxboro's tongue flicked along her collarbone, nipping and skimming until she shivered and arched closer.

Their lips caught, mouths clinging together. This kiss was…lazy but so…blatantly carnal in nature that Sophia's toes stretched in to the deep pile of the rug. His fingers carefully trailed over one breast, palm hovering over the nipple, barely brushing the hardened tip hidden beneath the lace.

Sophia whimpered. Pressed herself closer.

Threading her fingers through the silk of Roxboro's hair, she kissed him back with every bit of longing inside her. Sophia hadn't realized that she'd had any yearning for him at all, but—

Oh, I do.

Roxboro's hands mapped every curve through the silk and lace while his tongue teased along the bottom of her mouth, coaxing Sophia to open for him, which she did without hesitation. Sucking at her tongue, an altogether erotic sensation, two fingers trailed along the slope of her breast, before nipping at Sophia's bottom lip.

She tugged at his hair. She wanted more. Would beg for him to—

A pained, annoyed sound came from Roxboro. He grabbed Sophia's hands from his hair and placed them on her lap. "I can't," he said under his breath, pushing away from her. "I—cannot bed you." He turned away and swallowed the remains of his glass. "No," he said more firmly. "Absolutely not."

"I see." Roxboro's heat fell away from her body, leaving Sophia cold inside and out. His rejection after such a passionate embrace left Sophia's heart to beat shallowly in her chest. For a moment, she'd thought—

"That's—perfectly fine." It wasn't. This was a mistake. A miscalculation on her part. "I prefer a more…convenient marriage. One that is not muddled with physical relations. I would prefer, Roxboro, that you not ever touch me again," she said with more force.

"I won't."

"Don't so much as offer your hand to help me into the

bloody carriage. Or I will kick you in your well-lauded *cock*, Your Grace." Sophia jerked to her feet.

"Jesus, don't say that," Roxboro murmured, shifting on the sofa.

"I'm pleased we understand each other."

I am ever foolish about Roxboro. But I won't be again.

When he didn't reply, Sophia poked a finger in his arm. "Do you understand me, Roxboro?"

"I do." His body slid down along the leather of the sofa until his backside hit the floor. "Now, go away, Lady Salmon."

Sophia stumbled to the door, dropping the empty wine bottle on the rug. Timmons would clean it up. Or not. She didn't care.

"You've used that one more than once, Your Grace."

Chapter Seventeen

ALEXANDER SQUINTED AS the sunlight hit his face. He was rarely up this early and frankly, wished he was still in bed. His temples pounded so fiercely the beat had him a bit unsteady on his feet, and lord knows, Alexander needed no help with that.

As a lad, he was forever tripping or stumbling. Stubbed his toes on everything. Damon grew exasperated but Aunt May only hugged Alexander tight and whispered he would outgrow his awkwardness. But he never had. Several physicians were called to examine the Duke of Roxboro, but not one found anything wrong with Alexander. He was just…clumsy.

Good lord, his entire staff at The Pillory lived in fear that he'd trip over a rock and land in the pond at his estate and drown.

To be entirely fair, he had tripped into the pond. Damon eventually found him, thrashing about and covered with wet reeds, and fished Alexander out. An excess of spirits made the problem worse, but ironically, more acceptable. No one batted an eye at a *drunken* duke tripping about. Mostly.

"Headache powder, Timmons," Alexander ordered the butler as he came to the bottom of the steps.

"Yes, Your Grace."

The shiny black exterior of his carriage gleamed in the sunlight like a bit of onyx as it waited to make the trip to the train station. The Roxboro coat of arms stared boldly back at Alexander.

His steps paused.

Alexander had stayed roaring drunk since his wedding night, the best way to avoid his new duchess, who he was not averse to. *At all.*

Oh, he had heard her moving about in the rooms beside his own, the connecting door all that separated Alexander from temptation. Stone, his valet, was instructed to lock that damned door leading to the duchess and pocket the key, which his valet had done without question.

Good man, Stone. If he wasn't such an excellent valet, Alexander would make him butler, therefore ridding himself of Timmons, who he cared for less and less as time went on.

Alexander had stared at that door, ears cocked as Sophia spoke to her maid last evening, all the while swallowing copious amounts of scotch to alleviate his unwelcome desire. Why he had such...a thirst for his bride, Alexander had no idea. But when Sophia snapped that she would kick him in the cock if he dared touch her again, Alexander had been so aroused, his baser instincts had nearly overridden his common sense and caused him to break the vow he'd made to Damon.

Please don't let her say anything of the sort today.

Alexander might not be able to exhibit any sort of control in his weakened state. He'd end up fucking her in the carriage.

I cannot. I promised Damon.

Timmons reappeared with his headache powder, and Alexander took the packet in one swallow, washing away the bitter taste with the brandy his butler offered. Taking a deep breath, Alexander approached the carriage. Sophia was waiting inside. The remainder of the day was bound to be unpleasant.

The footman bowed and opened the door to reveal...the *empty* interior.

Alexander took in the black leather seats where Sophia should have been sitting and was not. He looked at the top of the carriage. Every trunk was his. "Timmons," he demanded. "Where is the duchess?"

Had she left him? Run back to her family?

A terrible, hollow feeling expanded inside Alexander at the sight of those empty leather seats. Of Sophia being gone. As unexpected as the desire he felt for her.

"The duchess has already departed for The Pillory, Your Grace."

That little shrew. "When?" He turned to his butler.

"Yesterday, Your Grace. I made the arrangements myself." Timmons cleared his throat. "Lord Damon suggested it might be best if the duchess left before you so that she might become more quickly acquainted with her new home. He suggested as much and the duchess agreed."

"And no one thought to inform me." Alexander was furious. He hadn't even known his uncle had called yesterday. Now the silence coming from Sophia's rooms today made a great deal more sense. He must have slept through her departure.

"Lord Damon," the butler stammered. "Said you were under the weather and did not wish to be disturbed, Your Grace."

"Under the weather," Alexander repeated.

Intoxicated. Drunk. A feckless sot.

"I assure you, Your Grace, Lord Damon—"

"Is not the Duke of Roxboro. I am," Alexander ground out. "A reminder, you are in my employ, Timmons. Not that of Damon Viceroy. If you dare circumvent me again, you will be sacked. I don't care if Lord Damon is carrying a note from Her Majesty."

The butler shrank back. "Yes, Your Grace."

His uncle handled a great many things when Alexander was 'under the weather,' most of which he didn't give a fig about. But in this *instance*—how dare Damon send Sophia on ahead without first consulting Alexander. She was his bloody wife. Instead of being pleased that his uncle had solved yet another obstacle by removing Sophia from Alexander's orbit today, he was furious.

I should be pleased Damon intervened.

Alexander climbed inside his lavishly appointed carriage and settled into well-oiled leather seats.

Yet, I am not.

The previous evening, Damon had accompanied Alexander to Binson's and failed to mention he had sent the *Duchess of Bloody Roxboro*—Alexander pressed his fingers into the seat, trying to tamp down his temper—to The Pillory without informing her husband.

He took a lungful of air, letting his chest expand.

Damon was only trying to help.

Alexander should stay in London. Not climb aboard that train. The only reason Alexander was visiting The Pillory at all was that he couldn't very well send Sophia alone. Canterbell would object.

He took a deep breath. Then another. The ache in his temples began to recede.

On his wedding night, Damon must have sensed his nephew might forget the vow to not touch Sophia. He'd suggested a visit to a brothel, Madame Lucret's, a favorite. But Alexander had declined, preferring to hole up in his study where a bottle of scotch sat awaiting him.

Then Sophia appeared.

Adorable in her stupid doily. Foxed on a bottle of wine she'd somehow managed to acquire. She'd been so...lovely to him. Allowing him to call her Lady Sausage and hurling insults. Taunting him with a list of his character deficits. Of which he had many. No one else dared speak to him in such a way. Damon or Violet on occasion, but mostly, everyone around Alexander treated him with an outlandish amount of deference.

The longing for Sophia dressed like a tea cake had been...*insurmountable*.

Damon must have guessed, or Timmons, *who was absolutely going to be sacked*, warned him.

Another deep breath and most of his anger receded.

His uncle, as usual, only sought to save Alexander from himself.

"John," he said to his driver. "I believe I won't be taking the train. We'll go the long way to The Pillory." Maybe, if he stayed away from Sophia for just a bit longer, the thirst for her would simply fade. The Pillory was overly large, like most ducal estates and he could go days without seeing Sophia. Alexander would stay for a week and return to London. Canterbell would be satisfied, after all, his daughter had made it clear she wished to be sent to the country. And there would be no danger of consummating the marriage.

"You've a hankering to visit The Sheepshead, Your Grace?"

John was a good man. He knew his duke well. This wasn't the first time Alexander had decided not to take the train but take the longer journey to The Pillory so that he might stop at the Sheepshead.

Timmons stood frowning at the bottom of the steps. "Your Grace?"

"I may even stay the night," he said to John, ignoring Timmons. "I'm in no rush." The Pillory was barely two days from London by carriage. Not a great distance and the passing countryside was appealing. The Sheepshead boasted an excellent lamb stew as well as a rather delicious barmaid, Nell. Both were favorites of Alexander.

He was hopeful the buxom flax-haired woman would renew his...enthusiasm for bedsport. Because since meeting Sophia, there wasn't a woman in London Alexander wanted to fuck *except* his wife. Which was entirely unacceptable considering he couldn't.

But I dearly want to.

Damon, thankfully, had been logical. Cooped up in first a carriage and then a train with Sophia. Sipping on a flask of brandy. The worst could transpire, ruining all their plans.

What had his uncle said as they entered Binson's?

Six months. I think that fair. Keep her in the country most of the time. What little appeal she possesses can be flaunted upon the cows and pigs.

Alexander pulled out his flask and took a sip before rapping on the carriage roof. "Let us be off, John."

Chapter Eighteen

Sophia paced across the drawing room of Roxboro's estate, barely noticing the gorgeously tufted rug beneath her feet. Every so often, she would stop, glance out the window, and then resume her marching back and forth.

Roxboro had yet to arrive at The Pillory.

She shouldn't even have had a shred of concern about the coward.

Roxboro couldn't even inform Sophia himself that he wanted her to leave without him, instead he'd had his devious, calculating uncle inform her. Staring down Damon Viceroy, she'd asked why the duke would bother coming to the country at all if that were the case.

Lord Damon merely raised a brow, looking down at Sophia without an ounce of emotion, handsome features as closed as a sphinx. "I doubt he'll stay long. There isn't much at The Pillory to interest him."

Sophia, to her credit, didn't flinch from the politely delivered insult.

"Give my regards to Lord Canterbell. Be sure and write to him of the joy you've found in your new home." Then Lord Damon spun on his heel and sauntered away, but not before instructing Timmons, who'd been lurking in the shadows, to make travel arrangements for the duchess.

So Sophia journeyed to The Pillory on her own the day before Roxboro, save for Ann and strangely enough, the duke's valet, Stone. Stone was a lovely man, spare and neat with a dry wit. He explained it wasn't unusual for him to leave a day or two before the duke when Roxboro visited The Pillory. His family lived in the area and the duke was gracious enough to relieve Stone of his duties for a short time so that he might pay them a visit.

Seemed out of character for Roxboro, to be so gracious, but Sophia accepted Stone's explanation.

The Pillory left Sophia awestruck.

Papa had a large country estate, a place Sophia had spent a glorious childhood before being forced to spend more time in London. It wasn't that The Pillory was only massive in size, stretching out along the top of a hill, but Roxboro's ducal seat was the most interesting, outlandish bit of architecture she'd ever seen.

Three stone towers, just as Roxboro had said. Two of the towers were barely more than rubble, but the third stood with its notorious cut holes in the stone. The Pillory, or parts of it, was old. The main house consisted of a hodgepodge of various styles, having been built in stages over the decades. Each generation of Viceroy's had left their mark, adding a new wing or extending a room, but the towers remained and were never torn down. The curved stone of the second tower, what was left of it, made up part of the wall in The Pillory's drawing room.

The estate was spectacular. Sophia did nothing but walk about and explore on her first day. A lifetime could be spent here and she might never find all of The Pillory's secrets.

When she found the library, Sophia squealed in delight, though upon further examination, there wasn't much to her taste on the shelves…but that could be fixed. One of the maids, Lizzy, helped her unpack the crates of books sent ahead from London, placing them carefully on the shelf.

Sophia took long walks through the extensive gardens, waving at the team of gardeners employed to keep every inch lush and green. The gardens turned to gentle rolling hills and if Sophia walked far enough, the hills eventually gave way to rugged cliffs overlooking the sea below.

If she were destined to remain here, Sophia could be happy. In fact, she wouldn't care if she never saw London again. Her family could visit her at The Pillory. Roxboro could continue to indulge in his gambling hells and courtesans. Maybe that was what had caused his delay, a visit to a brothel or an opium den.

Sophia decided she didn't care if he ever arrived.

But after a few days, when Roxboro should have appeared and did not, Sophia's curiosity got the best of her. Barstow, The Pillory's butler, would know the duke's…plans.

Barstow was nothing like Timmons, which meant she liked Barstow immediately upon introduction. He was tall and broad with the bearing of a man who'd once been a soldier, which Stone, who'd known Barstow for ages, assured her was the case. His craggy features softened at her approach.

"Your Grace," he bowed.

"Barstow. The duke," she'd started, unsure how to proceed. "Was due to arrive before now. I grow concerned. Have you received word on his delay?"

Difficult to admit her husband wouldn't send *her* a note, but Sophia supposed she and Roxboro would communicate through the servants going forward. When her parents argued, Mama left notes to be delivered to Papa by their butler.

"Do not worry, Your Grace," Barstow assured her. "The duke decides at times, to take the long way to The Pillory."

"The long way?"

"Not take the train. The journey by carriage is less than two days, which gives the duke ample opportunity to sample the shepherd's pie or lamb stew at the Sheepshead Inn which is located along the main road." Barstow cleared his throat. "At such times, His Grace invariably decides to stay the night. Rarely does the duke send word ahead, unless he'll be longer than two days. I've received no note. I expect him tomorrow."

"Thank you, Barstow." Sophia inclined her head and retreated. Fuming.

Ann informed Sophia, while preparing her for bed, that the scullery maid, Bertie, mentioned there was a barmaid at the Sheepshead, who Roxboro favored far more than the shepherd's pie.

Vile, drunken cur.

Sophia kept up a brave front until today, when she caught sight of Barstow staring out the window, his rough features drawn into lines of concern. Roxboro had exceeded his usual lateness by an entire day, which according to Ann, who heard it from the cook, was highly unusual.

Later, right before tea, Barstow sent two footmen out to see if the duke's carriage had gotten stuck or thrown a wheel.

"Or," she'd heard him say in a low tone. *"How long he meant to linger at The Sheepshead."*

That had been hours ago, while Sophia enjoyed tea in the elegant drawing room, a book in one hand. But the sun was starting to sink towards the horizon and Roxboro still hadn't appeared. Nor had the two footmen returned. Something was wrong. If Roxboro hadn't meant to come to The Pillory at all, Damon would have taken great delight in telling Sophia. Or Timmons would have sent word to Barstow so that she could be informed.

That was how things were done.

Counting her steps, Sophia paced across the large, rectangular rug, absently admiring the blue and gold swirls that made up the design.

Twenty. Twenty-one. Twenty-two.

She paused at the sound of shouts coming from outside. Carriage wheels struck the gravel of the drive.

Twenty-three.

Sophia took a shaky breath and smoothed her skirts, refusing to give Roxboro the satisfaction of knowing she'd been distressed at his late arrival. Her husband would probably fall out of the carriage, reeking of brandy and barmaid. Sophia planned to inform Roxboro that in the future, she objected to Lord Damon as an intermediary. She would not tolerate any further disrespect. Then she would make a rather grand exit and proceed to ignore the duke, which wouldn't be difficult given the size of The Pillory.

Resolve firm, Sophia stood before the window, watching as Roxboro's mud-stained carriage, missing one of the horses, halted before the front door.

Barstow stepped onto the gravel drive, hurrying toward the carriage, shouting instructions to the footmen who rushed outside.

Sophia pressed her fingertips to the window pane.

Servants swarmed the vehicle. A footman leapt down from the driver's seat, the same young man Barstow had sent out to search for the duke earlier today. Another bedraggled footman, his livery torn and dirty, arrived on the missing horse.

Stone appeared, sprinting towards Barstow as the carriage door was opened.

Roxboro's driver tumbled out, the side of his face bruised a deep purple, a thin trickle of red streaming down one cheek.

Blood. A great deal of it. On the driver. On the footmen. The carriage door.

Sophia didn't hesitate. She ran outside, heart in her throat, just in time to see Roxboro, unconscious, the fine lawn of his shirt, stained crimson as Barstow and Stone pulled him from the carriage.

"Your Grace."

Sophia looked up at the exhausted face of Dr. Reading. He'd been summoned while enjoying a pie his wife had made. Cherry, according to the stain dotting the napkin still suck in his collar as he arrived at The Pillory.

One footman, Milburn, dead. The driver, John, injured from a blow to the head. The remaining footman had been fortunate. He'd been stabbed but the wounds were shallow, according to Dr. Reading.

But Roxboro.

"I've done all I can for now, Your Grace." Dr. Reading placed a hand on her shoulder. "The rest, I'm afraid, is in God's hands. We'll be on the lookout for infection. Fever." He pressed his lips together in consternation.

"What is it?" she said, taking in Roxboro's pale, bloodless countenance. Her anger towards him was still there, sitting in her mid-section, but the sight of her husband like this had *torn* at Sophia in a way she hadn't expected.

"The duke's love of drink will make things worse. His body will notice the absence of spirits. It will make his recovery that much more difficult, Your Grace." Dr. Reading looked to Barstow.

"I had an uncle who required care when he gave up the bottle. I understand," Barstow replied.

"What must I do for both…illnesses?" Sophia asked. She'd never nursed a soul except for one of her dolls when Mara tore the arm off. That experience was unlikely to assist her in this instance.

You've the courage. Patience and comfort are required.

Lady Violet's whispered instruction to Sophia after the wedding breakfast. At the time, she hadn't known what to make of the words, but now, looking at Roxboro, she had some idea, although Violet could never have imagined this scenario.

"Your Grace," Stone said. "I'll stay with the duke."

"Yes," Dr. Reading agreed. "A lady such as yourself—"

"Forgive me, Dr. Reading," Sophia returned crisply. "But you don't know what sort of lady I am. I will nurse my husband, with Barstow's assistance. And Stone's." She glanced at the butler who appeared pleased by her demand. "Now, what must I do?"

"Of course, Your Grace. Send for me immediately if his wounds worsen. You know what I refer to, Barstow, do you not? Redness. Pus. Flesh not knitting together. There's laudanum for pain and his—other symptoms."

"I saw many fevers and putrid wounds while I served England, Dr. Reading. I'll send word immediately should the duke's wounds worsen. And as to the other, as I've said, I helped my uncle who loved gin far too much." Barstow looked at Sophia. "Begging your pardon, Your Grace."

"Putrid wounds. Fever. Some sort of symptoms caused by lack of spirits." Sophia jerked her chin. "Very well." The fatigue of the last few hours crept under her skin, but she pushed it aside. Roxboro would *not* die. She would make sure of it.

When Barstow had yelled to fetch Dr. Reading even as Stone helped him carry Roxboro from the carriage, Sophia had stood still on the drive, deathly calm. She followed his blood-stained form up the stairs as he was carried to his rooms. Didn't weep or collapse into a fit of tears, though she'd dearly wanted to. The entire household looked to her for guidance. Strength.

Because Sophia was the Duchess of Roxboro.

And even though she'd never wanted such a lofty title and had held it only little more than a week, Sophia would not fold. Nor crumple. A duchess was made of sterner stuff.

She had called for hot water and towels, instructing Ann and two of the maids, knowing instinctively that all that blood must be cleaned away.

"Your Grace," Barstow said gently, as he and another footman had placed Roxboro on the bed. "Stone and I can handle this."

"No. I'm staying. What must I do?"

Roxboro's entire shirt had been soaked with blood; his coat long gone and discarded. Cravat hanging by a silken thread at his throat.

Barstow held up a pair of scissors and cut off her husband's clothes, blocking the view of Roxboro from the others in the room. After pulling the sheet up to the waist, he said, "The worst of it is confined to the duke's chest and arms."

The worst of it...the large gaping maws across Roxboro's torso were so deep in places she could see—inside to the muscle beneath. Barstow instructed her to hold a clean towel to his side as it still seeped blood, which Sophia had done without question.

You will not die, Roxboro. I forbid it. I've not yet voiced my annoyance with you.

"Bring me brandy," Barstow ordered Stone. "You know where he keeps it. Where is Dr. Reading?"

Stone rushed to the armoire and threw open the doors. "For emergencies." He plucked out a bottle of brandy hidden in the back. "Reading has been sent for. He should be here any moment." The bottle was passed to Barstow.

"No," Sophia protested, thinking the butler meant to force some of the amber liquid down Roxboro's throat. "It will make things worse. I'm sure of it."

"Not to drink, Your Grace. To clean the wound," Barstow assured her. "We used it on the battlefield. It helps." He took the bottle of brandy Stone offered and spilled some of it into the gash on Roxboro's chest.

When Dr. Reading had appeared, he nodded his approval, cleaning every single cut on Roxboro and splashing each one liberally with brandy, before stitching up the largest. Disturbing to watch as Dr. Reading blithely used a needle on Roxboro as if he were a bit of embroidery.

She did not look away.

Six stab wounds. Two of them so near Roxboro's lungs and heart, Dr. Reading marveled at Roxboro's luck for having an assailant with such poor aim.

According to the surviving footman and the driver, the carriage had been attacked after leaving The Sheepshead for The Pillory. There was a long stretch of road which was rarely traveled except by those going to Roxboro's estate. Thick trees lined the route, the perfect cover to hide and waylay the duke's carriage. Two men, both wearing handkerchiefs over their faces to hide their features, jumped into the road, killing first the unlucky Milburn, and then taking a bludgeon to John, hitting him so forcefully that he fell from the driver's seat.

And the second footman?

I rolled off the carriage and into the woods, Your Grace. I knew they'd kill me too if I didn't. Ran alongside when they drove off. One of them jumped inside with the duke.

The young man, Samson was his name, took a deep breath and had looked away before continuing. He could be no more than twenty.

The carriage rocked back and forth. I knew—the duke was in danger. The door opened and—a body fell out before I could catch up. Not the duke, Your Grace, but his assailant. Dead. The man who'd taken John's place, pulled the horses to a stop and jumped off the seat cursing something fierce. I lunged and tackled him to the ground. His Grace threw open the door, a pistol in his hand as we fought.

"Don't worry, Samson," *the duke said to me.* "I'm a good shot."

Samson had swallowed, throat bobbing as he related to Sophia and Barstow what had happened. The poor footman had been horrified Roxboro might have died under his watch.

Shot him straight between the eyes, Mr. Barstow. The duke weren't wrong. He's excellent aim. He was bleeding so bad. I put him and John in the carriage. I unharnessed one of the horses, meaning to ride to The Pillory for help.

"You should rest, Your Grace," Barstow said in a quiet tone from behind her. "He won't awaken...for some time." The butler's words turned thick, the unspoken knowledge that Roxboro might not wake up at all sitting between them. "I'll have Mary come up and sit with the duke while you have something to eat."

"No, I want to stay with him," Sophia looked up at the butler. "Please see to the others. They'll need to retrieve...Milburn. Inform his family."

"Yes, Your Grace."

"Ensure that Milburn's family is informed and...give my

deepest sympathies," she croaked, closer to tears than she'd been since watching a bloodied Roxboro pulled from the carriage. "The duke owes them a debt for Milburn's devotion to duty. We will not forget. I will ring for you, Barstow, should I need assistance."

Once the butler departed, Sophia pulled up the stool Dr. Reading had used. She laid a hand on Roxboro's own. His skin was a sickly hue, the color of paste. Or soured milk. Dark lashes fanned across the striking cheekbones, not moving as he took shallow breaths.

"I'm so...annoyed with you, feckless sot," she murmured, dabbing at Roxboro's forehead with a cloth. The heat of his forehead burned her fingers, far warmer than he'd been an hour ago. The fever had started. "Having Damon send me ahead because you lacked the courage to tell me you didn't wish to endure my company on the journey."

Roxboro made a sound, head twisting as if listening to her.

"Did you know," Sophia said casually. "That 'three-legged stool' also refers to a gentleman's anatomy. My maid, Ann is her name, taught that to me on our wedding night. I wasn't going to use it, of course." She wrung out the cloth and dipped it once more into the basin of water.

A raspy noise came from Roxboro's chest. He panted slightly. Settled again.

"I'm sure, given I'm so bloody annoyed, you're probably wondering why I've chosen to sit with you. Well, you're my husband, whether you wish it or not. And I have come to the unwelcome conclusion; I don't dislike you as much as I should. But that could change at any moment once you are well. Also, and I will insist on this, but I think," her voice broke just a little. "That Samson deserves a bonus for saving your life."

Roxboro twitched once more, eyes moving beneath his eyelids.

"Good, you agree. I didn't want to argue over it."

Samson had the presence of mind to bind Roxboro's wounds

even as the duke instructed him to turn the carriage and retrieve John, a short distance behind them. The footman had only just decided to ride for The Pillory to seek help when the footmen Barstow dispatched arrived.

"No one was more surprised than I to discover you could handle yourself in a fight. Honestly, Roxboro, I was shocked. As is the entire staff."

Not entirely true. Barstow hadn't seemed surprised at all.

"Clumsy duke that you are," she halted and pressed a cloth to his forehead. "I would have thought it more likely you'd shoot your own foot off. I wouldn't have guessed you would remember there were pistols under the seat since your memory is spotty at best." A tiny sob escaped her lips. "And being able to aim properly while bleeding to death was truly inspired. Not to mention your use of a knife." A tear trailed down one cheek. "Roxboro," she choked.

Sophia laid her head down on the bed, cheek next to her husband's chest so that she could hear the rattle of his breathing. The terror and fear at the last few hours bubbled to the surface, no matter how she tried to stop it. She sobbed, wretchedly, against Roxboro, soaking the sheets with her tears while he stayed silent and unmoving.

I do not dislike him.

Quite the opposite.

CHAPTER NINETEEN

ROXBORO REMAINED UNCONSCIOUS all through the night and into the following day. At times, he thrashed about as the fever took hold, his big body trembling. Elegant fingers twitching in agitation. Sweat dotted his brow.

"The fever is from his wounds, Your Grace. But that jerking about is the withdrawal from spirits," Barstow informed her, while checking Roxboro's bandages. "My uncle did the same. It lasted…for some time."

Sophia refused to leave Roxboro's side. If anyone were to ask why she was so committed to caring for him after the circumstances of their marriage, she would have been hard-pressed to explain. She didn't know the reason, or rather, she did but decided now was not the time to examine those feelings.

Barstow asked if he should send word to Lord Damon, but Sophia decided against it. "I'll write to him tomorrow."

But she didn't. Nor the next day.

"Open your eyes," Sophia said to him, smoothing her hand over his forehead, brushing away the coffee-colored strands, now damp and clinging to his skin. Even barely alive, Roxboro was still the most beautiful thing she'd ever seen.

"I must confess, Roxboro, I don't have a great many suitors. None, in fact. I'm sure you find that surprising. Mara has dozens, though she's set her cap for Caster. Who I do not think is truly your friend. Maybe once. Your uncle is quite manipulative.

But...you appeared and I wanted to know what it was like to feel desired, by...someone like you." A self-deprecating laugh broke through. "When you said to me, on our wedding night, that I behave the way I do merely to shock and be seen, you are correct. I have been invisible most of my life. But the greatest tragedy of this entire affair is...the man in the Perswick gardens wasn't you." Sophia looked away, giving the truth to a man who should have heard it well before wedding her. "I should have—stopped our marriage, but it seemed so impossible that there was another man in London, or anywhere else, who looked so much like you. Exactly like you. I can't make sense of it. But—it couldn't have been you. There's no freckle. And I know about...the wine cellar."

On her very first night at The Pillory, Sophia had a tray brought to her prepared rooms, far too exhausted by the journey and her new life to dine alone downstairs. She had asked Ann to bring a bottle of wine as Sophia had decided a glass with dinner was appropriate. A short time later, Ann returned with her tray, but there was no fine French Bordeaux to enjoy with her roasted chicken.

"There isn't any burgundy at The Pillory," Ann explained. "The duke detests wine. There is nothing in the wine cellar except mice. If Lord Damon stays for any length of time or the duke has visitors, he allows wine to be procured. Barstow has placed an order for a crate of Bordeaux which should arrive tomorrow, Your Grace."

No wine at The Pillory. Nor at the duke's home in London. And Barstow had told Sophia why.

"You never drink wine. Not ratafia. Nor Madeira or port. Nothing of the kind. Yet the night of the Perswick ball, the Roxboro I spoke to held a glass and drank from it. His lips tasted of wine when he kissed me. And there was a large, purple stain on his coat." A sound of regret left her. "I cannot fathom how it is possible, Roxboro. But there is a gentleman who resembles you so strongly, right down to your eyes, that he fooled the other guests at the Perswick ball. Lady Brokeburst. My father. But especially me."

Sophia pulled up the sheets he'd kicked off in his thrashing, tucking them gently around his waist. She allowed her fingers to trail over the lines of Roxboro's torso, carefully securing the edge of a bandage that had come loose. She'd never seen a male unclothed before now. His body was so different from hers, all muscle and strength. More so than she'd expected from a libertine.

And so unbelievably beautiful.

"I'm not sure why anyone would want to pose as a sot of a duke," her words trembled as the worry for him blotted out everything else. "But someone is."

Sophia rose and stepped back from the bed, meaning to leave only long enough to fetch a pitcher of cool water. Dr. Reading said she must force some between his lips.

"I believe you, Roxboro. And I'm sorry I didn't before."

SOPHIA'S EYES SNAPPED open. She'd fallen asleep in the chair beside her husband's bed, neck bent at an uncomfortable angle. A low moan came from the bed where Roxboro twisted and panted, whether from the fever, which most definitely had taken hold, or the withdrawal of spirits, she wasn't sure.

Jumping up, she immediately placed a hand on his brow.

Burning. Roxboro was burning up.

Dr. Reading had visited just yesterday, leaving behind a mixture of herbs that should be given to Roxboro to help with the fever. The laudanum would help with the pain of his wounds, though since she wasn't certain whether Roxboro was addicted to opium or not, she cautioned Barstow on the medicine's use.

Keep him quiet. Don't get his wounds wet. Bathe him with cold water to keep him comfortable. Check for putrid skin.

She pulled back the sheet to examine the wound below his shoulder, and the others, across his ribs on his chest. Two looked far better than they had but the others were still an angry red. Sophia leaned in and sniffed, searching for the terrible odor of rotten flesh, but there was nothing but the aroma of sweat. No sign of infection.

"You don't get to die yet, Roxboro. I should be given a chance to make things right. Then, if you wish, fall into the Thames. Or trip down the stairs. So be it. But not yet."

Sophia stood and walked across the room, remembering Dr. Reading's instructions. Throwing open the door, she startled the maid just outside who nearly fell off her stool.

"Find Barstow and Stone," she said to the girl. "I need a tub with the coolest water you can find. Hurry."

"LOWER HIM IN. Slowly." Sophia checked the depth of the water, making sure it would go no further than his hips. The bandages above his ribs could not get wet.

Roxboro was completely naked save for the bandages and the small clothes covering his…male anatomy. She'd turned her back while Stone adjusted matters to give his employer some privacy. And while she didn't think her husband necessarily cared who saw his…*cock*…given his arrogance, Sophia did.

She declined to look herself.

It was hard enough to not ogle such a handsomely made, but unconscious man. Thick thighs, heavy with muscle. The sculpted torso dusted with dark hair. Long, elegant arms and legs. Hard to believe they tangled up so often to make him trip.

Sophia lowered her eyes, biting back a sob.

I don't want him to die.

"Your Grace," Barstow said quietly. "Stone and I can bathe the duke. You should rest. Eat and sleep."

"I eat. I sleep," Sophia returned, raising her chin. "Let's get on with this."

Roxboro's eyes, glowing green and laced with flecks of silver, snapped open in surprise as the cold water touched his heated skin.

"No," he snarled at Sophia. "It hurts. What is the meaning of this?" he choked out.

"Shh. You have a fever, Roxboro. We need to bring it down. You've been injured." She gently ran a cloth over him while Barstow held him down. He was so hot. Like touching a stove.

"That trollop tried to slash my throat," he mumbled, the rest unintelligible. A series of grunts and whimpers followed as Sophia bathed his heated skin. "Tell Oakhurst I am not ever coming to this establishment again."

"I will," Sophia said in a soothing tone.

"Oh," his eyes on her were unfocused as they took her in. "You aren't the trollop, are you?" He settled. Stopped twitching. "Maybe you'll join me in the tub?"

"Barstow," she said. "Please remain outside the door until I call. You as well, Stone."

The butler opened his mouth to protest but changed his mind and nodded instead.

Stone merely bowed.

"Thank you," Sophia murmured. "When I'm finished, I'll have you return him to the bed."

Roxboro was delirious. Not in his right mind. And while she was sure that Barstow and the rest of the staff were used to the duke and his antics, Sophia didn't want any of them to see him like this.

"Yes, Your Grace. Should I send for Lord Damon?" Barstow's eyes met hers.

"No, I'll write to him tomorrow." She wasn't sure what, exactly, kept her from sending for Damon Viceroy when Roxboro very well could be dying—

I won't let that happen.

—but something inside Sophia told her not to summon Lord Damon, and that something was rather insistent. She absolutely detested the man. Roxboro could be angry with her later.

"Better?" she asked, pressing the cloth to his uninjured side.

His head lolled against the rim of the tub. "I don't know why Oakhurst insisted on bringing me here. I already tupped Lady Hastings at Binson's. And taking me to that opium den, which I wasn't in the mood to enjoy at all, though it was lovely to see Lady Maxwell. She kept asking when I had time to change my coat. Said there was a wine stain. Can you imagine me, with a wine stain?"

"No," Sophia replied softly. "You don't drink wine."

Because of the wine cellar.

"Hate the stuff. Tastes of sour grapes and...the cold." His brow furrowed and he shivered. "Why is this bath so bloody cold? Can I have a scotch?"

"Not right now, Roxboro."

"You're a sassy wench. But I like you." He grinned at Sophia, closing his eyes. Taking one of her hands, he placed it firmly between his thighs. "As much as I'm enjoying the bath, there are other matters which need attending to."

Sophia went completely still.

Thanks to Ann, she had a decent description of male anatomy. Mama had been much less forthcoming with her talk of "lengths," leaving it to Sophia's imagination. All of which is to say, she had a vague impression of what lay beneath Roxboro's smallclothes.

"I'm—" Sophia attempted to move her hand, but Roxboro held fast. His...*cock* was hard, like a bit of stone beneath the fragile cotton of his small clothes. And as heated as the rest of him. A gasp left her as *it* swelled beneath her touch.

"Come now. I enjoy a good bath, especially the ending." His eyes opened to narrow slits, the gray green bathing her in wickedness.

Arousal, because this must be what the sudden throb taking up residence between her thighs must be, struck Sophia.

Oh. Dear.

Roxboro was delirious with fever, thinking her some trollop

at a brothel. He was ill. Could possibly die. Still entirely carnal in nature but that was no excuse for Sophia's...reaction. She tamped down every one of those delicious sensations.

"This isn't the time for such matters." When she pulled her hand away this time, Roxboro didn't try to stop her. "You aren't well at present."

"I'm not?" He shivered violently. "I want a scotch."

"Later, Your Grace." His skin had cooled, but his *cock* still twitched. She continued to bathe him until he no longer felt hot to the touch, studiously keeping her gaze averted from...matters.

"Barstow," she raised her voice so the butler, just outside the door, could hear her. "I require your assistance. And possibly Stone's."

CHAPTER TWENTY

THE FEVER RETURNED.
The baths helped, but only so much. Sophia poured cups of the potion Dr. Reading prepared down Roxboro's throat all while he screamed out his protests. She fed him sips of broth and water, worried as he ate little and the hollows under his glorious eyes deepened. Mopped his cheeks when he grew too warm between baths, which was near continuous. Listened to him ramble about a variety of subjects, most of which had her blushing. Roxboro's…exploits were colorful to say the least. Her husband had earned his reputation, though he was careful to remind Sophia that the sheep incident was completely fabricated.

Sheep?

Roxboro didn't slur or stumble over his words in his delirium, his speech remained cool and patrician, colored with arrogance. The only indication he wasn't in his right mind was the glassy, unfocused gaze and the sweat clinging to him.

At times Roxboro thought he was on the pleasure barge, the one he'd fallen into the Thames from, with Oakhurst. Or at Binson's waiting to play hazard. Usually, he thought Sophia to be a courtesan and spent a great deal of time listing the acts he wished her to perform.

Her cheeks flamed the entire time.

But the most unsettling hallucination, the one that had him shaking not from fever but terror, was the wine cellar. Roxboro thought himself a lad of ten once more. Locked in the wine cellar of The Pillory, screaming for help.

Barstow had found him. Curled into a ball and surrounded by broken glass. He'd drank the wine because he was hungry and thirsty. Cold. How Roxboro had come to be locked in the far recesses of the wine cellar was anyone's guess.

How had the staff lost a ten-year-old duke?

Had he followed in one of the servants? Lord Damon, perhaps?

Barstow's lips had pressed together so tightly his mouth disappeared. He refused to answer or say more.

"I'll probably die soon," Roxboro whispered. Taking Sophia's hand, her palm to his cheek. "Don't be sad, Nell."

Today, Roxboro imagined he was at the Sheepshead with his favorite barmaid, Nell. Sophia was so exhausted, so terrified he would perish if the fever didn't break, she didn't even mind. "I won't allow it."

"Sweet Nell. But we both know I'm destined for tragedy, as is every Viceroy. One need look no further than my parents." The green of his eyes, now dull with illness, tried to focus on her face. "Or my grandsire. We Dukes of Roxboro don't live long."

"I'm sure you're mistaken," she squeezed his fingers.

"My grandfather was hit on the head with a bag of grain while inspecting the new mill. Can you imagine? The blow didn't kill him, but his temple hitting the stone wall of the mill did the trick. Uncle Damon says it was…quite terrible."

"Lord Damon…witnessed his father's death?"

"He did." Roxboro nodded somberly. "Not a thing could be done. Just like my father."

Sophia placed her hand on his cheek. He was…a little cooler.

"Murdered as he left Parliament." Roxboro sounded tired. "By my mother's lover. Cotswold. Marianne boasted of it to Damon. But my scheming mother didn't get to be a merry widow. She died that night too." He took a shaking draw of air. "I killed her, you see. When I was born."

There was so much pain in his casual recitation. Years of it.

"You are not to blame, Your Grace." Sophia took his hand, lacing their fingers together. "You were an infant."

"Fragile and scheming. That's what my uncle says of Marianne." Roxboro's head lolled to the side. "That's why I prefer women like you, Nell. Sturdier and far less deceitful." A deep mournful sigh came from him. "I am the product of my parents' hatred for each other." His eyes started to close. "I must apologize, but I'm excessively weary. You'll have to do most of the work, I'm afraid." He pointed to his lower body. "I'll make it up to you later."

"Very well, Your Grace." Gently, Sophia released his fingers and smoothed the sheets, listening to the soft hum he made at her touch.

"Don't leave me—Sophie," came a broken whisper.

Her hands halted. Roxboro's eyes were still closed. A tiny snore came from him. Asleep. Her own exhaustion had her hearing things. He hadn't recognized her once during his entire illness, which was rather true to form. Nor had he ever called her Sophie.

She came abruptly to her feet.

Roxboro had said many things in his delirium, all of it interspersed with frequent requests for scotch or brandy. He'd begged for gin, just yesterday, instructing her he didn't even need a glass. But he'd never given a careless, yet deeply profound description of his life. Nor exposed how pained his soul.

Don't leave me, Sophie.

The urge to protect Roxboro from…what she wasn't entirely sure, had only grown stronger since he was brought bleeding and broken into The Pillory. That might be why Sophia had written to no one of his condition, especially not Damon Viceroy. All she could see in her mind's eye was Damon, waving for Roxboro's glass of scotch to stay filled. And she hadn't spent days nursing Roxboro only to have his uncle arrive and feed his nephew endless amounts of spirits.

"I won't leave you, Roxboro," she whispered fiercely. "I promise."

Another snore erupted from him. She leaned over to touch his forehead with a small sound of relief, fingers trembling. Definitely cooler. Calm. The thrashing about had stopped. His breathing was deep and even.

The fever had finally broken.

Sophia looked down at her skirts, unsurprised to see them covered in broth stains and lord knew what else. She turned her head to the window, watching as a bird alit on a tree just outside, blinking back the wetness gathering behind her eyes.

Roxboro would survive. He would not die. Sophia could make things right.

"Your Grace," Barstow said softly from the door.

"The fever has broken," she said, wiping at the dampness on her cheeks. "Send word to Dr. Reading to have him examine the duke. And…once Dr. Reading deems the duke improving, I'll write to Lord Damon."

Maybe tomorrow. Or the day after. She couldn't put doing so off much longer.

"Yes, Your Grace." The butler carefully came forward, offering Sophia his arm, and made a tsking sound when she stumbled. Now that Roxboro would survive, the strain of the last few days rose up to drown her. She was more tired than she'd ever been in her life.

"I'm a bit unsteady, Barstow." More wetness struck her cheeks no matter how she wiped it away. "The duke's fever is gone."

"So you've said, Your Grace. Do not fear, I'll watch over him." Barstow's words were gentle. "You've barely eaten since the duke fell ill. That must be remedied immediately."

"Someone tried to kill him," she whispered, afraid to admit such a thing out loud. Could it be the man in London who pretended to be Roxboro? "He didn't just trip and fall on a knife."

Yet Sophia had told no one of her suspicions. Not halted the wedding. Or confided in her father. Now this.... *pretender* may have tried to kill Roxboro. This was all her fault.

A sob left Sophia.

"I know, Your Grace. Your maid is preparing a bath for you."

A bath? Yes, she probably needed one. Sophia hadn't left Roxboro at all except to see to her immediate needs. "I am in need of one."

"I will stay with him," Barstow said firmly. "And will not leave his side until you return. I promise. But you must eat, Your Grace. Sleep." He opened the door connecting her rooms to Roxboro's. The rooms, done in the same colors as her chambers in London, seemed foreign to her now after sleeping for so long in a chair beside Roxboro.

"Barstow and I are in agreement." Ann came forward as the door opened and took Sophia from the butler. "Come, Your Grace. The bath is ready. Steaming hot."

"Oh, that sounds lovely." Sophia's limbs felt weighted.

"And there is fresh bread. Butter. Thick slices of ham. Oh, and scones. Currant. Which you adore. You can eat while I bathe you."

Sophia signed, heavy with exhaustion. Her stomach rumbled. "I do love a good scone."

CHAPTER TWENTY-ONE

Sophia paused outside of Roxboro's chambers, her hand lingering over the doorknob, listening to her husband throw a temper tantrum of which any child would be envious. She'd been in the library, searching through the books that had followed her from London. She read to Roxboro every day, mostly to pass the time and ease his boredom though he had no great love of the novels Sophia favored.

"I want a bloody scotch." A fist pounded on the mattress. "Right now, Barstow. You are in my employ, and you will do as I ask or I'll," Roxboro puffed. "Sack you."

Barstow murmured something in a low tone, not the least intimidated.

"I don't care what she says. *I'm* the duke."

Sophia opened the door and stepped through, book tucked under one arm. "Thank you, Barstow, for your continued tolerance of the duke's tantrums as he heals."

"Your Grace." The butler bowed to Sophia and hurried out.

"Brandy," Roxboro yelled after him. "If there is no scotch. Everyone knows brandy has healing properties." He turned to scowl at Sophia. "It is cruel to keep it from me."

"I see you're feeling better." She shut the door. "But I believe brandy can wait until you are fully recovered."

"Tyrant." He glared back at her, freshly bathed, the hollows of his cheeks starting to fill out now that he was eating solid food once more. Roxboro was still weak as a kitten, barely able to sit up without help despite his demands. The wounds were almost completely healed, scabbing over with no pus or infection. Dr. Reading was very pleased with the duke's progress, calling his recovery extraordinary.

After the fever finally broke, he slept for the entirety of one full day before waking up once more. And once Roxboro opened the shimmering green orbs with their streaks of gray, he eyed her with nothing but irritation.

"I'm a duchess," she answered. "The rules dictate that I may behave as such."

Roxboro made a frustrated sound, but one side of his mouth tilted in a sensual smirk, one Sophia had dearly missed. He had always been breathtaking in appearance, but now she'd grown to care for him. Incredibly unwelcome under the circumstances, though it was likely only a result of having nursed him back to health.

Oh, it's more than that.

Her heart, ever disobedient, thumped loudly in agreement.

"Completely unfair, Serafina. I demand a brandy."

Sophia bit her lip, trying not to laugh at his determination to address her by any other name than her own. Roxboro had quite a list.

"Life, Roxboro, is not fair in general. Stop behaving like a child. It is unbecoming of a duke."

"This is the problem with a termagant such as yourself, wife. You've gone mad with power." A wave of hair fell over his forehead and Sophia's fingers twitched with the need to brush it aside.

"What if I have?" She took a seat in the chair by the bed, while a wash of green trailed over her, intense and difficult to read. "Stop pouting."

"I do not pout."

Good lord, he did. Sensual lips slightly pursed. Hair mussed from days in bed. He was rather blinding at times.

"Are you going to read to me? Please, not that drivel from yesterday. I beg you, ...Susan."

"You've used that one twice in the last two days."

"I've been ill." He threw up his hands. "Tell me that is not the nun book. Nuns do not become countesses. It isn't done."

Sophia never gave Roxboro a choice in the books she read to him, which he liked to complain about endlessly.

Annoyance means he is better. That he is alive.

Now that he was going to live, according to Dr. Reading, Sophia could allow herself to feel the true terror at the thought of Roxboro dying. The fear she kept buried while ordering everyone about. She had nightmares about the blood, of Roxboro dead at her feet.

"*Lady White's Revenge.*" She held up the slim tome. "You were enjoying the story yesterday and I think we should finish it."

"I was not enjoying that bit of drivel."

"I like nuns." She shrugged. "I very nearly became one. But I wed you instead."

"Aha. You chose me over a convent." Roxboro grinned back at her.

Sophia's breath halted in her lungs at the sight of that smile.

"May I *please* have a brandy?" he winked.

Her heart skipped. "No. Stop acting flirtatious."

"I will only have one glass," he pleaded. "It isn't as if I can go downstairs and steal the decanter." Roxboro's eyes darted to the armoire across the room where Stone had fished out the bottle of brandy kept there for emergencies.

"Gone. You'll find nothing there."

His lips tightened. "You can even measure it out for me. I won't object."

"Still no." She opened the book and cleared her throat. "Chapter Twelve."

"Fine, you petty despot." Roxboro reached behind the pillow. "But if you are going to read to me, I'd prefer it be a book that is a favorite of mine. I had Barstow bring this up from the library."

He placed the tome covered in green leather on his lap. "It would bring me great comfort if you read it to me."

"Oh, I didn't realize you read, or even liked books, Your Grace."

"I'm not a heathen, Serendipity. Only a bit of a deviant." He nudged the book in his lap. "You'll adore it." A tiny smirk tugged at his lips. "I promise."

Sophia picked up the slim tome. *"The Lustful Turk?* I've never heard of it."

"A romantic novel. You're sure to enjoy it," he said, gaze dropping to her mouth. Roxboro seemed unusually interested in her lips as of late. Their conversations were still adversarial but each insult took on an intimate quality. Or shared a jest. Not a debauched duke and his unwanted duchess but…friends, possibly.

He merely wants a brandy.

She snatched *The Lustful Turk* from his hand, but not before Roxboro slid his fingers along her own. This time, the tingling along her spine stretched all the way to the small of her back and around her thighs. "A romantic novel?"

"Indeed." Roxboro laid back against the pillows, far too innocently.

Opening the book, Sophia scanned the first page. The story was written as a series of letters from a young lady to her friend in England. The young lady was sailing abroad for the first time. A travel journal of sorts. What an odd choice for Roxboro.

"Dear Sylvia," she started. "We arrived here early this morning after a melancholy journey."

Melancholy journey. Who uses such prose? This was bound to be some overblown bit of fluff. She glanced longingly at *Lady White's Revenge.*

"Keep reading," Roxboro instructed. "No nuns."

Sophia read through the first two chapters, delighted. "The young lady is captured by pirates. I stand corrected, Roxboro. This does sound rather more exciting than the revenge of a former nun."

"Doesn't it?"

Damn it.

Sophia wished Roxboro would stop smiling at her. Every time he did, her heart would tug hard in his direction. The very last thing Sophia wanted was to...become besotted by her husband. Her feelings would be unrequited, not to mention, she wasn't even sure Roxboro *had* feelings. Then there was the matter of fraud. She'd wed Roxboro knowing full well it hadn't been he in the Perswick gardens. And he'd nearly been killed, possibly by the man impersonating him, for which Sophia felt immense guilt.

How could I know?

Regardless, when Roxboro broke her heart, as he would if she allowed it, Sophia would once more be a fool. At best, given time, she hoped they would be friends. Partners. Or Roxboro would find a way to end their marriage, *which* they hadn't consummated, when Sophia confessed.

The very idea made her ill.

Sophia returned her attention to *The Lustful Turk* because she didn't want to think on any of it a moment longer.

Half an hour later, Sophia wished she had left Roxboro to his own devices.

Vile libertine.

Sophia had assumed the book to be a mildly scandalous tale of a young lady kidnapped by pirates, which was disabused the further she read. Especially as she came to the "letter" from the Dey of Algiers.

"I found a pure maid; her virginity I sacrificed on the Beiram feast of our Holy Prophet. To cull her sweet flower, I was obliged to infuse an opiate in her coffee."

To Sophia's credit, she barely stumbled over the *cull of her sweet flower*. Nor did she hesitate when reading, *"Whilst his lips were glued to mine, he forced his tongue into my mouth in a manner which created a sensation it is quite impossible to describe. It was the first liberty of the kind I ever sustained."*

But she did grow…overly heated.

Her eyes raised from the page to see Roxboro, lichen green gaze regarding her intently.

Wretch.

"Do you like the book, Your Grace?" he asked, with more of that false innocence.

Sophia should know better. She doubted Roxboro had been innocent of anything a day in his life.

"Delightful." She bit her bottom lip, fascinated when he followed the movement with his eyes. A deep well of something rather…*alarming* was cresting at that look from Roxboro.

"I should open a window. The fresh air will do you good." And hopefully cool this ache inside her caused by the book and Roxboro.

"Illness has affected my ears. I can't hear you clearly from the chair." An elegant hand patted the space next to him on the bed. "You'll have to sit closer."

ALEXANDER WAS A terrible, awful human being. That was not up for debate.

He was also lusting after his unwanted bride. His desire was not the result of forced companionship. Nor his illness. Alexander hadn't touched another woman since meeting Sophia and had no inclination to do so. He hadn't even bedded Nell at The Sheepshead, a disappointment for both of them.

And as to the annulment?

I don't want it any longer.

Sophia had *nursed* him. Wiped the sweat from his brow, among other…places. Not Stone or Barstow. Their hands were not slender and small. Soft and smelling of roses. It had all been Sophia, caring for Alexander as she would a newborn babe.

Without the suckling, of course. He meant to get to that later.

Thus, he'd decided to reward his newfound revelation and Sophia's devotion by forcing her to read *The Lustful Turk* to him. A highly erotic novel that no lady of good family should even know about, let alone read.

This was the most fun Alexander had had in ages. Or without a drink in his hand.

His first thought, once he was somewhat coherent again, was that he wasn't dead. Despite the best efforts of the idiots who'd dared to come after his carriage, Alexander had survived. Over the years, he'd attracted a great many thieves, pickpockets, and murderous trollops, and Barstow thought it prudent the duke learn to shoot a pistol. Also, wield a sword, and handle a knife. He might well be as doomed as the last two Dukes of Roxboro, but that didn't mean Alexander should make it easy for fate to dispose of him.

The second thought? When he'd realized the cool hands and gentle voice of his dreams belonged to his shrewish wife. Alexander had been so…elated at the sight of Sophia sitting by his bedside when he finally opened his eyes that a hum had started inside his chest.

The hum hadn't abated. Not one whit.

"Why?"

"I can't hear you."

Sophia, damn her, gave him a suspicious look. Raised her chin which had sunlight spilling over the bridge of her nose. The loose curls around her face glinted like honey. "I'm quite comfortable where I am, Your Grace." She regarded him as one does a predatory wolf. "But I'll speak louder."

Difficult chit.

"You held my hand while I was ill," Alexander reminded her. "It speeds my recovery to have you do so again."

So did all the instances when he pretended to be asleep and Sophia would lean over and fluff the pillows, putting her rather lovely bosom within inches of his mouth. He'd been tempted several times to nibble at a breast but restrained himself.

Slowly, she stood and made her way to his side, perching on the edge of the bed.

Alexander immediately unfurled his fingers, gratified when she placed her hand into his. "I am instantly comforted."

Sophia snorted in derision but did not move away.

"Continue, Your Grace, if you please," Alexander said.

"I felt his hand rapidly divide my thighs," Sopha choked over the words, attempting to regain her composure. A blush had taken up residence on her cheeks. Not a pretty pink, but more a violent crimson.

The lower half of Alexander's body stirred to life.

What a relief. I thought things might be dead down there.

Alexander stroked the top of her hand with his thumb, drawing small, deliberate circles on her skin. She was warm and smelled like a rose garden, a scent that had been constant through all his feverish dreams. The aroma had been caught in his nostrils as the knife the assailant wielded pierced his chest. An image of Sophia burned in Alexander's mind while he fought for his life. If he died, she would never admit it wasn't he who had been in the Perswick garden. Or that he didn't kiss like a puppy.

I...want to bed her.

The urge only grew by the day. Every bit of carnality in his body was focused entirely on Sophia which is why he hadn't been able to fuck another woman in weeks. Nell had tried, bless her, plucking at his trousers just the way he liked. But Alexander's cock refused to stand at her attentions.

Not the case at present.

"'And quickly one of his fingers penetrated that place which," Sophia's voice trembled. *"God knows, no male hand had ever before touched. If anything was wanting to complete my confusion, it was the thrilling sensation I felt, caused by the touches of his finger."*

The book abruptly slammed shut. Sophia kept her chin at an angle, refusing to look at him. "Wretch," she said under her breath.

He was a wretch, among other, less savory things. Alexander

tightened his grip on her hand. "Do you not like my taste in literature?"

"This book...is rather scandalous, as you well know, Your Grace."

"I would have said erotic." Entirely worth her annoyance, watching the way she avoided looking directly at him, only stealing looks at Alexander's lower body, though he was fully covered by the sheet and coverlet.

"You are a horrible man."

"I am," he agreed cheerfully. He squeezed her fingers. "Why didn't you just let me die, Sophia? You would have been free of me. Instead, you never left my bedside."

No one had ever cared for Alexander in such a manner, save possibly Aunt May.

"You are mistaken, Your Grace. That was Barstow, Stone, and the occasional maid."

"Untrue. I wasn't entirely out of my mind. And neither my butler nor my valet smell of roses. Also, Barstow has hairy knuckles. I would have recalled that."

"Your memory is faulty, Roxboro."

She pulled at her hand, trying to get away from him, but Alexander wouldn't allow it. "You would have been a widowed duchess. Still young. Wealthy beyond belief. Had property given over to you." He brought her fingers to his lips. "You would have had to suffer my uncle for a time, but eventually Damon would have left you alone. You could have pursued your own interests."

"Perhaps I have no hobbies of worth, Your Grace. You told me once that I was average and unexceptional in virtually every way."

"Except in the matter of your heart. I surmise that it is larger and far more generous than most," he said softly. "You hide very well, my wife.

She turned again to the window, pretending deep interest in the tree swaying in the wind outside the window.

"I'm not completely obtuse."

While Alexander had bedded some of the most beautiful women in London, there had been little feeling involved. Relationships with the opposite sex were shallow. Only one or two, like Lady Maxwell, could he claim as friends. He hadn't thought his mind, heart and cock would ever find themselves in agreement. Honestly, his heart had never made a peep before. Until Sophia.

He wanted more of her.

All of her.

Alexander nipped at the edges of her fingers.

"What are you doing, Your Grace?" She sucked in a breath as his mouth closed over her forefinger, his tongue swirling about the tip.

Yes, what are you doing? Uncle Damon's voice hissed in his mind. *If you seduce the chit, you'll never be rid of her.*

"Mmm." He hummed, ignoring Damon's counsel, before popping Sophia's finger out of his mouth. She sounded breathless. Aroused. So different from her usual chafing bluntness.

Then there was the matter of her...lips.

Decadent. Lush. Two delicate pillows begging to be put to all manner of wicked use. He imagined her begging him with those lips. Moaning out her pleasure along with his name. Perhaps taking his cock.

The sheet covering him twitched.

Alexander smiled.

Definitely not dead.

Chapter Twenty-Two

Roxboro's eyes had gone stormy. Murky. The streaks of gray nearly blotting out the shimmering green. He didn't release her hand, though his tongue was no longer wrapped around her finger.

What a strangely sensual experience, having your finger bitten and sucked by a handsome duke. The ache that had started as no more than a trickle of warmth, had now taken up residence between her thighs. The sensation teased along her calves, making her toes curl inside her slippers.

"You don't even like me," she whispered, struggling to maintain some control over the situation.

"I've changed my mind. And not because you've been fussing over me. Well," he shrugged. "Partially. But I liked you before, probably because you didn't like me. That rarely happens. Everyone likes me."

Sophia swallowed. She'd no idea that her lack of respect and ability to hurl insults would produce such an unexpected response in Roxboro. It certainly hadn't inspired any other gentleman. She tried to pull her finger away once more but was held fast.

"You are…terrible," Sophia breathed.

Also witty. Clever. Possessed of a teasing personality which kept Sophia…off balance. And judging by the books in the library downstairs, all of which Barstow claimed the duke had ordered himself and read when he came to The Pillory, Roxboro also possessed intelligence. One well-worn tome was on Roman aqueducts.

His looks and the ability to consume vast amounts of spirits were the least of Roxboro's talents.

"I am," he agreed. "Be awful and terrible with me." Roxboro tugged her closer, until Sophia was sprawled partially across his lap. He moved and took her hand, pressing the palm to his chest. "Please."

Sophia stretched her hand, feeling the play of muscles just beneath her fingertips. The lawn of his shirt failed to hide all those lovely hollows of sinew. Trailing her fingers down the expanse of his chest, her breathing quickened, because she knew what was beneath the shirt. And the sheet.

She'd bathed Roxboro when he was ill. But at the time, Sophia had been more concerned that he would die and she'd never be able to tell him—

"Your Grace." Her fingers reluctantly curled away. "You are…recovering." Sophia's heart refused to stop fluttering about in her chest, like some crazed bird beating its wings. The ache became need and insistent, spreading down between her thighs.

"Alexander." He caught her wrist.

"Alexander," she repeated, shivering when her breasts brushed along his arm, nipples peaking as they strained and begged to be touched. "What is happening?"

"I'm attempting to seduce you, and I would appreciate your cooperation. Don't worry; I haven't the strength to do too much. Regrettably." The tip of his nose pushed along the edge of her collarbone. "But I want to." His tongue flicked out, catching the lobe of her ear. "Taste you a bit." Teeth grazed her skin. "Perhaps nibble." His mouth sucked and licked down the slope of her neck.

"This is rather unexpected."

"Isn't it? No one is more surprised than I." One big hand cupped Sophia's breast, gently testing the weight before his thumb rubbed carefully along the fabric of her dress, searching and finally finding her nipple. "But I find you…*pull* at me,

Sophia."

"I pull at you?" The words came out in a soft moan. "Are you comparing me," she panted. "To a hook of some sort?"

"More like a tether. Annoying but I cannot fail to follow." A rumble of male appreciation came from his chest. "I'll wager these are lovely." He took hold of the small peak between his thumb and forefinger. "Pink and dewy."

Sophia arched slightly as a furious hum traveled from her nipple, straight down the length of her body. "That feels…"

"Good. Now, lift up your skirts," he growled, lips pressed to the corner of her mouth. "I realize I can be clumsy at times, but I'm rather good at this."

Given his reputation, he should be.

Shaking, Sophia obeyed, moving aside the skirts of her dress until her stockinged legs came into view. "Alexander," she gasped as those long, elegant fingers stroked the inside of her thigh.

"I'm not a Turkish lover, that's true. But you'll enjoy yourself." He sucked her bottom lip between his teeth. "I promise."

"You're…recovering."

"You keep reminding me," his voice lowered to a husky purr. A finger deftly found the opening to her underthings, which was no great surprise. He could probably have her completely undressed in under a minute.

"I think this improper," she struggled to take a breath.

The finger drew along her slit in a light, exploratory touch, teasing at the dampness there. Mama hadn't mentioned this part of physical relations. Only instructing Sophia to lie on her back.

"I'm your husband," his lips ghosted over hers. "Nothing at all improper about me touching you."

"The book was quite descriptive." Sophia let out a sigh as he caressed a particularly sensitive spot. A place that ached so desperately for his touch. "Roxboro."

"All in due time." Roxboro gave a wicked, deep-throated chuckle. "Patience, wife."

"Oh," she panted as he stroked the spot repeatedly, firm but gentle, drawing out an endless stream of sensation. Her thighs trembled, his forefinger circled her opening before slowly pushing inside.

Sophia's eyes slid shut.

Goodness that felt...as if it might be earthshattering at some point.

Another finger joined the first, stretching along her inner walls as his thumb...

Oh yes. His thumb.

Teased at that small, excited bit of flesh hidden in her folds.

Ann called it a button, but I don't think that's the anatomical term.

"Sophia," Roxboro murmured. "The next time, I'll use my mouth here." He tweaked the small bud. "And you'll scream the house down."

The very idea of Roxboro's dark head nestled between her thighs, his mouth on her quim—*lady parts*—sent another trickle of wetness. She squeezed her legs together, trapping his hand.

"Alexander," Sophia choked as her eyes flew open to see him watching her, stormy eyes focused completely on her and filled with...every thought in her head shattered.

Oh. Goodness.

Sophia broke apart, her hand covering his as pleasure, *dear lord, but this was magnificent,* flowed over her with sharp, brilliant intensity. The air seemed too thick to breathe, or possibly her lungs weren't working. This was so much more than Ann had described to her. More—

Roxboro let out a soft moan into her hair. "So wild, my terrible duchess."

Clever fingers pulled forth from Sophia another wave of pleasure, stroking a spot inside her that had Sophia shouting his name as Roxboro milked every bit of bliss from her body. When his fingers withdrew with one final caress, the fluttering pulse of her release beginning to ease, Roxboro pulled her close to the warmth of his body. His lips formed words along her neck, but Sophia couldn't make out the words. Her heart skipped once or twice before beating once more in a steady rhythm.

Roxboro's hand possessively covered her mound.

Sated but confused, Sophia sat up, pushing away from the smell of bergamot and duke.

She attempted to regain her composure, difficult with Roxboro twisting his fingers through the hair covering her...lady parts. His *cock* pulsed in his lap, just beneath the sheet, poking at Sophia with insistence.

"I'm ill, Sophia. Not dead."

She wiggled until her bottom was once more on the bed, not Roxboro. Drew her skirts down her legs. Her skin rippled with tiny pulses. This was supposed to be a marriage in name only. One forged by being compromised.

Except he didn't compromise me.

Guilt made her legs unsteady as she came to her feet.

"I should—"

Roxboro's fingers circled her wrist, surprisingly strong for a man who'd spent the last fortnight bedridden. "You should not." There was a somberness to him now, a sincerity Sophia wasn't sure what to do with.

"You've been ill and... well, any port in a storm, isn't that right, Your Grace."

Sophia wasn't sure what made her say those words, ones that reduced the last few intimate, beautiful moments to nothing but a physical release. When that wasn't what her heart thought at all.

"Alexander," he hissed back at her. "I want you to use my bloody name."

"Why? You rarely use mine."

"Untrue. Besides, I'm nearly out of names." He shut his eyes for a moment. "Sophie," his voice was soft, as he opened them once more, the shortened form of her name an endearment. "Come here."

Sophia shook her head and took another step towards the door. Straightened her shoulders. Buried her heart once more for protection. "Boredom, Your Grace. I understand and do not think less of you for it." Sophia sounded so calm. Rational. Mature.

Not the lovesick creature I suspect I'm becoming.

"Is that supposed to reassure me somehow?" he growled. "You truly believe—Sophia, if I wanted another woman in my bed, I could have one. *Any* one."

"How lovely for you."

"Very well." Roxboro sounded so...angry. "I agree with your low opinion of me." He closed his eyes. "You wish to be like the other women I take to my bed? Then you are dismissed," he said with an elegant wave of his fingers. "Your services are no longer required."

Sophia winced, falling back as if he'd slapped her. "Don't toy with me, Your Grace." Her voice was firm with no sign of the regret starting to seep into her skin.

I've ruined it. I speak before clearly thinking matters through.

"Toying? Go away."

Opening her mouth, Sophia considered whether now was the time to admit what she'd done. Offer to—have her father approach Parliament on Roxboro's behalf. Admit to the fraud she'd committed. But those words wouldn't come.

"I don't care to be your amusement until you return to London," she said instead, before marching out of the room, careful to hide her trembling hands in her skirts. "I'll send Stone in to see to your needs."

WELL, THAT HADN'T gone as Alexander hoped.

He looked down at his cock tenting the coverlet, too tired to do much more than will it to go down. Sophia's assessment of his character wasn't incorrect, which pained him. He *was* a cad when it came to women. A bit of a sot, although his longing for spirits had abated a great deal. His character was...questionable, but Alexander enjoyed being a libertine. Or at least, he had.

Nearly being murdered changes one's perspective.

Alexander came close to telling Sophia he'd made the decision to water down his scotch and brandy well before they'd wed, with the exception of his wedding night. The fact that he'd ruined a girl he couldn't remember had been the catalyst for his decision. He liked having his wits about him.

And yes, he missed brandy. Scotch. Good lord, even gin. Just the taste of it.

What he didn't miss was Oakhurst. London. Or Uncle Damon, though Alexander was curious why his uncle wasn't at The Pillory.

"Your Grace." Barstow appeared in the doorway. "Would you care for something to eat? Cook has made Cornish hens."

"Yes, I'm starving." Not only for food, but Sophia. "Where's Stone?"

"Gone to visit his mother. As you told him to do when he refused to bring you scotch, Your Grace."

"I'd prefer a brandy." The argument with Sophia had left Alexander unsettled. He didn't want to go back to the emptiness that threatened whenever she wasn't here.

"The duchess—"

"Is a dictator. Never mind." Alexander waved him away. "I'll wait and have a brandy with my uncle when he arrives. Has there been any word? I take it the duchess sent for him."

Barstow's lips rippled, pausing before he answered. "Yes, indeed. But Lord Damon is not in London at present, Your Grace."

"Not in town? Well, that explains his absence. My uncle likes to go off to fish for trout." When Damon was troubled, as he surely had been in the weeks leading up to Alexander's marriage. His uncle wasn't to be blamed for wanting a bit of peace and quiet, though they rarely went so long without speaking. "Try the hunting lodge in Hampshire. There is a stream nearby full of trout."

"Your Grace." Barstow bowed. "I'll send word immediately."

"And inform the duchess that I expect her to dine with me this evening. Read to me." Alexander knew he sounded petulant like some spoiled lord, but he didn't care. Sophia's parting words and her exit made him furious. Accusing Alexander of using her merely for amusement. Did she think she was the only bloody woman for miles? He could snap his fingers, and a half-dozen would arrive from the nearby village, all eager to—

Alexander tossed *The Lustful Turk* across the room.

"You weren't much help," he said to the book as it fell to the floor. "After all."

Chapter Twenty-Three

Sophia sat outside, the gentle breeze blowing through her hair, lifting the strands to tickle her cheek. The lavish gardens of The Pillory were a perfect spot to enjoy a book. Peaceful. Every blade of glass manicured. The roses, bright crimson and pink buds just beginning to unfurl, dotted the landscape, along with peonies, delphinium, and a wealth of wisteria.

She liked wisteria a great deal. The tight clusters of flowers reminded her of grapes.

Turning, Sophia looked up to the open window of Roxboro's rooms, wondering if he could see her out here sitting amongst the flowers. Or even if he cared. They had not spoken again since their argument, because Sophia was studiously avoiding her husband. Whether over embarrassment from the intimacy they'd shared or her own behavior in saying such cruel things to him, Sophia wasn't sure.

Which did not stop Roxboro from demanding her presence.

Hours after the reading of *The Lustful Turk*, Barstow informed Sophia that His Grace expected her to dine with him that night.

She politely declined, citing a headache.

Roxboro snarled his displeasure as he hurled a series of books, possibly a porcelain figurine and what sounded like a boot at the closed door separating their rooms.

Though her husband could hardly get about on his own yet without toppling over, Sophia made sure the door stayed locked.

Just in case. She wasn't ready to…face him.

Over the course of the following day, Roxboro insisted Sophia present herself, more than once. He attempted bribery, suggesting Barstow tell Sophia the duke had relapsed into illness.

Stubbornly, she did not go to check on him.

Stone wasn't available, as he was still visiting his mother, but Barstow could deal with Roxboro.

The butler said little in relaying Roxboro's messages to Sophia, but she could read the censure in his eyes well enough since Barstow made no effort to hide it. She did not bother to explain her avoidance of the duke, because as a duchess, there was no need to explain herself to anyone. Putting some distance between she and Roxboro seemed prudent. A matter of self-preservation. Sophia's emotions were far too unwieldy where her husband was concerned.

The only bit of good news, in addition to Roxboro's recovery, was that Lord Damon had still not been located. According to his staff, Lord Damon had gone to join Lady Falmouth and his daughters at yet another house party. But when a note was sent, Lady Falmouth replied that Damon was not with them. She wanted to come to The Pillory immediately, but Sophia assured her that Roxboro was on the mend and would return to London shortly.

His Grace says his uncle may have gone fishing in Hampshire, Barstow informed her.

Sophia's delay in sending word to Damon had mattered not a whit, it seemed, so she decided not to feel guilty over doing so any further. He was bound to arrive eventually, much like potato blight.

Gravel crunched on the path winding through the garden, stopping behind her. A throat cleared.

"Forgive me, Your Grace," came Barstow's voice. "But the duke requests you attend him. He is quite insistent."

"Roxboro is always insistent. Has…the fever returned? His wounds reopened?"

"No, Your Grace."

"Has he had any brandy? Scotch?"

"No, Your Grace, though he continues to ask."

She'd made sure Barstow and the rest of the staff was informed that Roxboro was not permitted spirits. Not until he was healed. Anyone handing him so much as a thimble of brandy would be sacked immediately. She hadn't nursed him—*her heart clenched*—only to allow him to fall back into his old habits. Barstow had explained to her that his uncle had been truly addicted to spirits, body and soul. But Roxboro didn't seem as far gone.

Still, Sophia was not willing to take the chance. Roxboro could be angry all he wished. He would hate her soon enough when she confessed. Plenty of time to become a sot again.

She returned to her book which had been open to the same page for the better part of an hour because Sophia couldn't seem to concentrate. "Then please inform the duke that I am busy at present. I shall attend him another time. Tell him I've gone for a walk. Or...into the village."

Barstow clasped his hands before him. "Your Grace—" He nodded towards the house. "He has been watching you since you came into the gardens. He ordered me to pull a chair to the window. I do apologize. As I said, he is most insistent."

Dear God.

"Duchess," Roxboro's dark rumble echoed over the lawn to where she sat. "I see you."

Sophia snapped her book shut. It wasn't holding her interest, at any rate. She was going to have to face Roxboro, it seemed, or he'd scream the house down.

"Inform the duke I shall be along presently."

Behaving like a child. *Again.* Yelling into the gardens. Did he have not an ounce of respect for his status? Dukes did not summon their wives in such a manner. Admittedly, there was some gratification in having him demand her presence. As if she were...important to him.

I can't possibly be.

Yet, she'd seen the way he'd looked at her when Sophia came apart in his arms, only she didn't trust it.

"Yes, Your Grace." The butler bowed, lips twitching.

"This isn't the least amusing, Barstow." Sophia stood. "Not at all."

A HALF HOUR later, Sophia stood before the door connecting her room with Roxboro's. She'd thought to delay longer, but Ann had arrived only moments ago, whispering that His Grace was becoming quite annoyed and threatening to pound on her door until Sophia appeared.

She took a deep breath, preparing herself.

Sophia knew the time had come for her to confess she'd known the day they wed that it had not been Roxboro in the gardens. She could have halted the ceremony though Mama would have fainted and Papa furious. But Roxboro didn't have a freckle. He didn't drink wine. And the impossibility of there being…another man who so closely resembled him became real. She should have been honorable and fled the church. Accept her status as a pariah. Society meant little to her.

After much consideration, Sophia had decided that in the spirit of honesty, she would contact her father and have him use his influence in Parliament to have her union with Roxboro dissolved. The marriage had not been consummated. She was still a maid. Lord Damon would be ecstatic. Sophia would learn how to become a nun and tend bees.

Her palm pressed against her mid-section, willing the scones she'd eaten to stop pitching about. Food always seemed to settle her nerves. Not today, it seemed. But usually.

Roxboro was bound to be unpleasant once she confessed.

Any liking for her would immediately disappear, as would be expected. Papa would make sure the annulment was secured.

Roxboro could remarry someone far more suitable than Sophia. Parliament would *never* deny him an annulment under the circumstances. He was a duke after all.

It's the right thing to do.

She couldn't live with the guilt for the rest of her life simply to stay a duchess. She'd been wrong and it was time for Sophia to admit her mistake.

Swinging open the door, Sophia came to a stop, mouth opening in surprise.

"Finally," Roxboro snapped. "The water has almost cooled."

She tried to avert her eyes from the sight of Roxboro in his bath. One in which he was no longer ill and *completely* unclothed. The tub had been turned to face the bloody door connecting their rooms. Where he knew she would appear and see…. everything.

Damn him.

The steam from the bath had the dark tendrils of his hair curling about Roxboro's temples. Not so much as a bubble floated across the surface of the tub's water. Every inch of his magnificent form was…on display.

Wretch.

It was difficult, no, impossible, not to admire him. Her eyes, against Sophia's will, traced down his chest dusted with dark hair, pausing only at the newly formed scars now decorating his torso, before lowering to—

She jerked her chin away.

"Something wrong?" Roxboro lifted a brow as if his nakedness was of no consequence to either of them. "You appear to be unsettled, Sahara."

"Not at all," Sophia snapped back.

"Good, because I had an interesting conversation with Barstow and Stone. Neither of whom bathed me while I was ill and feverish."

Damn. She should have sworn both men to secrecy.

"I also put spoonfuls of broth between your lips." Sophia looked him in the eye. "What of it?"

"Well, I don't understand your shyness. You've already seen everything." A lazy grin pulled at his lips. "And you are my wife. We should have no mystery between us." His voice lowered. "Come. Here."

Sophia's body.... arched towards Roxboro at the command. Dear God, the blood was fluttering beneath her skin.

"Is there a reason you've summoned me, Your Grace? I was enjoying the gardens. Reading," she managed to croak.

"You haven't read a book to me in several days. Not since I pleasured you on the bed. You appeared to enjoy having me touch you, which is why I find your absence untenable."

"Untenable?"

"Intolerable. Unacceptable. Unfathomable. Do I need to go on, or do you take my point?"

Dear God. He sounded entirely ducal. She wanted to beg his forgiveness. And the ache for him? It was everywhere, especially between her thighs, where he'd put his terribly elegant fingers.

"Was it necessary to yell at me from the window, Roxboro?" she countered. "Such behavior is unbecoming of a duke."

"How would you know, Sophia? You've not been a duchess for very long. Nor are there any written instructions on how best to be a duke." He cocked his head. "And before becoming a duchess, you were merely the far too direct, thumb your nose at society, much too forthright daughter of Lord Canterbell. I'm the only one brave enough to stand my ground with you. I'm told the other gentlemen lacked courage."

All true. Every word. "I found them unintelligent."

"But not me. Not when you ran out into the Perswick gardens with the most debauched duke in London." He leaned forward. "Which means you've more than a bit of wickedness in you, *Your Grace*. At any rate," he motioned to the soap sitting on a chair beside him. "I require my back washed." Roxboro fixed a flat, arrogant stare on her.

"No. I do not care to be dictated to." She trembled, clutching her skirts, knowing she would comply. There could be no repeat of what had transpired before. Allowing such a thing would...doom Sophia. She hadn't confessed to him and—

"Not another word, Sophia." He slapped the edge of the tub. "You will address me as Alexander when we are alone. Which I intend us to be," there was a thread of menace in his tone. "with increasing frequency."

A tiny bit of vulnerability flickered in the shimmering green, the streaks of silver flashing at her.

I've hurt him by staying away.

That knowledge that she possessed the power to harm such a magnificent being had a tremble go through her. Her heart took a small leap before she forced it down. Roxboro would feel differently later.

Sophia came around behind him and picked up the soap. "Fine. Demanding, petulant duke." Her eyes widened as she looked down.

Dear lord, I can see...well, it is larger than I imagined.

"Shoulders first," Roxboro commanded. "You forgot arrogant."

"I think that to be given." She picked up the cloth and dipped it in the bath. "You're put out with me."

The shoulders tensed. "I am."

She rubbed a good amount of soap on the cloth and drew it over the breadth of his shoulders. How unfair that one man had been gifted with such startling looks, a title and great wealth. Though Sophia thought the Lord had a sense of humor, because he'd also bestowed a great deal of clumsiness on Roxboro. Enough to keep him humble, perhaps.

Taking a seat on the stool at his side, Sophia glanced into the water. A mistake because—well, his *cock* bobbed back at her.

"I thought we had come to an agreement, of sorts." Roxboro shut his eyes. "Don't you dare miss a spot."

Absently, Sophia drew the cloth over his arms and shoulders, all the while her attention fixated on his *cock*. Yes, she'd caught a glimpse, once or twice after that first bath, but...he'd been ill and—honestly, Sophia had made sure *it* was covered. Roxboro had been sick. She hadn't wanted the distraction.

"This avoidance of each other must stop, as amusing a chase as it has been." Reaching back, he took Sophia's hand, flattening her palm across his chest. "Don't make me yell through the window for you again." The words were gentle. "You'll upset Barstow."

"Roxboro—"

"Alexander. I need you to address me as Alexander." His hand pushed hers more firmly into his chest. *"Please.* I—nearly dying—well, your view of the world changes. Oh, I realize that almost dying is something of a hobby of mine. Usually accidental. Sometimes for my purse. And all those instances took place when I was foxed…so not entirely unexpected. Oakhurst might be there to laugh at my misfortune. The society pages would write of my latest brush with injury. But this time was different because there was someone who cared whether I survived and fought for me."

"Lord Damon—"

"Bears me a great deal of affection. As do Rose and Violet. But none of them would ever sit by my bedside and read to me. Mop my brow. Bring me comfort. I think the last person who did so was Aunt May when I had a terrible cough one winter." His brows drew together. "Laugh with me and—" The words halted.

"You are what?" she whispered.

"Not alone," he rasped. "Because you are here."

Sophia looked down to Roxboro's hand, holding hers to his heart, realizing what he meant.

Oh. Her heart expanded sharply, leaning towards his.

"More importantly, I desire you. Greatly. Perhaps more than you can comprehend and definitely far more than I should." Roxboro moved her hand from his heart to his stomach, then still lower, until Sophia's fingers caught in the thatch of hair surrounding his *cock*, which was now…so stiff the tip pointed directly at her.

The green of his eyes glinted up at her, the heat, unmistakable. And longing. So much of it.

Her breasts grew heavy and taut with arousal, because now Sophia knew exactly what desire felt like. The sensation spilled along her mid-section to sit throbbing between her thighs until she pushed them together.

Roxboro's free hand lifted from the water, looping around Sophia's neck, dripping water and staining her dress. He brought their mouths close, mere inches apart before his tongue flicked out, tracing along the seam of her lips.

Sophia whimpered.

"Sophie," he whispered her name against the corner of her mouth. "A bad start does not mean that we cannot have a good ending." He kissed her carefully, his lips lazy and sensual, full of promise.

A sound left her. Soft with surrender.

Sophia dropped the cloth with a plop into the water. He pushed her hand further, encouraging her to touch and explore. His skin was slick with soap as her fingers slid along his stomach, daring to come close to his *cock*.

"Yes," he groaned. "My terrible bride."

The desire between her and Roxboro plucked insistently at her skin, reminding Sophia that it was there, no matter how unlikely. She wanted to give herself over to it. And him. *This feeling is real*, her heart whispered. *Why have you been avoiding this marvelous—*

Oh, yes. Nearly forgot.

"There is something I must tell you." Sophia almost wept at having to push away from him. Here was Roxboro, shocking her with his sincerity which made her own deceit all that much worse.

"And there is a place you must touch me," he returned in a silky tone. "No talking right now. None. I don't want to hear a word unless you are screaming my name as you climax. Or giving me specific instructions on where to place my mouth."

"Alexander." She tried to force her confession out, but the

words refused to come though she'd practiced them in her mind often enough.

Coward.

"Are you always so direct in such matters?"

"Yes, I am," Roxboro answered. "Now, this is my cock. There are other names for it, but I like that one best. But if I'm truthful," he grabbed her hand once more, positioning her fingers over the hard length, silky and heated beneath the water. "You may call it anything you like as long as you place your fingers just so."

"Ann told me to call it a cock." At his look, she said, "My maid. Ann. I—not specifically your—male anatomy—but in general." Sophia attempted to sound...confident, even with her cheeks burning.

"I'm glad to know Ann is not peeking at my *cock*." A wry smile pulled at his lips. "When I'm asleep. Now, wife. I am yours to do with as you like."

"I don't know what to do. My mother told me to lay on the bed and obey you."

"Hmm. We'll get to that presently."

Fingers curling around him, Sophia tested the size before stroking gently down his length. "Like this?"

"Sophie." Roxboro's mouth on hers became more demanding with each stroke of her fingers beneath the water. His large body trembled, sending ripples across the bath water as her thumb rubbed along the tip, dipping into the seam at the top. A growl came from him.

"Is that wrong?" she whispered.

"Nothing you could possibly do is wrong." Roxboro's hand tightened over the top of her fingers, showing Sophia exactly how to caress him. "More." He nipped the side of her neck. "Harder." His mouth found the slope of her neck, biting gently until she gasped. Then his lips found hers once more, kissing Sophia as if his life depended on it. Tongues twined together. Breaths mingling as Roxboro groaned into her mouth.

He stiffened. Held her hand with a forceful grip as he jerked beneath the water.

"Sophie," he gasped. Hips thrusting up, forcing his cock further into her hand, Roxboro found his pleasure.

He was beautiful when he climaxed, though Sophia had never witnessed such a thing before. A feeling of power surged through her. She had given him such pleasure. Not some courtesan or a barmaid at a tavern. But Sophia.

Roxboro's eyes were closed, lips parted as he panted softly. "Well, imagined I would last longer considering I'm a notorious libertine, but I've been dreaming of you, Sophie."

"You dream of me?"

"I do. Mostly wicked things." He winked. "I'm going to get out of this tub before I completely wrinkle, because I've been soaking for some time. I spent so long waiting for you, my terrible wife, that the footmen had to bring me more hot water." Roxboro stood, water sluicing off his chest, stomach and along the globes of his muscular backside.

Rather splendid considering he doesn't ride.

Taking up a towel, he dried himself, while a smug smile crossed his lips. "You look warm, Sophie. I'll need to get you out of your dress as soon as possible. I don't want you to…swoon in the heat."

Wretch.

"No—" She shook her head and pulled back from the tub. "I need to tell—"

"Yes," he said in that ducal tone that had her humming inside. "We are consummating our marriage. Now. Today. Admittedly, having not done so previously is mostly my fault, but your avoidance hasn't helped matters. But as much as I've enjoyed the bath and your attention to my instructions on how best to bathe me, I have other plans."

"We—we cannot." Sophia blurted, knowing that she must tell him. Especially now. Roxboro would want an annulment and she would…tend bees. Possibly.

"Yes we can." He regarded her for a moment. "I would wager

that your lovely quim is wet."

Sophia's mouth popped open. "Roxboro," she protested.

"Alexander. Turn around." He leaned closer, nose trailing along her neck. "Please. So that I may take off this dress. Or I can rip it off if you prefer. In either case, it is coming off."

"You've been ill," she said weakly.

Roxboro cocked his head, a curl falling across his brow. "Not entirely true. I've been pretending for the last few days, hoping you'd rush to my aid. Which you did not. I'm greatly disappointed, Sophie."

"You—" she stammered as his hands ran up and down her body. "Did climb from the tub with a great deal of surprising agility."

"Do you not desire me, Sophie?" His hands stopped their roaming, all his teasing tucked away. Fingers twisted the buttons at her back, but went no further. "Am I wrong?" There was an odd note in his tone. "Because I have felt it for quite some time, though I didn't wish it. Nor expect it." He pressed his forehead to her back. "It consumes me." His palm landed on her stomach. "Do you not feel it? That we are meant to be together?" There was pleading in his tone.

"But you won't be able to annul the marriage, Alexander," she half-sobbed, blinking away a tear. "If we do this. Our marriage forced upon you."

"Sophie."

"I—knew," she announced loudly.

A sigh came from him, his clever fingers moving once more to make short work of the buttons trailing down her back. "I see."

The dress slipped over her shoulders.

"I realized it wasn't you," she said in a rush, desperate for him to understand. "Not the night of the Perswick ball but…when you kissed me after dining with my parents. And again, when we stood before the vicar because there was no bloody freckle," she wailed. "I should have stopped the wedding. Recanted. Right there in front of the vicar and all of London."

Fingers brushed along the edges of her corset. Tugging at the strings. He didn't even struggle with the ties. "You aren't listening to me."

"I am," he hummed against her neck.

"It would have been terrible for me, recanting at the altar and an enormous embarrassment for my family. I am Lord Canterbell's daughter, after all. But your uncle would have been overjoyed. You would have been pleased. But I couldn't—I'd been so sure and then I was not. Because of the freckle. And it all seems rather impossible. The other guests *saw* you."

"Shush, Sophie." His arms went around her, nose in the crook of her neck.

"And I was afraid." Sophia tried to push him away, knowing she would lose him now. How could she not? "To make such an insane declaration."

Roxboro turned her to face him.

"I couldn't imagine anyone had the audacity to go about London pretending to be you, Roxboro," she pleaded. "Who would be brave enough to do such a thing, with no worry of being caught?"

"Alexander."

"And how does this man look so much like you? Lady Brokeburst," Sophia stepped over her corset which had fallen to the rug. "She curtseyed to him. Lord Lacton bowed and addressed him as Your Grace."

"I agree it is a mystery." Roxboro stood naked and stunning before her, watching as she stormed about in her chemise with a bemused look. "One we will need to look into further but not at present."

"And of course, the freckle. I hadn't really looked at your nose until we stood before the vicar. There was no freckle." Sophia threw up her hands.

"I was wondering when we'd get back to the freckle. Come. Here."

"You had one at the ball. A freckle." A surprised gasp came

from her as Roxboro grabbed Sophia around the waist. "Just on the end." She pointed with her finger. "And now you do not."

"Is that why you were staring at me all through the wedding breakfast like I was some bloody insect? I did wonder."

"I convinced myself it was a drop of wine," she tried to explain as his fingers plucked at her chemise. "But there is no wine at The Pillory." She let out a small whimper. Not from distress but because Roxboro was tearing at the thin layer of cotton covering her.

"I hate wine," he finished. "I would never drink it, not even were I dying of thirst. Because I did once—and it soured my stomach for all time."

"It reminds you of the cold. And being…trapped."

Roxboro grunted. "I should sack Barstow. Now, I suppose I can rip off your underthings. I'd rather enjoy that."

"It isn't entirely Barstow's fault. When you were not…yourself, you spoke of many things. The wine cellar was one of them. I only asked him for clarification."

A tearing sound met her ears. Roxboro was on his knees shredding her underthings.

"This marriage was made under false pretenses," Sophia whispered. "Please forgive me. I will make things right, I promise. I'll confess to my father that it was not you. I'll write to him today." Cool air struck her between the thighs, mixed with the warmth of his fingers.

"No, you won't." He straightened, a strip of cotton in one hand. Water from the bath still dripped from the ends of his hair and down his chest. "And you will cease this nonsense. Because I also knew." An open-mouthed kiss met her shoulder. "Not about the freckle." He frowned. "Though I'm now concerned you would think a drop of wine would resemble a freckle, which leads me to believe you may need spectacles."

"The lighting was rather poor at the Perswick ball," she replied tartly while Roxboro tugged on her chemise. "Goodness," she exclaimed when one breast was exposed. "Was that entirely necessary?"

"This seduction is taking far too long."

"You're taking this rather well considering I've trapped you in marriage, Roxboro. Which I'm trying to correct."

"I am not inclined to rid myself of you, Lady Sacrifice." He cupped her breast and pressed a kiss to the skin above her heart. "I want this. I want *you*."

"But—" the last word came out in a breathless whisper as his thumb pinched the tip of her breast.

"No, Sophie." Roxboro's lips brushed along hers, making Sophia shiver with want. "You may have mistaken that imposter for me, but there is no mistaking this." He nipped at her bottom lip. "I've kissed dozens of women—"

"Likely hundreds," she said against his mouth.

"But I've never had—the only thing I could compare it to is the euphoria of several glasses of brandy, before one becomes unsteady."

"I'm not sure what to make of the sentiment."

"It is meant as a compliment. So yes, I knew. After I kissed you properly and not like a slobbering puppy." He shrugged and pinched the nipple, rolling it between his thumb and forefinger a bit more forcefully.

A lightning bolt shot straight from her breast to nestle at the apex of her thighs.

"And yes, Damon has political aspirations. Lord Canterbell can ruin them. So at first, our marriage was for my uncle." He tossed what was left of her chemise over one shoulder. "Now it is for me. I don't want to spend the rest of my days stumbling about filled with scotch. Incapable of little more than playing cards and bedding women." Regret hung in the air. "You've helped me realize I am—Alexander. More than a sum of my brandy-soaked parts."

"You are not brandy-soaked." She cupped his face.

"Not any longer, thanks to you. Unfortunately, sot or not, I'm still going to trip over things. Bump into tables. That will never go away. Society is so much more accepting of your limbs tangling up or slipping off a horse when they think you're foxed. Won't everyone be surprised when I return to London. Especially Freeman."

"Freeman?"

"My secretary. He and my uncle have been managing my entire existence for as long as I can remember. But that is now at an end. I don't even care whether Oakhurst returns. Probably best he doesn't. And since we are being completely honest, Damon had already advised me to never bed you." His mouth lowered to hers, stealing the air from her lungs as he backed Sophia towards the bed.

"Lord Damon was going to sue for an annulment." Sophia wasn't shocked.

"Yes, on the grounds that my cock doesn't work. But now you've gone and ruined that, Sophie." He lowered her carefully to the bed, naked now, save for her stockings. "Because." Hardness pushed along her thigh. "I'm keeping you."

CHAPTER TWENTY-FOUR

*H*E'S KEEPING ME.

"Why?" Sophia said, hands running up his arms, feeling the flex of sinew as he shifted. Roxboro, for a feckless sot and a somewhat clumsy duke, had a finely honed body. He was lean, yes, but—"Do you...fence?"

"And risk putting an eye out?" He chuckled as he climbed over Sophia's naked body on all fours, pausing only to lower his mouth to one breast, sucking at the tip. "You taste so much better than I imagined and these...dear lord...magnificent."

"You don't ride, at least not well, so there must be something—" her words caught as Roxboro's teeth grazed the hardened peak, alternately sucking and grazing her nipple with his teeth.

"Barstow. He was in the army, once. A long time ago. I made him teach me how to defend myself. We practice, he and I, when I am here. There is a footman in London who indulges me as well. When I've been sober."

"I don't think you are so clumsy after all, Your Grace," she breathed as his fingers dipped between her thighs.

"No, I am. But Barstow's training has helped the worst of it, and most definitely saved my life as this latest incident proves. Now, no more talking. Only moaning. Begging. Panting." He pressed his mouth between her breasts, slowly gliding down Sophia's body. "Whimpers of pleasure." He nipped at the skin of her stomach, fingers gliding over her slit. "Cries of bliss." Roxboro's head moved lower and the pad of his tongue found without err the one spot aching for him most.

"A lovely quim, my duchess," he breathed, breath tickling her aching flesh. "One I plan to enjoy over and over." Two large fingers gently pushed inside her, while his tongue continued to tease and explore. Roxboro took hold of one buttock, murmured something about it being "nice and plump" and then spread her open, tossing one leg over his shoulder.

"Oh god." Pleasure had her legs twitching.

"I thought," he paused in his efforts. "I insisted you call me Alexander." A dark, wicked sound came from him as a third finger joined the first two, stretching Sophia while his tongue continued to do the most amazing things, lapping at her wetness. Toying with the small bud in her folds.

"Please, Alexander."

"Say it louder, Sophie. I can barely hear you." He bit that sensitive spot, oh so gently.

"Alexander," she screamed. Her hips arched off the bed, knees trapping his head, as pleasure ripped through Sophia, threatening to break her apart. She clutched at the thick locks of his hair, pushing herself more fully into his mouth, unaware of anything in the moment except the blinding pleasure cresting over her in waves. When the last of the bliss ebbed from her limbs, Sophia took a deep breath, her body relaxing into the bed.

"Are you now more agreeable to this union?"

Sophie's eyes were closed, but she could feel Roxboro smiling. She released the hold on his hair, running her fingers through the still damp locks. "Possibly. Not bad for a vile cur."

"Oh good. We're back to hurling insults, you miserable chit." He licked up one hip, pausing to press a kiss on her ribs. "It's arousing. I think because… it reminds me that I am more a man and less a duke." His lips brushed over hers. "I'm told it hurts, but only the first time." He tugged on a loose curl of her hair. "I've tried to prepare you."

"Get on with it." She shifted, biting his neck, gratified when he made a low, deep masculine sound. "You don't scare me, Your Grace."

"You see, my little shrew," he kissed her forcefully. "This is why I'm keeping you. I'll be careful. If I'm not, tell me." Concern flashed across his handsome features. "I've never bedded a virgin before."

"I've never bedded a duke. So I suppose that makes us even."

Dark laughter came from him before Roxboro kissed her again...in a positively decadent, possessive manner that left no doubt as to what he felt for her. Sophia felt the press of him between her thighs as he settled between them. And with one thrust, Roxboro buried himself inside her.

A cry came from Sophia, because, well, it did hurt. And the fullness was rather...unusual.

"I'm sorry," he murmured, holding perfectly still.

Sophia smiled up at him and shifted her hips. "I was only surprised, you arrogant rogue." No one had ever...desired her before. Not like Roxboro. "I'm keeping you too," she said, kissing his cheek. Her hands roamed down his back, clutching at his hips. "It barely pains me. Do your worst."

"That mouth, Sophie," he snarled, retreated a few inches and then pushed once more inside, so deep, her back arched to take him all. "I have better uses for it." His lips fell to the curve of her ear. "I want it on my cock."

The idea sent a twist of wickedness through her, but Sophia had no time to contemplate the thought further because Roxboro was taking her hard. Nothing gentle about it at all. Every stroke skimmed a spot deep inside Sophia that..."Oh, please don't stop."

"Now," he hooked one of her legs over his elbow. "That's better."

Sophia's body...clenched. There was no other word for it, grasping him as she stretched towards that peak of pleasure. She clawed at his back, unraveling as stars burst before her eyes. His name came from her, in a low erotic moan.

"Jesus, Sophie."

Roxboro bit into her shoulder, and a second release tightened her body. She screamed, not caring if the entire household heard her. The bed creaked and battered the wall, bringing footsteps down the hall, which quickly retreated. Sophia became a wild, mindless thing, mad with the sort of passion she'd only read about. Roxboro thrust once more, pushing her halfway off the bed before a breathless sound came from him and warmth spilled inside her.

THE LATE AFTERNOON sun streamed through the open window, dappling the floor of Roxboro's room. The curtains fluttered in the breeze as it cooled the sweat on their skin. Sophia and Roxboro lay entwined; his long limbs stretched around her own. The entire staff must now know that the duke had pleasured his duchess given how loudly Sophia had screamed out his name. She wondered if she'd ever be able to look Barstow in the eye again.

Physical relations with Roxboro were...far more athletic in nature than she'd anticipated. His mouth, hands and tongue had been everywhere at once, bringing Sophia to such heights...and well, she hadn't known a person's body could...contort in such a fashion.

Every moment had been earthshaking. Monumental. Brilliant.

"Are you well, Sanctimonious?" Trailing a finger along her arm, he drew his tongue over her shoulder, swirling it over her skin.

Sophia smiled. "I am. You did decently for a libertine. And a sot."

"I'm not either of those anymore, I don't think." He wrapped his arms more tightly around her. "My Sophie. You'll be sore. A bath will help. I wasn't as careful as I should have been."

"I didn't complain. Save your concern for Barstow's sensibilities and that of the upstairs maids."

"And Palfrey." He nuzzled her ear.

"Palfrey?"

"The head gardener. The window is still open," Roxboro chuckled. "If he's run off, Sophie, you will have to find someone else to prune the rose bushes. And Barstow has been in my employ for ages. If I haven't scared him off yet, I doubt you will."

"That's not as reassuring as you think it is." Sophia snuggled deeper into his arms, her thoughts finally quiet, as they had never been before. She and Roxboro were an unlikely pairing, to say the least. But a good one.

CHAPTER TWENTY-FIVE

THE NEXT DAY, Alexander woke his wife in the most pleasant manner possible, with his head firmly wedged between her thighs. She yelled his name and beat her fists on his shoulders when reaching the peak of her pleasure, which was immensely satisfying.

He intended to keep his wife so happy and sated so that she might forget what a terrible human being he'd been and possibly still might be. They would have to return to London eventually, which meant Sophia would be faced with a herd of former paramours along with Alexander's tattered reputation, not to mention those who assumed she'd trapped him in this marriage, which to be fair, she had, no matter how unintentionally.

Yes, but I don't mind.

He would let none of it touch her. He wanted nothing to hurt Sophie.

Alexander had never been in love. Not once, unless you counted an expensive bottle of French cognac. But he mused, gazing at his wife all lovely and pink after climaxing on his tongue, he was in love with Sophia. Why, exactly, he'd no idea. Nor was Alexander certain when he'd fallen in love with her, only that he was. She was not beautiful, though Alexander thought her the most marvelous creature in existence. Ordinary in every way, yet Sophia made him feel the most extraordinary things.

Damon would not be pleased. Not about Sophia, nor anything else Alexander meant to do. His mind was clear. His thoughts focused. There was no Oakhurst to demand his attention. Whether his uncle approved or not, Alexander was going to be the bloody Duke of Roxboro. Going forward, he would handle the affairs of his estate and title, whether Damon assumed he was capable or not. He would release his uncle from all responsibility in regards to the dukedom. Not because his uncle had mishandled matters. Quite the contrary. But it was far past time for Alexander to take the reins of his own legacy.

The careless, arrogant libertine he'd been died in that carriage weeks ago. Well, somewhat. He'd try to be good. For Sophie.

So, several days ago, while his wife was being difficult, Alexander summoned his secretary, Freeman, to The Pillory.

Damon might have complained, but his uncle was nowhere to be found.

Sophia rolled out of bed with a groan, clutching the sheet and searching for the remains of her chemise. Her lips wrinkled at the torn pile of clothing. "It looks as if I were attacked by a wild animal."

"You were." Alexander stood, naked, and walked to the center of the room, holding up a few tattered bits of linen. "I fear everyone will know of your depraved nature, Sophie. Stone is a terrible gossip."

"You should...cover yourself." She averted her eyes, a blush on her cheeks.

"I don't think so." Sophia was ogling him and didn't want to admit to it.

I adore her.

She hissed, like an irritated cat. "I'm taking the sheet with me." She marched to the door adjoining their rooms. "I believe I'll bathe."

"A grand idea." He'd let her do so alone. This time. "Join me for breakfast on the terrace, my terrible shrew, once you are dressed."

She gave him a saucy wink, which sent a glowing ember to

flame inside Alexander's heart.
Yes, I'm definitely in love with her.

LESS THAN AN hour later, Sophia and Roxboro were settled in comfortable chairs on the terrace, sharing a leisurely breakfast. Birds chirped and flew overhead. Butterflies floated above the blooms in the garden. Entirely peaceful.

"I've sent a messenger to Hampshire," he said. "I think my uncle must have gone trout fishing."

Sophia set down her tea. "I should have summoned him the moment you were brought home after—the incident. But I was so worried you'd—and I suppose it slipped my mind and—"

"You didn't want him here, because he doesn't like you."

"Also, yes."

"Don't trouble yourself. I didn't die. Damon wasn't in London even had you sent a note immediately after I was brought home. I've written to Lady Falmouth and my cousins. I'm sure they'll descend upon us in due time.

"You've been busy."

"Well, there wasn't much for me to do while I was pretending illness to force my wife back into my orbit but send letters." He shot her a bemused look. "Damon is unlikely to be pleased with me, but not entirely due to bedding," his voice lowered to a seductive purr. "You." His eyes dropped first to her mouth then to the tops of her breasts.

"Why?" She lowered her cup of tea, scorched by that look. The love for Roxboro hummed inside her heart, it had been there all along, but afraid to be heard.

Roxboro had told her while they lay in the darkness last night, whispering to each other, that his uncle had wanted a more advantageous marriage for his nephew. He'd planned on choosing the bride himself.

"Because he's planned a match for you. I can still—no one

need know." She bit her lip, afraid of what he might say, even after their night together.

"Are you insane?" Roxboro tossed a grape at her. "No." An exasperated sound came out of him. "You might already be carrying my heir. But even if you weren't, I don't want an end to our union. I thought I made my position clear, several times over the course of the evening. But if I must spend the rest of the day and night convincing you with my tongue on your—"

"Roxboro," she whispered, somewhat horrified. "The servants."

"Alexander," he countered. "Besides, Damon would pick someone...tedious. Terrible women such as yourself who know how to hurl a good insult *and* detest embroidery are in short supply in the *ton*. Where would I find another?"

"Hmm." A lovely glow filled her heart.

"Damon will barely notice you once I make my announcement." Roxboro's eyes glinted deep green in the morning light, so dark she could barely make out the striations of gray around his pupils. "I plan to take over the management of my own estates. Damon has been doing so for years, first because I was far too young and then after," he shrugged. "Well, I was far too busy enjoying my immoral lifestyle. But I owe it to my father to take a firm hand. And Damon deserves to enjoy his own life. He has his own properties. He's got to find husbands for Violet and Rose, which will be a great challenge, to say the least." He regarded her with a lifted brow. "That pleases you, doesn't it?"

"Yes. You are intelligent, Alexander, as your library suggests. *The Lustful Turk* notwithstanding."

"It is historical in nature."

"But not the volumes on mathematics. Nor engineering. I know you read such when you come to The Pillory, which you do far more regularly than I'd first guessed."

"Barstow is nothing more than a gossip. Worse than an elderly matron of the *ton*."

"I'm not quite so bad, Your Grace." The butler appeared on the terrace.

"Good God, Barstow. Announce yourself." But there was no bite in Roxboro's words. "Do you have word from my uncle?"

"Not yet, Your Grace, however, this has arrived for you." Barstow's features remained bland, but the corner of one eye twitched.

Roxboro took the travel-stained envelope from his butler, surprise lighting his features. "This is Oakhurst's writing. I suppose he's finally decided to write to me."

Barstow pulled a newspaper from beneath his arm. "The London papers."

"I'll read them later."

"I'm sorry, Your Grace, but I must insist you read them now."

Dread filled the air. The news, whatever it happened to be, wasn't good.

Roxboro narrowed his eyes. He set down Oakhurst's letter and picked up the newspaper. "New bill introduced to Parliament." One elegant finger flipped the page. "Lord Waller is suspected of falsifying an investment opportunity and thus bankrupting several of his peers. No surprise there. My uncle has always said he couldn't be trusted. All very boring. Sophie, pass me another piece of toast."

"Your Grace," Barstow intoned. "May I direct you to the second to last page?"

Sophia drizzled a bit of honey on the toast and pushed the plate to him, alarmed when he paled dramatically at whatever he read. He glanced at the letter, then back to the paper in his hands.

"Oakhurst is dead. As is Lady Maxwell."

"What?"

Roxboro jerked to his feet and walked to the end of the terrace, gazing out over the lawn, fingers stretched over the balustrade, gripping the stone.

Sophia reached for the newspaper, which was over a week old. The news that Alfred White, the Earl of Oakhurst had died, was much older. His body, and that of Lady Maxwell had been found at the home of Comte Deleon in Paris. There was a brief mention of a large gambling debt. And how honorable Oakhurst had been in taking the gentleman's way out.

Her stomach pitched as she took in her husband. *Suicide.*

"I'll handle this, Barstow," she said.

"Yes, Your Grace." He gave Sophia a sympathetic look and bowed, before exiting.

"This is unexpected," Roxboro said to her once Barstow and the other servants had gone.

Sophia approached, letter in hand. "You should read it," she offered, not daring to get too close. Roxboro was…rather brittle in the morning light. She wasn't sure what to do to comfort him.

"The gentleman's way out. You understand the meaning, don't you, Sophie? Though I can't imagine why he would shoot Felicia."

Sophia tamped down the jealousy at the use of Lady Maxwell's given name. It spoke of intimacy between the two. "Maybe the letter will explain matters."

"Will you read it to me. I don't think—" Roxboro shut his eyes. "Please."

"Of course." Sophia tore open the envelope and pulled out one thin sheet of paper. The letter wasn't long. Only a few paragraphs.

"*Roxboro*", she read. "*I've shot Lady Maxwell.*"

"Well, I suppose that confirms matters," Roxboro said, his voice etched with grief. "Continue."

"*She lies mere feet from me, dead as I write this. Soon, I will turn the pistol on myself once I post this letter. Confession, they say, is good for the soul. Felicia insisted, you see. She was always more consumed with guilt over our actions than I. I would have confessed sooner, Roxboro, but I assumed you'd be dead and I wouldn't have to. But, you've always been far too lucky. Damon Viceroy has found me out.*"

Roxboro sent Sophia a questioning look.

"There's more." She cleared her throat.

"*You see, dear friend, I've been pilfering bits of your fortune for several years. It was rather easy to do considering your love of drink, and I was quite desperate. You seemed an easy mark, and I could tolerate being in your company. At first, I merely stole your purse. Cheated you at cards. Hazard. Had you sign off on my markers at Binson's after telling you they were yours. Do you recall the emerald cufflinks?"*

Roxboro went still, hands clutching the stone. "My father's. Rare and valuable. I stupidly," he shook his head. "Well, it doesn't matter."

"I could have lived off you for years, but you were exhausting. I wanted away from you. So I forged your signature on a handful of bank drafts. Decent sums but far less than you usually spend. I never imagined Lord Damon and your secretary would look too closely. My mistake."

A deep, horrible sound came from Roxboro. Sophia took two steps towards him, but he held out a hand. "No, Sophie. No. Finish it."

"I had truly hoped that trollop at the brothel would kill you and I could flee to the Continent in peace, but your uncle was not so easily fooled. He has men looking for me, chasing me about until I realize I can run no further. So I'll salvage what is left of my honor the only way I know how and I couldn't allow Lady Maxwell to confess my sins to your uncle. Pity. She was a lovely woman."

"That's all," Sophia choked out, wishing there was something she could do or say to take the sting of Oakhurst's betrayal away, but there was nothing. "Save for his signature."

"I'd no idea," Roxboro's chest rose and fell, pained by the news. "That he was destitute. Or that he hated me. I thought Oakhurst—it never occurred to me I was being used. We were always wallowing in drink. No wonder Uncle Damon couldn't stand Oakhurst. He must have suspected."

Sophia refolded the letter, touching his arm. "Alexander."

"I want a brandy, Sophie. Desperately."

"Alexander—"

"But I'm not going to have one." He leaned down to kiss her forehead. "I promise. You need not worry." He gave her a wobbly smile before walking off the terrace and into the sweep of lawn. She watched him go, until he disappeared near a cluster of oak trees.

Chapter Twenty-Six

"Lord Damon will arrive within the hour, Your Grace," Barstow intoned. "A footman was sent ahead to alert you. I've prepared his usual rooms."

Sophia's mouth halted mid-bite, eyes raised to take in her husband. She'd done that quite a bit recently, mainly because it was hard to know that every day Alexander, glorious duke and former sot, *was* her husband.

"Splendid. Don't you agree, duchess?" The green of his eyes heated as they settled on her mouth, bringing with it a rather vivid image of Sophia, naked, on her knees. His hands in her hair as he—

"I do," she managed to say.

My God, he's turned me into a trollop.

Gone was the somewhat gentle lover who'd taken her virginity, and, in his place, the Duke of Roxboro had taken up residence. Every ounce of ducal arrogance that had been bred into Alexander, no longer hidden beneath endless frivolity and brandy, had risen to the surface. The careless charm was still there, the overt sensuality, but he was now…commanding in a way he hadn't been before.

Rather thrilling, all things considered.

When he'd returned later that night, after leaving her on the terrace, worrying Sophia and Barstow half to death because he'd been gone the entire day, she'd been sure she'd find him with a bottle of brandy in his hand. Instead, he'd been furious to find Sophia sleeping in her room. Snarling, he'd picked her up while she protested, and carried her to his bed.

We do not sleep apart. Is that understood, Your Grace?

And Sophia, being well...*Sophia*, had snapped at him for waking her up, declaring that duke or not, she would sleep where she wished.

A miscalculation.

Roxboro did not agree. He made his feelings on the matter known that night, as well as the following morning. Last night, he'd tied her up with his cravat, taking her so savagely that Sophia was having trouble sitting this morning. All of which was terribly exciting and left her feeling like one of the heroines in the romance novels she so adored, though admittedly, it was becoming increasingly difficult to meet the eyes of the household staff. Sophia's voice...carried.

Mama had been incorrect. The marital bed, at least if it contained the Duke of Roxboro, was no duty.

Most importantly, Roxboro hadn't touched a drop of brandy, scotch, or anything else.

"Freeman made his train?"

"Yes, Your Grace," Barstow replied.

Mr. Freeman, the duke's secretary, had appeared at The Pillory the day after Roxboro received that terrible, awful letter from Oakhurst. Her husband stayed closeted with Freeman for nearly two days in his study, barely speaking to Sophia unless they were in bed. Roxboro spent the entire time with a pen stuck behind one ear, as he marched about with a stack of ledgers in his arms.

Freeman, poor man, scurried about, uncertain how to proceed with this different Roxboro. He'd been sent back to London just after breakfast.

"You will heed *me*, Freeman," Sophia had heard Roxboro say, as the secretary climbed into the carriage waiting to take him to the train station. "Or you will find other employment. Your salary is contingent upon my largesse, not Lord Damon's. Do we understand each other?"

"Yes, Your Grace," Freeman's throat had bobbed about before he departed.

"Lord Damon is bound to be...unsettled by...certain changes," she said, taking a bite of roasted chicken. Roxboro's uncle was not going to be pleased to see that she and the duke had come to terms with their marriage, but in a way he wouldn't have considered.

Roxboro drew one finger along the edge of his goblet, one filled with well-watered wine, which was all he allowed himself. Given his dislike of wine, he only took a few tiny sips, mostly for appearances sake.

Everyone will still assume I'm a sot. Let them. It is an advantage.

"My uncle has much to answer for," Roxboro said from his side of the table. "He was aware of Oakhurst's deception, yet he never informed me." Anger laced his words.

That much had been confirmed by Freeman. The bank drafts, dozens of them, that Roxboro couldn't recall signing. Markers with his signature. A house in a corner of Mayfair, with Roxboro's name affixed to the lease. Sophia did not blame her husband for being furious.

"Yes," Roxboro continued, watching her. "Damon put an end to it, but I deserved to know. Instead, he allowed me to go stumbling about like the drunken village idiot."

The betrayal of Oakhurst had wounded her husband deeply. But there was also immense guilt over the way he'd abused his father's legacy and that of every Duke of Roxboro who'd gone before him. He was fumed, quietly, at what he saw as his uncle's coddling. Lord Damon had treated Roxboro like a child. Encouraging his excesses. Handling Roxboro's affairs. He was convinced that had his uncle not been so accommodating, he would have seen through Oakhurst's scheme.

"I do not think that was Damon's intent," she voiced quietly, though Sophia didn't know. She didn't care for Damon Viceroy, but she refused to allow her opinion to color Roxboro's feelings towards his uncle. "I am firmly on your side, Your Grace."

"I know, you tedious chit." Roxboro stood, tripped over the leg of the table, cursed, and made his way over to her. "I've two left feet. Or perhaps," he nuzzled along her neck. "It is only that I am so well endowed, my balance is off."

"An understatement," Sophia replied.

"Naughty." His teeth nibbled at the lobe of her ear. "Terrible." His tongue teased along the edge. "Thing." A kiss was pressed to her neck. "I adore you. Come, be terrible with me."

"Your uncle—" she giggled, leaning into him.

"Has arrived," came the coldly patrician tone of Lord Damon Viceroy from the doorway.

And he didn't look pleased at all.

CHAPTER TWENTY-SEVEN

ALEXANDER CROSSED HIS legs and took in Damon, waving at Barstow. "A brandy, Uncle?"

"Yes, thank you." He looked askance at Alexander. "You won't be joining me?"

"I'm enjoying this fine, French vintage." He held up his glass of well-watered wine. Terrible tasting. He'd no desire to indulge further which was the point. Alexander could sip on one glass the entire evening and no one was the wiser, but brandy? He was deeply afraid he'd drink an entire bottle.

"You detest wine."

"I've acquired a taste for it as of late. The duchess approves. Tell me about Oakhurst." Alexander wanted answers. Why hadn't Damon told him he suspected Oakhurst of such deceit?

"I'd hoped—that is to say, I meant to tell you of my suspicions," Damon paused. "But I wasn't certain, not for some time. I didn't want to bother you with it. And frankly, I could hardly believe it myself. I confronted him—" Damon's words grew thick. "I think he hoped the trollop at that brothel—"

Alexander's eyes widened. Oakhurst tried to have him murdered?

"At any rate, the girl admitted as much to the man I had following Oakhurst about. I hadn't thought he'd flee abroad so quickly. Or that Lady Maxwell was helping him. And then you compromised Canterbell's daughter and I had more pressing matters than chasing Oakhurst."

The scent of the brandy filled Alexander's nose. If ever there was a time to have a brandy, it was now. Finding out your closest friend not only stole from you, but also planned to have you killed would make anyone drink.

But Sophie would be disappointed.

I wish to never disappoint her.

"You were already at The Pillory when I received word that Oakhurst was in France. My man was searching for him, and I was so distraught over the entire affair, I thought I would do a little trout fishing to clear my mind after everything that had happened. I could have sworn I told Lady Falmouth of my whereabouts."

Alexander said nothing for a moment. "He sent me a letter. Oakhurst. Confessed everything."

Damon placed a hand on Alexander's arm. "At least he was honorable at the end. I'm truly sorry. I should have told you of my suspicions. But, frankly, I'd hoped you'd never find out. He betrayed you horribly."

"You never did like him." Alexander gave a bitter laugh.

"No. I never did. He hung off your coattails. Encouraged your poor behavior. And now it appears I've failed you again in the matter of your unwanted duchess. She's manipulated you, hasn't she?" Damon shook his head. "Cut from the same cloth as your mother, Marianne."

Alexander heartily disagreed.

Sophie was the only thing that had ever eased the lonely ache inside him, that vast hole inside that spirits, trollops and cards used to fill. Her presence calmed him. Aroused him. Made him…*purposeful.* Sophie did not treat him like an overgrown child, plying him with liquor and indulging his every whim, something he decided not to point out to his uncle.

If anything, Alexander's wife was a small, plump force of nature who refused to back down, even when they argued. Flippant. Disobedient. *Terrible.* And Sophia had absolutely no reservations when it came to the marital bed. If anything, Alexander found her to be highly creative and open to any manner of suggestion.

"She isn't," Alexander said softly. "Manipulating me."

"You're a poor judge of character, nephew. Just look at Oakhurst." Damon sipped his brandy, something unkind flickering in his eyes. "I'm sure her ruination was well planned. I'll try to fix it, but I'm not sure if I can. It's obvious you've bedded her."

"The ruination was not a grand scheme, Uncle. Sophie was as much a victim of circumstance as I. Nor does it matter any longer."

I love her. Madly, as it happens. Who knew I was capable of such emotion?

"She failed to inform me about your accident." Damon's lips pursed. "Deliberately, I think."

Well, that much was true. "I'll remind you, Uncle, that you weren't in London, thus it would not have mattered if she wrote you right away or not."

"Bah," Damon waved his hand. "You could have died, Alexander, and I wouldn't have known. Her behavior is deceitful. Possibly...murderous."

"Are you suggesting Sophia had something to do with the attack on my carriage?" Alexander laughed. "You've got to be joking. She would never do such a thing."

Damon swallowed down the brandy in his glass. "She is capable. How could you be so stupid? I warned you not to bed her or I would not be able to secure an annulment. There might be another way, perhaps. I will not allow you to—perish in the same manner as your father. At the mercy of a scheming woman. One who seeks to control our dukedom. Send her away."

"Hmm." Alexander watched as his uncle fretted over Sophia, annoyed. Damon was not his keeper. And Sophia might murder him one day, but she'd be blunt about it.

Control. That was what this entire conversation was about. What *Damon Viceroy* was about.

Freeman stated plainly that Damon reviewed every line of every ledger. He knew where every pound went, which is likely how he discovered Oakhurst's thievery. But why not confront Oakhurst sooner? Why allow him to do more damage? And while Alexander was grateful for his uncle's oversight and appreciated his counsel, Damon was *not* the Duke of Roxboro. The estate did not belong to *him*. Roxboro was Alexander's birthright.

And I mean to make it my own.

"I promise you, Uncle. Should I suspect Sophia of any deceit, you will be the first to know. I'll have her drawn and quartered on the lawn."

"This isn't a jest, Alexander."

"I am quite satisfied in my marriage." An edge of command bled into his words, unintended, but there all the same. You could dictate to a sot, but not a duke.

Damon's face reddened. "You don't mean that." He placed a hand to his forehead. "This is the same as Charles. Again, I must relive it. Marianne had him convinced as well of her affection. Do not be stupid, Alexander. The girl has ambitions."

Alexander's lips pressed together, afraid of what he might say. "You will not disparage Sophia to me. I realize I've given you every reason to treat me as a child, but I am no longer your libertine of a nephew who stumbles about inviting disaster. I am not stupid. Cease behaving as if I can barely feed myself without your direction." He slapped the arm of the chair.

Damon fell back, sputtering.

Interesting. I've never seen him at a loss for words before.

Damon had raised Alexander as his own. Given him Aunt May, Violet and Rose to be his family. But Damon had also kept him isolated save for Oakhurst. Ignorant of matters Alexander should be familiar with, out of the need to protect him. He understood, he did. Damon had loved his older brother Charles and despaired endlessly that he had not stopped his murder.

But Sophia was not Marianne.

"No, of course not. It is only that—" he turned away. "I do

not wish to lose you as I did your father. It would be the end of me, Alexander. I couldn't bear it. You are…my son." His face fell between his palms. "I simply could not bear it."

"I know, Uncle." Alexander stood. "But I am the Duke of Roxboro, and it is time I behaved as such." He placed a hand on Damon's shoulder. "I would be lost without you and your guidance, but I have matters well in hand. I've met with Freeman."

Damon lifted his chin. "Freeman? He came to The Pillory?"

"Yes, and I've explained that I will be handling my affairs with your guidance. I don't want to—disregard everything you have done for me. I am deeply appreciative. Nor could I continue without your help," Alexander said in a rush. "I am not my father, Damon. Nor is Sophia Marianne. Besides, stepping back from my affairs finally allows you the chance to pursue your ambitions in politics, which you have put aside on my behalf for far too long. Lord Canterbell can be a useful ally, don't you think? Prime Minister Viceroy has an excellent ring to it."

"It does," Damon agreed, pouring another glass of brandy. "I—suppose it's time. If you're sure."

"I am," Alexander insisted. "Now, your rooms are ready. Barstow will bring you something to eat. We can talk more in the morning."

Chapter Twenty-Eight

Sophia wandered out into the gardens, grateful to be away from the house and dark cloud of Lord Damon's presence. He was polite to her, of course. Smiled. Said mildly charming things. But those gestures were only meant to hide his obvious dislike of Sophia from Roxboro. The last few days had been uncomfortable to say the least.

Thankfully, Damon was returning to London today.

"Not a moment too soon," she said into the breeze. "He is like the plague hovering over Alexander."

Damon had received the news that Alexander was taking up his own affairs with a thinly veiled smile, less than eager to give up control of the estates he'd managed since the Duke of Roxboro was an infant, but Sophia's husband would not be dissuaded. She'd caught Damon, more than once, deliberately trying to entice Alexander to share a brandy. Which her husband resisted. He seemed firm in his belief that the attack on the duke's carriage had been two desperate thieves and nothing more, suggesting Alexander hire more footmen.

"Yes, well," Sophia said to herself. "When your nephew is a sot, it is easier to maintain control over him and his wealth. Dictate his days. You'll have to find something else to occupy your time, Lord Damon."

A squirrel ran across the path, stopped, chirped at her, then veered to the left, a part of the trail that had fallen into disuse, overgrown with weeds and brush.

"See," she said after the squirrel. "Even you agree. I suppose you think I should go this way."

The squirrel circled a tree a few steps to the left, pausing every so often to chirp at her. He started up the rough bark of the giant oak, watching Sophia with the small black beads of his eyes, tail twitching. Then the squirrel moved, revealing a scarred portion of bark. It...looked like letters.

Sophia approached, hands running over the gnarled tree which looked to be nearly ancient. Branches stretched overhead, enveloping her in a canopy of green.

M and C was carved into the bark. Along with a crudely drawn heart.

She stretched to trace the letters.

Marianne and Charles?

Sophia jerked back her fingers as if burned.

She knew the tragic tale of the previous Duke of Roxboro, along with the ridiculous tale that all the dukes were notoriously short-lived. Easy to believe when one is well on their way to drinking far too much brandy in the middle of the day, but far less certain now. Alexander had told her once that his mother had been a devious creature who after securing an heir in her belly, had her lover murder Charles Viceroy, Alexander's father. Her husband claimed there had been no affection between his parents.

If they cared nothing for each other, why carve such a symbol with their initials into a tree at The Pillory?

"Sophie!"

Turning from the tree, Sophia lifted her skirts, running back the way she'd come. Her husband was searching for her, and she wished to be found. Stepping back onto the main path leading to the gardens, Sophia stopped at the sight before her.

Breathe, Sophia.

Alexander, in only his shirtsleeves, striding towards her, the color of his eyes matching the leaves above her head. Nearly. There was still a hint of stormy gray around his pupils. Her husband. The magnificent Duke of Roxboro. Sophia thought her heart might burst.

"I'm here," she dipped into a curtsey, gratified to keep her balance.

"Oh, stop doing that. You're awful at it," a slow grin stretched across her husband's face. "Mara is much better."

"Pity you didn't ruin her then, Your Grace."

He wrapped an arm around her waist, spun her about and then lowered her to the grass. "I was missing you, Sophie."

"I thought to leave you and Lord Damon alone before he departs."

"Oh, he's already gone. Didn't even wait to bid you goodbye." Alexander's eyes widened, pretending great surprise. "How impolite."

"I'm quite hurt," she cried. "Devastated."

"You aren't. Damon is quite put out that I insist on bedding my wife and do not plan to stop." His hands tugged at her skirts, lifting them until her stockings and underthings were exposed. "I've not yet fucked you under a tree, Sophie."

"Well then, don't waste this moment, Your Grace." She pressed her lips to his, feeling the honey spill languidly between her legs as she stretched them wider in a plea for his touch.

"Little harlot."

"I am what you've made me, Your Grace."

"True." He stopped tugging at her clothing, his hand running up the side of her hip and long one breast until she sighed. Cupping her cheek, Alexander regarded her intently, his thumb brushing along her lip. "Sophie," his voice broke just a bit before his mouth caught hers.

Oh, Alexander could kiss a woman senseless.

"I love you," he whispered against her mouth. "I love you. I am so—shamefully lost without you, my unwanted duchess. Whoever has been impersonating me, I owe him a debt I can never repay because he brought you to me."

Sophia shut her eyes to hold back the tears gathering. What a somewhat sweet but rather perfect thing to say.

"You don't have to love me back." He pressed his forehead to hers. "I'm rather lovely on the outside, but the inside requires a great deal of work. Not many would be up to the task. But don't give up on me. Don't—"

"Stop being an idiot, Your Grace." A tear trickled down her cheek as she opened her eyes. "Your affections are returned tenfold."

EPILOGUE

ALEXANDER CIRCLED THE theater box, glancing at the stage with little interest. He didn't really like the theater, but Sophie preferred it to the opera, which she likened to torture. Lord and Lady Canterbell had joined them this evening, as well as Mara and Lord Caster, who if Lady Canterbell had her way, would be betrothed soon. Violet and Rose, along with Lady Falmouth, rounded out the evening.

Damon, however, had declined the invitation, citing a previous engagement.

Probably not the last time his uncle would decline to join him. He and Damon had butted heads continuously, as of late. Alexander tried for patience, but Damon was having a great deal of difficulty letting go of the control he'd exerted over every aspect of Alexander's life for nearly three decades. Lady Falmouth offered to speak to Damon on Alexander's behalf, but considering how his uncle felt about her, that was a poor idea, though he appreciated the effort.

Damon continued to insert himself into every business transaction involving Alexander's estates and other financial matters. His uncle refused to compromise. The final straw was when Timmons let Damon into Alexander's study and he found his uncle going over a ledger he had no business reviewing.

Timmons was sacked. Sophie took care of the matter herself and sent for Barstow. Two butlers were unnecessary.

Perhaps Lady Letitia, the Marquess of Dunhill's daughter, would distract Damon from further interference. The gossips said his uncle was courting her, though Damon hadn't admitted as much. But every politician needs a wife to further his ambitions, after all.

"Your Grace, there you are." His Sophie slid her arm through his as a pleased Lord and Lady Canterbell watched in approval.

Alexander pulled her to his side, already considering the things he would do to her later, all of which she would allow. "What do you think of the performance, Lady Saffron?"

"A bit overblown." Sophia gave him a swat of her fan. "A dead rodent appears to have taken up residence beneath the leading man's nose."

"Terrible thing." He squeezed her tight. "But I must agree. The mustache is atrocious. Perhaps you can swat me with that thing later, you naughty chit."

"Alexander," she whispered, making round eyes at Lord and Lady Canterbell. "My parents are here. Behave."

"Never."

A commotion started at the entrance to the box as a woman, clad in a gown of dark indigo at least two seasons out of date, pushed her way in and marched up to Alexander. She was pretty. Somewhat matronly. He'd never seen her before in his life.

"You." She pointed with one gloved finger.

"Me?" He and Sophie exchanged a look. "I'm sorry, but have we been introduced?"

"You vile—I knew you were a libertine. A rogue. But even for you, this is beyond the pale. It isn't as if you need the money. Good lord."

"Former libertine." He held up his glass of well-watered wine. "And sot. But I am enormously wealthy, thank you for noticing. Would you like some lemonade? Miss…?"

She flushed a deep red, glancing around the box, tugging at the lace edging her gown that had seen better days. Something Alexander always noticed. Clothing. After all, he considered dressing well to be one of his better character traits. Possibly the only one. Sophia had lately taken to calling him a sniveling dandy, but it wasn't nearly as arousing as *feckless sot*.

His duchess, fierce and terrible—

Oh, I adore her.

—stalked forward, placing herself between Alexander and this incredibly brazen woman like a shield. He found it adorable the way Sophia wanted to protect him from the world.

I love her madly.

"Who, may I ask, do you think you are to invade the Duke of Roxboro's box during a performance of—" she snapped her fingers at Alexander.

"*A Cousin's Request*," he supplied, delighted she'd come to his defense like an avenging Valkyrie.

"Yes, well, the play is terrible." Her brows drew together. "I'd forgotten the name. But I," she took a step towards the woman, who was now eyeing her with a great deal of trepidation, because his duchess was something of a menace. "Would like yours. I'm the Duchess of Roxboro. Who might you be?"

The woman made a sound of distress. Not at Sophia, but Alexander. Her gaze was fixated on the end of Alexander's nose. She shook her head, muttering to herself, then took a step back. "Impossible."

"Louder," Sophia demanded. "No muttering in the duke's box."

Good lord, she was magnificent. Alexander was becoming highly aroused. First the fan and then this. He might tell Barstow to give the staff the night off.

"I think I've made a mistake," she said slowly. "But..." The woman's eyes never left Alexander's nose. "There's no freckle. There's no *freckle*," she said louder. "Do you have it covered?"

"I what?" Alexander stared down at her, the pieces slowly coming together.

The woman looked at Sophia. "But how can there be two of them? You are the Duke of Roxboro. There's only one and he said…" Her words trailed away, a stricken look coming over her pretty features. "I've—please excuse me."

"You've seen him." Sophia grabbed the woman's arm. "The man who pretends to be the Duke of Roxboro. Because that," she pointed at Alexander. "Is my husband and I can most definitely confirm he has no freckle on his nose. Or anywhere else on his person."

Lady Canterbell made a sound, hand clutching her throat.

Glorious, my duchess.

"You aren't going anywhere," Alexander commanded in his most ducal tone. "Until you tell us who is going about London claiming to be me."

About the Author

Kathleen Ayers is the bestselling author of steamy Regency and Victorian romance. She's been a hopeful romantic and romance reader since buying Sweet Savage Love at a garage sale when she was fourteen while her mother was busy looking at antique animal planters. She has a weakness for tortured, witty alpha males who can't help falling for intelligent, sassy heroines.

A Texas transplant (from Pennsylvania) Kathleen spends most of her summers attempting to grow tomatoes (a wasted effort) and floating in her backyard pool with her two dogs, husband and son. When not writing she likes to visit her "happy place" (Newport, RI.), wine bars, make homemade pizza on the grill, and perfect her charcuterie board skills. Visit her at www.kathleenayers.com.

www.ingramcontent.com/pod-product-compliance
Lightning Source LLC
LaVergne TN
LVHW011931070526
838202LV00054B/4594